Incendiary

Incendiary

Chris Cleave

 ALFRED A. KNOPF   NEW YORK   2005

This Is a Borzoi Book Published by Alfred A. Knopf

www.aaknopf.com

Published simultaneously in Great Britain by Chatto & Windus, London.

Knopf, Borzoi Books, and the colophon are registered trademarks
of Random House, Inc.

Library of Congress Cataloging-in-Publication Data
Cleave, Chris.
Incendiary / Chris Cleave.— 1st American ed.
p. cm.
ISBN 0-307-26282-0 (alk. paper)
1. Terrorism victims' families—Fiction. 2 Terrorism—Prevention—Fiction.
3. Working-class families—Fiction. 4. Working-class women—Fiction.
5. Loss (Psychology)—Fiction. 6. Suicide bombings—Fiction. 7. London
(England)—Fiction. 8. Widows—Fiction. I. Title.
PR6103.L43I53 2005
813'.6—dc22   2005044078

Manufactured in the United States of America
First American Edition

For Louis and Clémence

. . . a most terrible fire broke out, which . . . not
only wasted the adjacent parts, but also places
very remote, with incredible noise and fury.

—Inscription on the Monument to the Great
Fire of London, north side

Spring

Dear Osama they want you dead or alive so the terror will stop. Well I wouldn't know about that I mean rock 'n' roll didn't stop when Elvis died on the khazi it just got worse. Next thing you know there was Sonny & Cher and Dexys Midnight Runners. I'll come to them later. My point is it's easier to start these things than to finish them. I suppose you thought of that did you?

There's a reward of 25 million dollars on your head but don't lose sleep on my account Osama. I have no information leading to your arrest or capture. I have no information full effing stop. I'm what you'd call an infidel and my husband called working-class. There is a difference you know. But just supposing I did clap eyes on you. Supposing I saw you driving a Nissan Primera down towards Shoreditch and grassed you to the old bill. Well. I wouldn't know how to spend 25 million dollars. It's not as if I've got anyone to spend it on since you blew up my husband and my boy.

That's my whole point you see. I don't want 25 million dollars Osama I just want you to give it a rest. AM I ALONE? I want to be the last mother in the world who ever has to write you a letter like this. Who ever has to write to you Osama about her dead boy.

Now about the writing. The last thing I wrote was N/A on an income support form that wanted NAME OF SPOUSE OR PARTNER. So you see I'll do my best but you'll have to bear with me because I'm not a big writer. I'm going to write to you about the emptiness that was left when you took my boy away. I'm going to write so you can look into my empty life and see what a human boy really is from the shape of the hole he leaves behind. I want you to feel that hole in your heart and stroke it with your hands and cut your fingers on its sharp edges. I am a mother Osama I just want you to love my son. What could be more natural?

I know you can love my boy Osama. The *Sun* says you are an EVIL MONSTER but I don't believe in evil I know it takes 2 to tango. I know you're vexed at the leaders of Western imperialism. Well I'll be writing to them too.

As for you I know you'd stop the bombs in a second if I could make you see my son with all your heart for just one moment. I know you would stop making boy-shaped holes in the world. It would make you too sad. So I will do my best with these words Osama. I suppose you can see they don't come natural to me but I hope this letter reaches you anyway. I hope it finds you before the Americans do otherwise I'm going to wish I hadn't bothered aren't I?

Well Osama if I'm going to show you my boy I have to start with where he lived and I still do. I live in London England which I agree with you is a bad place in lots of ways but I was born here so what can you do? London looks like a rich place from the outside but we are most of us very poor here. I saw the video you made Osama where you said the West was decadent. Maybe you meant the West End? We aren't all like that. London is a smiling liar his front teeth are very nice but you can smell his back teeth rotten and stinking.

My family was never rotten poor we were hard up there's a difference. We were respectable we kept ourselves presentable but it was a struggle I don't mind telling you. We were not the nice front teeth or the rotten back teeth of London and there are millions of us just like that. The middle classes put up web sites about us. If you're interested Osama just put down that Kalashnikov for a second and look up *chav pikey ned* or *townie* in Google. Like I say there are millions of us but now there's a lot less than there were of course. I miss them so bad my husband and my boy especially.

My husband and my boy and me lived on Barnet Grove which is a road that goes from Bethnal Green to Haggerston. There are 2 kinds of places on Barnet Grove. The first kind are very pricey old terraced houses. The estate agents call them Georgian Gems With Extensive Potential For Conversion To Fully Appointed Executive Flats With Easy Access To The City Of London And Within A Stone's Throw Of The Prestigious Columbia Road Flower Market. The second kind of places are places like ours. They are flats in dirty brick tower blocks they smell of chip fat inside. All the flats in each block are the same except that the front doors don't match on account of they get kicked in as often as they get opened nicely. They built our tower blocks in the fifties. They built them in the gaps where the Georgian Gems had incendiaries dropped on them by Adolf Hitler.

Adolf Hitler was the last chap who hated London as much as you do Osama. The *Sun* calls him the MOST EVIL MAN IN HISTORY and he made the gaping hole in Barnet Grove that they built our tower block in. I suppose it was thanks to him we could afford to live Within A Stone's Throw Of The Prestigious Columbia Road Flower Market so maybe Adolf Hitler was not all bad in the long run.

Like I say our flat was in one of those tower blocks. It was a small flat and you could hear the upstairs neighbours on the job. They used to start uh uh uh very soft at first and then louder and louder uh uh oh my god UH and after a bit you could listen as hard as you liked and still not know if you were hearing love or murder. It used to drive my husband crazy but at least our flat was warm and clean and it was ours. It was an ex–council flat which is to say we owned it. Which is to say we didn't have to struggle to pay the rent. We struggled to pay the mortgage each month instead there is a difference and that difference is called EMPOWERMENT.

I didn't work I looked after our boy. My husband's wages paid the mortgage and not much else so by the end of the month things were always a bit wobbly. My husband was a copper and he wasn't just any old copper he was in bomb disposal. You might reckon bomb disposal wages would of stretched a bit further Osama but you'd reckon wrong if you didn't reckon with the horses the dogs the cockfights in the back room of the Nelson's Head and whether it was going to be a white Christmas. My husband was the sort of bloke who'd take a punt on anything so thank god he had a better track record with bombs than the 11:31 at Doncaster. When we were behind on the bills I used to get teeth-chattering scared of the bailiffs Osama. Whenever I could squeeze a fiver out of the shopping money I used to stash it under the carpet just in case my husband blew everything one day and they chucked us out on our ear. There was never more than a month of mortgage under the rug so we were always less than 31 days away from the street or only 28 days if my husband blew the lot in February which sod's law he would. But I couldn't hold his flutters against him on account of he needed a thing to take his mind off the nerves and his thing was no worse than mine Osama I'll tell you about my thing in a minute.

In bomb disposal the call can come at any time of the day or night and for my husband it often did. If the call came in the evening we would be sitting in front of the telly. Not saying much. Just sitting there with plates on our knees eating chicken kievs. They were Findus they were more or less okay they were always his favourite.

Anyway the telly would be on and we'd probably be watching *Top Gear*. My husband knew a lot about motors. We never could afford a new motor ourselves but my husband knew how to pick a good secondhand one. We mostly had Vauxhall Astras they never let us down. They used to sell off the old police Astras you see. They'd give them a respray but if the light was right you could always see POLICE showing out from under the paint job. I suppose a thing can never really change its nature Osama.

Anyway we'd be watching *Top Gear* and the phone would go and my husband would put his plate down on the sofa and take the phone next door. He wasn't supposed to tell me anything about the job but when he came back through the lounge there was one sure way to tell if it was serious. They always knew which were the real bombs and which were most probably just hoaxes. If it was a hoax my husband would sit back down on the sofa and gobble the rest of his chicken kiev before he left the flat. It took him only 30 secs but he never did that if it was serious. When it was serious he just picked up his jacket and walked straight out.

When it was serious I used to wait up for him. Our boy would be asleep so there was only the telly to take my mind off things. Not that it ever would of course. After *Top Gear* there was *Holby City* and then it would be *Newsnight*. *Holby* made you nervous about death and chip pan fires and *Newsnight* made you nervous about life and money so between the both of them they could get you in a right state and leave you wondering why you bothered with the licence fee. But I had to keep the telly on in case anything happened and there was a news flash.

So I used to just sit there Osama watching the telly and hoping it would stay boring. When your husband works in bomb disposal you want the whole world to stay that way. Nothing ever happening. Trust me you want a world run by *Richard & Judy*. At night I always watched the BBC. I never watched the other side because I couldn't stand the adverts. A woman with nice hair telling how this or that shampoo stops split ends. Well. It made me feel a bit funny when I was waiting to see if my husband had got himself blown up. It made me feel quite poorly actually.

There's a lot of bombs in London these days Osama on account of if you've got a message for the nation then it's actually quite hard to get on *Richard & Judy* so it's easier just to stick a few old nails and bolts into a Nike bag of fertiliser. Half the poor lonely sods in town are making a bomb these days Osama I hope you're proud of yourself. The coppers make 4 or 5 of them safe every week and another 1 or 2 go off and make holes in people and often as not it's the coppers on the scene who get the holes put in them. They don't show it on the news any more on account of it would give people the screaming abdabs. I'm not big on numbers Osama but once late at night I worked out the odds on my husband getting blown up one day and ever since then I had the screaming abdabs all on my own. It was practically a dead cert I swear not even Ladbrokes would of taken your money.

Sometimes the sun would be up before my husband came home. The breakfast show would be on the telly and there'd be a girl doing the weather or the Dow Jones. It was all a bit pointless if you ask me. I mean if you wanted to know what the weather was doing you only had to look out the window and as for the Dow Jones well you could look out the window or you could not. You could please yourself because it's not as if there was anything you could do about the Dow Jones either way. My whole point is I never gave a monkey's about any of it. I just wanted my husband home safe.

When he finally came in it was such a relief. He never said much because he was so tired. I would ask him how did it go? And he would look at me and say I'm still here ain't I? My husband was what the *Sun* would call a QUIET HERO it's funny how none of them are NOISY I suppose that wouldn't be very British. Anyway my husband would drink a Famous Grouse and go to bed without taking his clothes off or brushing his teeth because as well as being QUIET he sometimes COULDN'T BE ARSED and who could blame him? When he was safe asleep I would go to look in on our boy.

Our boy had his own room it was cracking we were proud of it. My husband built his bed in the shape of Bob the Builder's dump truck and I sewed the curtains and we did the painting together. In the night my boy's room smelled of boy. Boy is a good smell it is a cross between angels and tigers. My boy slept on his side sucking Mr. Rabbit's paws. I sewed Mr. Rabbit myself he was purple with green ears. He went everywhere my boy went. Or else there was trouble. My boy was so peaceful it was lovely to watch him sleep so still with his lovely ginger hair glowing from the sunrise outside his curtains. The curtains made the light all pink. They slept very quiet in the pink light the 2 of them him and Mr. Rabbit. Sometimes my boy was so still I had to check he was breathing. I would put my face close to his face and blow a little bit on his cheek. He would snuffle and frown and fidget for a while then go all soft and still again. I would smile and tiptoe backwards out of his room and close his door very quiet.

Mr. Rabbit survived. I still have him. His green ears are black with blood and one of his paws is missing.

Now I've told you where my boy came from Osama I suppose I ought to tell you a bit more about his mum before you get the idea I was some sort of saint who just sewed fluffy toys and waited up for her husband. I wish I was a saint because it was what my boy deserved but it wasn't what he got. I wasn't a perfect wife and mum in fact I wasn't even an average one I was what the *Sun* would call a DIRTY LOVE CHEAT.

My husband and my boy never found out oh thank you god. But I can say it now they're both dead and I don't care who reads it. It can't hurt them any more. I loved my boy and I loved my husband but sometimes I saw other men too. Or rather they saw me and I didn't make much of an effort to put them off and one thing sometimes led to another. You know what men are like Osama you trained thousands of them yourself they are RAVENOUS LOVE RATS.

Sex is not a beautiful and perfect thing for me Osama it is a condition caused by nerves. Ever since I was a young girl I get so anxious. It only needs a little thing to get me started. Your Twin Towers attack or just 2 blokes arguing over a cab fare it's all the same. All the violence in the world is connected it's just like the sea. When I see a woman shouting at her kid in Asda car park I see bulldozers flattening refugee camps. I see those little African boys with scars across the tops of their skulls like headphones. I see all the lost tempers of the world I see HELL ON EARTH. It's all the same it all makes me twitchy.

And when I get nervous about all the horrible things in the world I just need something very soft and secret and warm to make me forget it for a bit. I didn't even know what it was till I was 14. It was one of my mum's boyfriends who showed me but I won't write his

name or he'll get in trouble. I suppose he was a SICK CHILD PREDA-
TOR but I still remember how lovely it felt. Afterwards he took me
for a drive through town and I just smiled and looked out at all the
hard faces and the homeless drifting past the car windows and they
didn't bother me for the moment. I was just smiling and thinking
nothing much.

Ever since then whenever I get nervous I'll go with anyone so
long as they're gentle. I'm not proud I know it's not an excuse and
I've tried so hard to change but I can't. It's deep under my skin like
a tat they can never quite remove oh sometimes I feel so tired.

I'll tell you about one night in particular Osama. You'll see it isn't
true I always used to wait up for my husband. One night last spring
he got called out on a job and while I was waiting up for him the
telly made me very anxious. It was one of those politics talk shows
and everyone was trying to talk at once. It was like they were on a
sinking ship fighting over the last life jacket and I couldn't stand it.
I ran into the kitchen and started tidying to take my mind off things
only the problem was it was already tidy. The trouble is when I get
nervous I always tidy and I get nervous a lot and there's only so
much tidying a small flat can take. I looked around the kitchen I was
hopping from foot to foot I was getting desperate. The oven was
clean the chip pan was sparkling and all the tins in the cupboards
were in alphabetical order with their labels facing outwards. Apple
slices Baked beans Custard and so on it was a real problem it was
effing perfect I didn't know what to do with myself so I started biting my nails. I can bite till my fingers bleed when I get like that but
very luckily just then I had a flash of genius I realized I never had
alphabetised the freezer had I? I'm good like that Osama sometimes
things just come to me. So I opened up the freezer and dumped out
all the food onto the floor and put it back in its right order from top
to bottom. AlphaBites Burgers Chips Drumsticks Eclairs Fish Fingers I could go on but the point is all the time I was doing this I was
very happy and I never once imagined my husband cutting the
wrong wire on a homemade nail bomb and being blown into chunks

about the size of your thumb. The trouble was as soon as all the packets were back in the freezer that's exactly what I started seeing. So then I did what anyone would do in my situation Osama I went down the pub.

Actually that isn't quite true. What I did first was open up the freezer again and take out the bag of AlphaBites and open them and put all the AlphaBites into alphabetical order and put them back into the freezer and *then* I went down the pub. There was nothing else for it I just had to get out of that flat and close the door behind me.

I know they say you should never leave a child alone in the home but there you go. The people who say that I wonder what they would do if it was them left all alone and it was their husbands making a bomb safe and all their laundry was done already and all their AlphaBites were in perfect order. I think they might of popped out to the pub like I did. Just to see a few friendly faces. Just to drink a little something to take the edge off. So off I toddled down the road to the Nelson's Head and I got a G&T and I took it to the corner table nearest the telly projector and I sat there watching Sky like you do. They were showing all the season's greatest goals which was fine by me. I know you'd rather watch blindfolded lads having their heads hacked off with knives Osama well that's the main difference between you and me I suppose we have different opinions about telly. If you'd ever spent an evening in front of the box with me and my husband there'd of been a lot of squabbling over the remote control. Anyway my point is I was happy minding my own and I sat there all alone good as gold and the old granddads sat at the bar talking about the footie and everyone let me be.

Now I may be weak Osama but I am not a slut. I never asked for Jasper Black to sit down at my table and interrupt me gawping at action replays. I never came on to Jasper Black he came on to me there's a difference.

You could tell straight away Jasper Black had no business being in the East End. He was one of those types who fancied a spot of

Easy Access To The City Of London And Within A Stone's Throw Of The Prestigious Columbia Road Flower Market. The *Sun* calls them SNEERING TOFFS. Usually they live about 3 years in Bethnal Green or Shoreditch then move to the suburbs to be with their own kind. I watched a documentary once about salmon swimming up rivers to spawn and that's what they're like those people. You turn around one day and they've upped sticks and gone and all you're left with is this fading smell of Boss by Hugo Boss on your nice T-shirt and a Starbucks where the pie shop used to be.

Including him there were 3 SNEERING TOFFS on Jasper Black's table it didn't take Sherlock Holmes to spot them. I was looking at Sky trying not to catch their eye but I could feel them looking up from their pints and giving each other these little secret grins on account of I was a bit of local colour. Like it was okay I was wearing a Nike T-shirt and trackie bottoms but they'd of preferred it if I'd been dressed as a Pearly Queen or maybe the little match girl from *Oliver! The Musical*. If they'd been just a bit more pissed they'd probably of taken a photo of me on their mobiles for those web sites I told you about. They thought they were very clever. My whole point is they weren't very nice and you could of blown up as many of them as you liked Osama you wouldn't of heard any of us complaining.

Anyway Jasper Black left his table and came over to mine and it was quite a surprise. Normally I'd of told him where to shove it but I couldn't help noticing he had nice eyes for a SNEERING TOFF. I mean most of them have dead eyes like they've been done over with electric shocks like Jack Nicholson in *One Flew Over the Cuckoo's Nest*. Or some of them have these little excited eyes like they've got a chinchilla up their bum like Hugh Grant in. Well. All his films. But Jasper Black wasn't like that. He had nice eyes. He looked almost human. I looked back at the slow-motion goals on Sky. I knew it was dangerous to look at Jasper Black at least give me that much credit.

—Football fan are you? said Jasper Black.

—What do you think?

—I think you're beautiful, said Jasper Black. So do my friends. They bet me 20 quid I couldn't get your name. So tell me your name and I'll split the cash with you and never bother you again.

He was smiling. I wasn't.

—20 quid?

—Yes, he said. 20 English pounds.

—Listen carefully. I'll say this slowly. Your friends are WANKERS.

Jasper Black didn't even blink.

—So help me take them for the money, he said. We'll go halves. 10 quid each. What do you say?

—I don't need 10 quid.

Jasper Black stopped smiling.

—No, he said. Neither do I really. Well maybe I can just talk with you?

—I'm married. I'm waiting for my husband.

I picked up my G&T and I made sure he got an eyeful of my wedding band. My wedding band is not silver actually Osama it's platinum it's a cracker. My husband chose it himself and it cost him a month's wages. There are some things you just can't skimp on he always used to say. I still wear it today on a little silver chain around my neck. It's as wide as runway number 1 at Heathrow Airport and it flashes like the sun but apparently Jasper Black couldn't see it at all.

—Are you here all on your own? he said.

—No. Well yes I suppose I am. Like I say I'm waiting for my husband he's a copper he's a rock he's never let me down we've been married 4 years 7 months we have a boy he is 4 years 3 months old he still sleeps with his rabbit the rabbit is called Mr. Rabbit.

—Are you okay? said Jasper Black. It's just that you seem a little overwrought.

—Overwhat?

—Overexcited.

—Oh really what makes you say that?

—Well, said Jasper Black. I only asked you if you were here alone and now I know everything about you with the possible exception of your mother's maiden name.

—Knowles.

—Excuse me? said Jasper Black.

—Knowles was my mother's maiden name. In fact it always was her name she never was married to my father.

—Oh, he said.

—I'm sorry. I don't know why I'm telling you all this. I'm never normally like this. Spilling my guts to strangers down the pub.

—Please don't apologise. Talk if you feel like talking. Get it all off your chest. I'm a good listener.

—Are you sure? You seem very kind you have a kind face my husband is in bomb disposal.

—Whoa there, said Jasper Black. Whoa whoa whoa. Just one cotton-picking minute. I'm going to go to the bar and get us both another drink and you're going to take a deep breath and count backwards from ten and when I get back from the bar you're going to start at the beginning and tell me all about it.

—Okay.

—Alright, he said. What are you drinking?

—G&T please.

—G&T it is, he said.

—Last orders, said the landlord.

So Jasper Black went up to the bar and his 2 SNEERING TOFF mates got up from their table and went in to the gents for a wee and I got up and locked them in there on account of they'd been gawping at me and Jasper Black and making blow-job faces at us ever since he sat down with me. It couldn't of been easier. There was a padlock on the outside of the door to the gents and I just clicked it shut through the metal ring that was there and went back to my table nearest the telly projector and sat down good as gold. The landlord and the old grand-dads up at the bar saw the whole thing and they were all nudging each other and smiling at me which would of been nice except that their teeth were a right state so it was a bit like a horror film actually like *Night of the Smirking Cardigan Granddads*. When Jasper Black turned back from the bar with our drinks he looked around for his mates and made a question mark face at me with his eyebrows.

—What happened to the blokes I was with? he said.

—They disappeared up their own arses. You should of seen it. It was amazing.

Jasper Black looked at me and frowned. Then he shrugged and sat down. We just drank our drinks for a little bit then. We didn't look at each other we looked at each other's drinks like they were effing fascinating. The way 2 people only do if they've known each other less than 25 minutes or more than 25 years. So I stared at Jasper Black's lager and Jasper Black stared at my G&T and after a while this loud banging started coming from the gents now his mates had found out they'd been locked in there. It got louder and louder. You might of thought the landlord would of let them out but he didn't because we do things a bit different in the East End. There are mysteries in this patch between Bethnal Green and Haggerston Osama that would of had your prophets scratching their heads I should think.

Jasper Black nodded his head at the door of the gents where all the banging was coming from.

—That's them is it? he said.

—They started it.

Jasper Black frowned again and then he started laughing.

—Good girl, he said.

—Yes I am a good girl as a matter of fact so don't think you can try anything fancy.

Jasper Black grinned.

—Last thing on my mind, he said.

—My husband is in bomb disposal he got called out on a job tonight I'm waiting for him to come home.

—Bomb disposal, said Jasper Black. The red wire or the green wire eh? That must be one hell of a job.

I shrieked when he said that about the red wire or the green wire I couldn't help myself.

—Oh god, he said. I'm so sorry that was bloody insensitive of me. Sometimes I can be such a prat oh now I wish the ground would just swallow me up.

—It's not your fault. I feel like a bomb myself tonight I'm all nerves I'm ready to explode I feel like I could go off at any moment.

—Oh you poor thing, he said.

He put his hand on my hand and I trembled.

—Will you drink up now please, said the landlord.

He meant it. 5 minutes later we were out on our ear and the banging from the door of the gents faded out when the barman locked the front door behind us.

—Will they be okay in there? said Jasper Black.

—Your mates?

—Yes.

—Do you care?

—No.

—Fine then.

We stood there looking at each other's shoes. It was raining. This is London Osama so if I do ever forget to mention the weather you just imagine it's raining and cold and you won't be far off.

—Will you be okay? he said. I'm worried about you.

—Worried about me? You don't even know me. I'm not your problem.

—There is such a thing as compassion, he said. We're all in this together. You're having a stressful night. Why don't you let me at least walk you to your house?

—Cause I don't have a house. It's a flat isn't it?

—Flat then.

—It's just round the corner. Don't worry about me I'll be alright I'll just go home and put the kettle on.

—Where are you living? he said.

—On the Wellington Estate on the corner of Wellington Row. With my husband.

—That's funny, said Jasper Black. You live right across the road from me. I see the Wellington Estate from my window.

—Bet that hasn't done anything for your house price.

—I'm sure it's nice inside, he said.

—It's alright. At least we don't have a view of the Wellington Estate.

He smiled.

—We'll walk that way together, he said.

He put his arm around my shoulders as we walked. I didn't know how to stop him doing it. I thought he was maybe just being kind. I was nervous in case my husband came past and saw us walking that way. I was nervous in case my husband got himself blown up. Oh actually I was just nervous.

When we reached the estate my husband's car wasn't parked in the road outside. The lights weren't on in our flat it was obvious he wasn't back yet.

—He isn't back yet.

I don't know why I said that. It was stupid of me. I don't know why I said anything at all to Jasper Black he hadn't even told me his name.

—Your husband isn't back? said Jasper Black.

—No. The lights are off.

—Well why don't you come to my place? said Jasper Black. I'll make you a coffee.

—I don't drink coffee.

—A tea then, he said.

—No thanks. I really should be getting back.

—But what on earth for? he said. It's not as if anyone's waiting up for you.

—I suppose not.

Even though my boy was waiting in there for me. But I couldn't tell him that could I? I couldn't tell him I'd gone out to the pub and left my only boy all alone in the flat. They might of taken the boy off me. Social Services I mean. So I froze up. I didn't know what to do. The rain was falling harder now and I was so nervous I couldn't speak or even think. Jasper Black did all that for me.

—Come on then, he said. Come back to my place. You shouldn't be alone in your state. A nice cup of tea will do you good I insist.

Jasper Black never did make me that cup of tea Osama. We went back to his place and it was one of those Georgian Gems. It was very nice and tidy inside I suppose he must of had a cleaner. His house was the other side of the road from ours and fifty yards down. He wasn't lying about that. In his lounge he put on some of that new age music with monks and no drummer. He said it would relax me but it didn't. I just kept looking out the window to see if my husband was home yet.

—My girlfriend's away, said Jasper Black.

—Oh.

—Yes, he said. She's in Paris.

—That's nice. On holiday is she?

—On business. We're journalists. She's doing a piece on Paris Fashion Week. Her name is Petra Sutherland. Maybe you're familiar with her work?

—Mmm?

—*Sunday Telegraph*? he said. We're both with the *Sunday Telegraph*. It's how we met.

—That's nice. Listen I don't know what I'm doing here I must be out of my mind I think I'll be getting back now.

—Please don't go just yet, said Jasper Black. For your own sake why don't you just stay a while and let me help you to relax.

—You don't understand.

—Oh I think I do, he said.

He stroked my neck all soft and gentle. It was like an electric shock I could feel it all up and down my body. He took my clothes

off very delicate while I just stood there shaking and then he took
his own clothes off too all of them.

—This isn't like me.

—This isn't like me either, he said. Oh god you have such lovely
breasts.

—What did you say?

—That you have lovely breasts, he said.

—Oh. My husband doesn't call them that.

He took me into the bedroom and we lay down on the bed and we
had sex ever so gentle it felt like everything was flooding out of me it
was lovely I cried all the way through it.

When I got home my husband still wasn't back. I ran a bath and
I lay in it with just my eyes and nose sticking out the water. I was
thinking nothing much. When the bath went cold I put on my pink
dressing gown and wrapped a towel round my hair and I went to
look in on my boy. He looked so peaceful. I felt very peaceful too I
lay down on the floor beside his bed and went to sleep. When I woke
up the room was full of pink light from the sun through the curtains. I heard my husband's key in the front door and I went to meet
him in the lounge.

—How did it go?

My husband was drinking his Famous Grouse. He looked up
at me.

—I'm still here ain't I? he said.

I smiled at him.

—Yeah love. Yeah you still are.

He went to sleep with his clothes on. I lay down beside him with
my arm over his chest. I listened to him breathing. I was very happy
I was still thinking nothing much.

*   *   *

They say you are a FIEND Osama but like I say I don't believe a
word of it. I've seen you in your videos. You give me the shivers and

you look like a gentleman. My husband was a good man he was a gentleman too. You would of liked him. Maybe you should of thought about that before you blew him up. They say you believe in paradise. They say you believe that if your people kill anyone innocent then you're doing them a favour because they will go to be with Allah. I wouldn't know about that. My husband didn't believe in Allah he believed in his kid and Arsenal football club.

I always liked the football but my husband and my boy were mad for it. My husband used to take the boy to all the home games. The fun used to start the night before. Before we put the boy to bed my husband would run around the flat with the boy on his shoulders. They would sing 1 NIL TO THE ARSENAL till the upstairs neighbours banged on the ceiling. They were Chelsea fans upstairs. You live in the mountains with your Kalashnikov Osama sending god's fiery vengeance down on the heads of the prophet's enemies so you might think football isn't that important. Well it is.

Sometimes the upstairs neighbours would come down and bang on our door. It drove them crazy when my husband and my boy sang 1 NIL TO THE ARSENAL. The neighbours would scream at us to eff off and bang on the door with their fists. Well that just made it worse because my husband and my boy would start singing 2 NIL TO THE ARSENAL. The more fuss the neighbours made the worse the Arsenal was going to beat them to nil. All of it gave me the jitters I don't mind telling you.

After the singing the boy would be overexcited and laughing and giggling like a lunatic. We couldn't get him off to sleep for love nor money. Mum he would say mum mum mum come quick there's something in my room. I'd rush in. What is it? I'd say. Nothing he'd say I fooled you ha ha ha. He was 4 years and 3 months old. You couldn't be cross with him. That boy had such a beautiful smile. He was just pleased to be alive.

—Go to sleep little monster or you'll be tired for the big game. Arsenal can't win without you they need the support.

—But I'm not sleepy mum, he'd say.

—Go to sleep or I'll have to fetch your father.

—I'm not scared of him, he'd say. My dad is the best dad in the world he's better than. Than. Than.

—Than what? Eh little monster? What's your dad better than?

—Monkeys, he'd say. My dad is better than monkeys and and and.

—And what?

—Tizer, said my boy.

It sounds silly Osama but sometimes I'm pleased your people blew them both up together. If my boy had survived he would of missed his father. It would of made him so sad. I never could bear for my boy to be sad so if someone has to be sad now I suppose it might as well be me.

When the boy would finally go to sleep it was always late and we would sit on the sofa drinking beers. Just me and my husband. One Friday night we had an argument about the football. I came right out with it.

—I wish you wouldn't take the boy to the game. He's too little. It makes me nervous.

—Nervous? said my husband. What is there to be nervous about?

—Well you know. The violence.

—Ha ha, said my husband. Crowd violence at a football game. That's a laugh considering I defuse bombs for a living.

—I know. Well that makes me nervous too.

—Listen love, he said. Football crowds aren't how they used to be. It's a family game now and anyway I'm a copper I'm a big bloke I can handle myself.

—It's not you I'm worried about. It's the boy. He is 4 years and 3 months old he still sleeps with Mr. Rabbit.

—Oh for Christ's sake, said my husband. You think I don't look after him? You think I'd let anyone touch a hair on his head? I'd kill them first.

—Alright. But it still makes me nervous.

—Everything makes you nervous, he said.

And he was right oh god he was absolutely right I could feel death rushing towards us.

That night my husband was exhausted he'd had a hell of a day and to top it off he'd blown 250 quid on the wrong horse at Doncaster. I shouldn't of got him to make love to me I should of just let him be but my nerves were screaming and I thought maybe he could bring it out of me. But no it was miserable sex and the terror stayed inside me my husband just made it worse. He was full of fear himself I could feel every one of those 250 quid he lost knotted in his muscles when he held me. Afterwards we just lay in the dark looking at the ceiling. Neither of us could sleep. The upstairs neighbours had mates over.

—I'm going to kill those bastards, said my husband. Drinking and shouting all hours of the night. Don't they understand there's families in these flats? What the hell is that they're listening to anyway?

—It's Beyoncé.

I knew the names of all the singers Osama I watched a lot of telly in the daytime you see.

—I don't mean who is it, said my husband. I mean what kind of music do you call that?

—It's R&B.

—It's a horrible bloody racket is what it is, said my husband. Look at this. The bass is so loud you can see the ripples in my water glass.

—I wish we were rich. If we were rich we could live in a house not a flat. It's only the poor who have to suffer each other's music.

—What are you on about? said my husband. We're not poor.

—Yeah alright but I mean look at us.

—Don't start, said my husband.

—Start what?

—Don't start on about money, he said. You think I need bloody reminding?

I sighed and I stroked his face in the dark.

—No love. I'm sorry.

—No, said my husband. I'm sorry. You deserve better than me.

—Don't ever say that love I'm so proud of you. You're a good man. You never think twice when you get the call. You go out and you save people's lives.

—Yeah, said my husband. But it shreds my nerves to buggery and when I get home those same people whose lives I saved are making our flat shake with what was her name again?

—Beyoncé.

—Yeah that's it, he said. Beyoncé. Sometimes I wish we just let the bombs explode.

I stroked his hair he didn't mean it. We lay there for a long time with the neighbours' music banging through the ceiling. My husband's eyes were open. He was all feverish and sweaty looking up at the ceiling.

—Fuckers, he said.

—You don't have to swear love.

—I'll fucking swear when I fucking well want to.

—Don't swear it makes me jumpy when you swear.

—Calm down love, said my husband.

—No you calm down. You're the one who lost 250 quid. How am I meant to feed the boy and put clothes on him when you carry on like that? Why don't you effing well calm down?

My husband looked at me like I'd slapped him round the face. I suppose it was a shock on account of I've never been a moaner but I was losing it and Beyoncé wasn't helping by shouting CRAZY RIGHT NOW down through our bedroom ceiling so loud it made my back teeth buzz.

—Oh fuck this, said my husband. I don't think we can carry on like this. My nerves are shot and you're half mental with worry all the time. You're turning into a hysterical woman.

—I am not hysterical.

—Yes you are, he said.

—NO I AM EFFING WELL NOT HYSTERICAL.

I grabbed my water glass and I smashed it against the wall. The water and the glass burst all over the carpet and I burst into tears. My husband held me very tight and stroked my hair.

—It's alright love, he said. It's not your fault. Anyone would be the same with all this stress.

I turned on the bedside light and I lit one of my husband's ciggies. My hands were shaking. The music from upstairs got even louder. The ceiling was heaving. Now the bastards were dancing up there. They were the NEIGHBOURS FROM HELL. I smoked the ciggie down to the filter and I threw it across the room like I never would of done in my right mind. I may not be a saint Osama but I am very house proud.

My husband stared at me like he was seeing something for the first time. The ciggie landed where the carpet was soggy from the broken glass water and it hissed out. I suppose that's when my husband made his mind up.

—You know what I'm going to do? he said.

—No. What are you going to do?

—I'm going to quit the force, he said. I'm going to get out while I've still got my health and you've still got your marbles.

—Oh god love. That's brilliant do you really think you could? What would we do for money?

—I know a doctor, said my husband. A police doctor. I did him a favour once back when I was in uniform. His boy got arrested for drugs. It wasn't anything really. Just a few pills. The lad was no worse than anyone his age. I flushed the pills down the khazi. No sense in making trouble for them. They were a nice family. Anyway. This doctor. If I go and see him and tell him my nerves are shot. Well. He owes me a favour. He can write me a ticket.

—Ticket? What do you mean a ticket?

—Well, said my husband. A ticket means you go on sick leave indefinite. I'd still get 3-quarters pay so there'd be no pressure. I could find another job.

—Oh god love could you really?

—Yes of course I could, said my husband. I'm 35 years old I could retrain.

I smiled in the dark. My husband. Leaving the force. I couldn't believe it. It was so wonderful.

—Oh god love imagine it no more call-outs no more stress. You'll lay off the bookies and we'll move into a nicer place and we'll laugh all the time and watch the telly together in the evenings. We'll watch whatever you like okay? And we'll make a brother or a sister for the boy. Okay?

—Okay, said my husband. Yeah. Okay.

I smiled at him.

—Come on love.

—Come on where? he said.

—Just come with me.

I took him into the lounge and I pulled him over to the stereo.

—Come on love. Help me choose a CD that'll drive the neighbours mental. We'll turn it up really effing loud. Give 'em a taste of their own medicine.

My husband started laughing.

—Oh you crazy cow, he said. I love you. How about Phil Collins?

—Phil Collins. Yeah that would wind them up alright but I was thinking of something even more annoying how about Sonny & Cher?

—Christ love, said my husband. We only want to piss them off we don't want to make them lose their will to live.

—Okay then. How about Dexys Midnight Runners?

—Perfect, said my husband. You are an evil genius.

We took the speakers and we turned them on their backs so they pointed straight up at the neighbours. My husband switched on the stereo and he turned the volume to max. My husband knew how to pick a good secondhand stereo. Ours was a monster. It used to be in a police pub in Walthamstow. Just the roar it made without a CD in it was brilliant. It was like a plane taking off.

We giggled at each other. The upstairs neighbours were in for it alright.

—Ready? said my husband.

—Ready.

—Contact! said my husband.

My husband put the CD in. He pressed PLAY and we ran into the kitchen. We held hands and crouched on the floor. It was scary. It was like an earthquake the way the plates rattled when Dexys Midnight Runners sang COME ON EILEEN.

When the song was over we went back in the lounge and we switched off the stereo. Everything went very quiet. Then one of the neighbours shouted from upstairs.

—Don't ever try that again you bastards, he shouted. Or I'm calling the police.

—They won't do nothing, my husband shouted back. The police love Dexys Midnight Runners and I should bleeding know. I'm a copper myself.

The neighbours went quiet after that and they didn't turn their music back on.

—Ah peace at last, said my husband. Thank fuck for diplomacy.

Then I remembered something. I put my hand up to my mouth.

—Oh god. We forgot all about the boy. All that racket. He must of been terrified.

We went to his room we opened the door we thought he'd be howling but he wasn't. He was just lying there fast asleep. He'd kipped through the whole thing hugging Mr. Rabbit I swear the ordinary rules of sleep did not apply to that boy.

We went next door and lay down on the bed. It was lovely and quiet now. My husband went to sleep straight away. I lay awake for a little while just feeling so happy. My husband was going to leave the force. No more waiting up for him watching *Holby City*. No more worrying my boy was going to lose his dad. It was so wonderful I couldn't believe it was true. I shook my husband awake again.

—Oh Christ what is it love? he said.

—Did you really mean it? What you said about leaving the force?

—Of course I meant it, he said. You ever known me not to do what I said?

—No. When are you going to do it?

He looked at me and sighed.

—First thing Monday morning, he said. Now will you let me sleep?

I smiled. I started to fall asleep myself. You can see I had my downs but I was often so happy in those days. I've gone through a lot of changes since then Osama but if you looked very carefully and the light was right I expect you could still see the memory of that happy time in me. Hidden but not quite invisible like the POLICE letters down the side of our old Astra.

*   *   *

They say you visited London when you were young Osama. I suppose you saw the nice bits did you? Did you see the Houses of Parliament? Did you walk down Knightsbridge on a sunny Saturday afternoon? Did you shop at Harvey Nick's? Did they politely ask you to leave your Kalashnikov at the cloakroom?

And I expect you watched the homeless in the squats and the subways? Did you see the crack girls on the game? Were you amazed how cheap the girls sell themselves in London? They'll let you do them for the price of a Happy Meal for their kids most of them. Does it worry you like it worries me?

So if you saw both Londons Osama then tell me this. Which London is it that Allah especially hates? I'm asking because I don't see how a tourist could hate both Londons. The SNEERING TOFFS London and the EVIL CRACK MUMS London I mean. Sorry Osama for calling you a tourist I don't mean to cause offence I'm just saying I don't see how you can hate the whole of London unless you actually live here on less than 500 quid a week.

One thing you start to hate when you live in London is the way rich people live right next to you. They'll suddenly plonk themselves right next door and the next thing you know your old street is An Upcoming Bohemian Melting Pot With Excellent Transport Links which means there are posh motors boxing in your Vauxhall Astra every morning. My husband always noticed the motors.

It was the morning after he promised to quit the force and he spotted a really nice one. We were outside in the street in front of the estate. It was May 1 and the sky was blue and it was nice and warm just like you want it to be on May Day. My husband was carrying the boy on his shoulders and both of them were grinning like idiots. They were wearing their Arsenal shirts because it was Saturday and it was the big day. Arsenal were at home to Chelsea. The upstairs neighbours were out too and they were wearing their Chelsea shirts. We were walking to our Astra and the neighbours were walking behind us. They were giving it the old mouth but we ignored them.

The good motor was parked in front of our old Astra.

—Look at that, said my husband. Aston Martin DB7. Hell of a vehicle.

He took our boy off his shoulders so he could look in the windows. The little chap pressed his nose up against the glass. It was all black leather in there.

—0 to 60 in 5 seconds flat son, said my husband. 400 horsepower. Take her up to 170 maybe 180. The force don't have anything that goes that quick. If a villain wanted to give us the run around in one of these things we'd have to go after him in a chopper.

—Chopper, said our boy. Chopper chopper chopper.

He grinned. He loved that word.

Then they climbed in our old Astra and drove off. The boy pressed his nose against the window glass and I waved him goodbye. I don't even remember if he waved back. I wasn't really watching I was thinking about what we needed from the shops. It's funny but you don't think about death you think about running out of crisps and toilet roll. I never saw my husband or my boy again.

I went to the shop and I bought toilet roll bacon eggs choc-chip ice cream crisps chicken kievs butter bin bags and beer. The ice cream was a treat for my chaps when they got back from the game. It was my boy's second-favourite thing after his dad. On the way back from the shop I saw Jasper Black and he was about to get into the Aston Martin DB7.

—Hello there, he said.

—Alright. That's a nice motor. I'll bet it does 0 to 60 in 5 seconds flat. I'll bet it does 170 maybe 180.

—Gosh, said Jasper Black. I didn't know you knew cars.

—Well that just goes to show you don't know anything about me at all.

—I'd like to get to know you better, said Jasper Black.

—I'll bet you would but I'm afraid that won't be possible.

—Excuse me? said Jasper Black.

—You heard. The other night was a mistake. My husband's a good man I should never of cheated on him.

—Well can't we at least talk? said Jasper Black.

—Nope. My choc-chip's melting.

—I suppose I should really be going too, said Jasper Black.

—Well off you trot then. Wherever you're going I reckon you can still make it if you get a wriggle on. Your motor does 180 miles an hour after all.

Jasper Black laughed.

—I'm off to a football match actually, he said. Arsenal are playing Chelsea.

—Yeah I had heard. My husband and my boy are there.

—They say it's going to be quite a game, said Jasper Black.

—I didn't have you down for a football fan.

—Oh I'm really not. Not in the slightest.

—So why now?

—Petra, said Jasper Black. My girlfriend. She insists I must at least try to get up to speed with the game. I seem to be the last man in England who isn't. I'm failing to hold my own at dinner parties.

Last week Petra gave me an ultimatum. For god's sake Jasper she said. Do you have to be such a snob? If you don't drag yourself out of your ivory tower and along to a football match this very weekend I'm moving back to Primrose Hill. Petra does that sort of thing you see. Drama. She's not like you.

—So what did you say to her?

—I couldn't say anything. It was all a bit awkward. We were having supper with two of Petra's girlfriends. Sophie and Hermione. They're painters.

—Good for them. Good steady trade. People will always need painters.

—Ah, said Jasper Black. Well they're not that sort of painter actually. They paint canvases. Mainly post-representational. They're very Hoxton. They're the kind of girls who'll talk about football and cook you something ghastly like eel pie. Which one's expected to find deliciously ironic. Rather than actually delicious if you see what I mean.

I was standing there holding my shopping bags with my mouth half open.

—I'm sorry, said Jasper Black. I'm boring you aren't I?

—Yeah you are.

In fact Jasper Black was boring me so much I was trying not to dribble.

—You're very plainspoken, said Jasper Black. You say exactly what you think don't you?

—Yes I do. You should try it. Saves a lot of brain work.

—Alright then I will, said Jasper Black. Here goes. I think you are the most original woman I know.

—You don't know me you twat.

Jasper Black looked up and down the street and lowered his voice.

—We slept together, he said.

—Doesn't mean anything.

—You really believe that? said Jasper Black.

—Nah.

Jasper Black looked down at my shopping bags.

—So we do know each other a little bit. And I think you're a very original woman.

—You can't know many women.

—Oh but I do, said Jasper Black. I really do. I work on a national newspaper. The office is absolutely hissy with women. Do you know the *Sunday Telegraph*?

—Well I don't know. Has it got big red letters across the top and lots of girls with massive melons?

—Um no, said Jasper Black. That would be the *Sun* or possibly the *Mirror*.

—I know. I'm only pulling your leg. Of course I know the *Sunday Telegraph*. It's the big pompous one.

—Oh ha ha ha, said Jasper Black.

—Yes. I am poor but I am not completely thick there is a difference.

—I never thought you were thick, said Jasper Black. I think you are very real. What? Why are you laughing?

—Well. I've been called a lot of things by a lot of people but no one's ever called me real before. They probably thought that was bleeding obvious.

—I'm sorry, said Jasper Black. You must think I'm an idiot.

He blushed and fiddled with his car keys. I thought I might of overdone it.

—Nah. You're not an idiot. You're sweet. You're an idiot for not liking the football though.

Jasper grinned.

—I suppose I've just never seen football's appeal, he said.

—It's cheap and people like you aren't into it. Next question.

—What about you? said Jasper Black. Aren't you going to the game?

—Me? Oh I never go to the games it makes me nervous. I just watch on telly. Don't get me wrong though. I love the Arsenal. Have done ever since I was a girl.

—I don't think I could ever get behind a team like that, said Jasper Black. I'm too fickle. Still. I do have a hell of a nice car.

He nodded his head at the Aston Martin DB7 and laughed. I laughed too.

—There's something nice about a man who doesn't take himself too serious.

Jasper shrugged. I would of shrugged back at him only shrugging isn't easy when you're holding 2 Tesco bags so I just said something stupid instead like I know how.

—Listen. If you really don't give a monkey's about the game you might as well come up with me and watch it on telly. I'll tell you everything you need for your next bloody dinner party. I'll talk you through why the Arsenal are the greatest team on earth.

—Are you serious? said Jasper Black. I do hope you are because I'd love to.

—It's just for the company. I want to get that clear. I mean you can talk if you want but we aren't going to have sex again.

—Really? said Jasper Black. What a shame.

—Yes. I mean it was lovely and everything but there isn't going to be any more. I was in a state when it happened. I was a bundle of nerves but now I'm over it. I love my husband and he's getting out of bomb disposal first thing Monday morning. So I'm not going to get in a state any more. And now that's clear as mud do you still want to come up?

—Well that depends, said Jasper Black. You're not going to feed me eel pie or anything are you?

—No. I'm making fish fingers. It isn't irony it's lunch.

Up in the flat I stuck the telly on. It was the buildup for the big game. Viv Anderson and Andy Gray were moaning on about how the new stadium didn't have the same atmosphere as Highbury. Then they started joking about what Gunners fans were really calling the place instead of Emirates effing Stadium and it was a laugh on account of Gunners fans have a terrible mouth on them so they weren't allowed to actually say it. They were showing a shot of the new ground from the air and you could see the supporters arriving in 2 big rivers 1 red 1 blue. They never let the fans mix in the roads round the stadium. Well you wouldn't would you? You think you've seen jihad Osama but I'm telling you you haven't seen anything till you've seen what happens if they let Arsenal and Chelsea fans mix going into a game.

The atmosphere was incredible even Jasper Black was gawping at the telly. There was a huge roar coming from the supporters already inside the ground but more and more were arriving all the time. 60 thousand they reckoned the new stadium could hold and it looked like it was going to have to. It was May Day and it was lovely and sunny and it was the last game of the Premiership for both clubs and the Gunners were only 1 point ahead of Chelsea so no prizes for guessing half of London wanted in to that game.

I left Jasper Black in the lounge while I put the fish fingers under the grill. I always loved fish fingers ever since I was a little girl. I love watching them turn from yellow to browny gold always exactly the same.

—4 alright for you?

—Yes, said Jasper Black. 4 is perfect.

—Good. We'll have them with chips.

I got the chips out of the freezer and into the microwave. Jasper came in from the lounge and just then his mobile rang. He flipped it open and said hello Petra and held the phone a bit away from his ear. I heard Petra's voice coming out of Jasper Black's phone and it sounded posh and tinny like the Queen of England wrapped in BacoFoil. Jasper Black looked straight at me.

—Yes, he said. Yes I'm on my way to the match now. What? Oh god Petra don't you have enough shoes already? Well alright then. Do try to leave a little something in the bank account. Just in case we need to buy anything tedious like food or electricity. Yes. Yes I will fuck off now. You be a good girl. Kiss kiss. Bye.

Jasper closed the phone back up and looked at it for a second before he put it in his pocket.

—So that was Petra, he said.

—Shopping.

—Yes, said Jasper Black. She does that.

—Do you love her?

—Yes.

—So what the hell are you doing here?

—Can I look around your flat? said Jasper Black.

Jasper Black started walking around the flat looking into the other rooms. It didn't take long there were only 4 of them. The bathroom the lounge and the 2 bedrooms.

—So this is your little boy's room, he said.

I supposed it was. I mean I couldn't see where he was looking I was still in the kitchen with my eye on the fish fingers.

—You've done it up terribly nicely, he said.

—Yes it's a cracking room my husband built the bed and I sewed the curtains.

Jasper Black came back into the kitchen. He was carrying a photo of my boy.

—You must be ever so proud to have such a handsome son, he said.

—Yes he's a pretty little boy. Takes after his mother ha ha ha.

—Yes, he said. I can see where he gets the looks from.

—You want kids?

—I'd love kids, said Jasper Black. It's just that Petra would take them out shopping and I don't think the global economy could survive the adrenalin rush.

—Hmm?

The microwave pinged. The chips were ready. Jasper Black looked out of the kitchen window down into the grubby backside of the estate where the plastic bags swirled.

—Seriously though. I'd love kids, he said.

—What's stopping you?

—It's not the right time in Petra's career, he said.

—On the up-and-up is she?

—We both are, said Jasper Black.

I put the chips out onto 2 plates.

—So what do the pair of you actually do for your living?

Jasper Black shrugged.

—Petra does fashion and I do social comment, he said. We're columnists. We write the first thing that comes into our heads.

I looked at him funny.

—What? he said. You think all that bullshit writes itself?

—No I mean I wouldn't of thought you'd say that.

—I'm sure Petra wouldn't, he said. I'm sure she'd tell you her lifestyle column constituted a useful social barometer and a zesty forum for the exchange of invigorating ideas.

—But you don't reckon?

Jasper pushed out his bottom lip and held up the photo of my boy.

—I reckon it would be different if I had a child, he said. I reckon I'd have a hard time convincing myself that my 800 words a week were making his world better. I wrote a piece about AIDS in Africa last month. I don't know anyone with AIDS. I've never been to Africa. But my piece won a prize. So fuck it. Is that going to be enough chips?

—It's going to have to be.

I served up the fish fingers next to the chips and we ate off our knees in the lounge watching the telly. Kickoff was at 3. The stands were already packed and the crowd was deafening it always made me jumpy.

—I'd forgotten how delicious fish fingers were, said Jasper Black.

—It's no trouble it was all frozen.

The telly roared. The players were out of the tunnel now. They were warming up on the pitch.

—So talk me through it, said Jasper Black. Tell me what's going on and what would be a good result.

—Well we're in red and Chelsea are in blue and a good result would be if we thrashed them so bad they never felt like kicking a football ever again in their pathetic little lives.

—Wow, he said. You really care about this don't you?

The telly was showing the starting lineups. I cleared the plates away. Jasper Black followed me back into the kitchen. I turned around when I got to the sink and I looked at him standing there in his smart clothes all fidgety.

—Look. I don't know what this is all about. What exactly is it you want with me Jasper Black?

—See? he said. There you go again getting straight to the point. Clearing the air. It's very original.

I ran hot water into the sink. I gave it a squirt of original green Fairy Liquid.

—Well? I asked you a question. What do you want from me?

—I don't know, he said. I've been asking myself the same question endlessly since the other night.

—Because if you need a new girlfriend then that isn't me. And if you want a child you're going to have to sort that out between you and Petra aren't you? I've already got a family and I love them. All I need for the rest of my life is to fall asleep with them every night and wake up with them every morning.

—I know, said Jasper Black. I would hate to do anything to spoil that.

—Don't flatter yourself. I won't let you do anything to spoil it.

—God, said Jasper Black. You're so different from Petra.

—Yes I can imagine. About 100 grand a year different I should think.

—Not what I meant, said Jasper Black. You're not into all the endless bullshit. You're strong.

—Strong? Don't make me laugh. I'm a bundle of nerves. You've seen what I'm like.

—You were just having a stressful night, said Jasper Black. What I mean is you're strong because you know what you want.

—Don't you have what you want? Posh newspaper job. Aston Martin. That'd be enough for most people I should of thought.

—I thought that was what I wanted, said Jasper Black. You make me think I want different things. Simple things. Fish fingers. You bother me.

Well that made me laugh.

—I think I quite like bothering you Jasper Black.

My heart started hammering Osama I couldn't believe what I'd just said I would of done anything to take it back but it was out now wasn't it? I could hear my voice inside me screaming here you go again you terrible bloody girl. Your husband hasn't been out of the house half an hour and here you go again.

Jasper Black grinned. I took off my trainers and my socks and I handed them to him. He reached out and took them like a lemon.

—Does this bother you?

—Um, said Jasper Black.

I took off my jeans and my T-shirt. I folded them over Jasper's arm. The one that was holding my trainers.

—What about this? Does this bother you?

—Yes, said Jasper Black. Look at me I'm getting all flustered.

—Well then. See what happens when you get yourself mixed up with the hoi polloi.

I stuck my tongue out and I took off my bra. It was brilliant watching his eyes go wide. It's true what the *Sun* says. THEY ONLY WANT 1 THING. I handed my bra to Jasper Black and he reached out and took it. He held it up and frowned like he didn't get what he was supposed to do with the thing. It's the same way you'd hold a tax demand from the Inland Revenue Osama. Just after you took it out of the envelope and just before you shoved it down the back of the sofa along with all those letters begging you for mercy.

—I don't know what to say, said Jasper Black. This really isn't what I had in mind.

—Yeah. Well listen don't take this the wrong way but you're one of those people who if we waited till we knew what you had in mind we'd be here all day and then it wouldn't matter what it was you had in mind because my husband would be back home and he'd kick your teeth in.

Jasper Black swallowed.

—Fair point, he said.

—Yeah. I do try to be fair.

I took off my knickers and I tucked them into his shirt pocket. I was grinning like an idiot. On the telly next door the ref blew his whistle. The crowd gave a roar. The game was starting. I skipped into the lounge and lay on my tummy on the sofa watching the telly in the altogether.

Robert Pires made a long run down the left side and Jasper Black laid his hand on my bum. I shivered. Pires gave it to Cesc Fabregas. Fabregas ran the ball between 2 blue shirts. Jasper Black ran his fingers down between my buttocks. Fabregas looked around for support. I raised my bum up a bit and Fabregas found Thierry Henry. Jasper Black found my clitoris and Thierry Henry struck it on the half volley and I gasped. Thierry Henry's shot went in sweet and low and so did Jasper Black the crowd went wild. Chelsea walked the ball back to the centre line Jasper Black was working his fingers in and out of me the crowd on the East Stand were singing 1 NIL TO THE ARSENAL. I smiled I was so happy. We were going to win the Premiership it was obvious. I knew my husband and my boy were singing their hearts out there on the East Stand. They would of been feeling great. I was feeling great too.

Neither side had many chances in the next 10 minutes. The game went all scrappy. I looked out at the street through the net curtains. Jasper Black was inside me all the way in very smooth and nice. I watched the street so calm and quiet in the sunshine. I sighed it was all so perfect. I half closed my eyes. Out on the street 3 kids were mucking around on their bikes. Turning in slow circles with the sun flashing on their spokes. An old dear was walking back from Tesco with her shopping trolley. She swerved to go round some dog mess. It was a perfectly ordinary day. My husband and my boy were happy. Jasper Black was moving inside me and there were hot shivers shooting all through my guts while I watched those kids turning circles on their bikes. It was a perfectly ordinary day in heaven.

I started to moan. The shivers were all through my body now flashing up and down my spine and exploding in my fingertips. I had to bite on the sofa cushion to stop myself screaming. There was a roar from the telly. Gael Clichy and Pires were playing 1-2s fast up the left. Jasper Black was moving quicker inside me it was obvious Arsenal were going to score again I was going to explode I couldn't stand it. Pires lifted the ball across to Robin van Persie then van Persie struck it on the volley then Jasper Black was gasping. I felt gorgeous and you could see van Persie's shot looping high and wide then curling back in towards the goal mouth. The Arsenal fans were coming to their feet behind the goal in their red shirts red hats red scarves their mouths were open they were screaming and I was screaming too. Everyone knew it was going in. The keeper was beaten and my whole body was in convulsions and you could see the ball curl in towards the goal tighter and tighter and then the whole East Stand exploded in flames.

*   *   *

At first I thought the telly was bust. There was a flash and I thought the tube was blown. But the ball was still there and the goalposts were still there. It was just the stand behind the goal that had disappeared in a white cloud. It looked like a fog bank. I wondered how fog had suddenly got itself into Arsenal's brand-new stadium like that.

All those fans that had been standing up to scream for the goal. Well. They were just gone. I couldn't work it out. I was watching the ball. It was still curling in towards the goal and then it slowed down in midair. Now it was shooting back the way it had come. It was flying backwards from the goal and I couldn't work it out. I started counting. I know it's daft really but I just started counting the way you do when you see lightning. The picture on the telly wobbled. The camera was shaking. The sound cut out. Everything went very quiet. Jasper Black stopped moving inside me. Oh fuck he said oh fuck oh fuck oh fuck. One, I said. Two three four.

I was just counting. I was thinking nothing much I was watching the telly. The fog bank faded into a big dirty ball of smoke and orange flame boiling up where the East Stand used to be. The keeper was flat on his face he wasn't moving. The flames rolled over him. Van Persie was still looking where his shot had gone. He followed the ball with his eyes. The ball flew back towards him and bounced right beside him and so did a man's arm. It was a strong hairy arm. A chippie's arm maybe. You could see the tats on it. The hand was open like it was reaching for something. The arm hit the ground hand first. It tumbled end over end for a bit and then it stuck into the turf. There must of been a spike of bone or something sticking out of the arm and the spike jammed in the ground. It looked like some chippie was trying to climb out of the earth. Van Persie was just staring at it. Fuck fuck fuck said Jasper Black oh my fucking Jesus Christ. Five I said. Six seven eight.

Some of the players were down and the rest were running now. They were running for the tunnel ahead of the waves of smoke and fire and some of them didn't make it. The other players had their arms up to cover their heads because half the Gunners fan club was falling down around them in bits. There were feet and halves of faces and big lumps of stuff in Arsenal shirts with long ropes spilling behind them like strings of sausages I suppose it was guts. All of it was falling out of the top of the screen. It didn't seem real. I looked out at the street. It was still very sunny and quiet out there. The old dear was shuffling off up the road and the 3 kids were still turning slow circles on their bikes. Nine I said. Ten eleven twelve.

Then the windows of the flat started to rattle. There was a low boom and then a sharp bang and the windows shook harder. After the first boom was over it echoed and rumbled all up and down the street. It went on for the longest time this thunder. The kids stopped their bikes and looked up into the blue sky. They couldn't work it out. I couldn't work it out myself. I only found out later that the telly pictures travelled faster than sound.

Jasper Black pulled out of me. I felt so empty. There had been something inside me but now there was nothing. I thought about my husband and my boy in their Arsenal shirts and I looked back at the telly. The smoke was everywhere now. The picture had gone almost dark it was like night had fallen on the stadium. The crowd was bursting onto the pitch. They were running in all directions. It was a total panic under this rain of blood and chunks. The crowd couldn't see where they were going with all the dark and the blood. They didn't have a chance. Lots of them fell and the ones that were still running ran over them. Then it all stopped.

Sky put on their test card. It was just a black background and the Sky logo and a message that said WHY NOT UPGRADE TO SKY DIGITAL? Yes I thought. Why not?

Jasper Black was pulling his trousers on. He tripped over and stood up again he was saying Oh god this is just too horrible. He tripped again he couldn't make his arms and legs do what he wanted. I stood up and I went over to the telly and changed channels to the BBC. I was cold. I was wearing only my birthday suit.

It was *Grandstand* on the BBC and they were showing the racing. It was nice to see those horses scampering round on the soft green grass. Things looked very neat and tidy at Lingfield or Chepstow or wherever it was. No blood no fire just miles and miles of nice clean white fence. It was like fish fingers it was a great comfort always the same round and round forever and ever amen. But then the horses vanished and Sophie Raworth was just sitting down in the newsroom. Her skin was very pale. She didn't have her nice orange makeup on and she looked like the ghost of Sophie Raworth it made me nervous. She looked at the wrong camera and she fiddled with the thing in her ear. News is just coming in she said.

—Come on. Let's go.

—Go where? said Jasper. I must get to the paper it'll be all hands to the pump this is huge.

—Bollocks to the *Sunday* bloody *Telegraph*. My husband and my boy are at that game.

—Oh my god, said Jasper. Yes of course they are.

—You can take me in your car.

—I'm afraid there's no chance, said Jasper. All the roads will be completely blocked.

—I don't think you heard me. My husband and my boy are at that game. I need to get them home.

I was crying now and I couldn't see straight. I was shaking I was thinking please god don't let them be hurt. Jasper Black looked at me standing there all skin and pubes and tears. Then he looked at Sophie Raworth on the telly and he looked at the clock.

—3:30, he said. We don't go to press for another 6 hours.

I was thinking please god don't let them be hurt or if they must be hurt please make it so it's only a little bit. Please god it would be alright if one of them had a cut or something. Even a broken arm. But not the boy okay? I don't want him hurt. If there must be a broken arm oh god it ought to be my husband he's a strong bloke he could handle it. He'd make the best of it he'd have a plaster cast and all his mates would sign it. I looked at Jasper Black.

—Please. Please. I need you to take me to the stadium.

—Look, he said. The emergency services can handle this. They don't need people getting in their way.

—You don't understand. My husband's leaving the force. He's going to tell his boss first thing Monday morning. We're going to be safe. Please help me get them home. Him and the boy. So I can make them their tea. Please please please.

I was howling now I was standing in front of the telly with my arms crossed over my tits and there was snot coming out of my nose.

—Oh god, said Jasper. Look at you you poor thing. I'm being a complete prick of course I'll drive you there. You mustn't worry I'm sure they're both fine.

—Thank you oh thank you I just need to get them back here that's all.

—Yes of course, said Jasper.

He looked very serious. I went to the front door.

—Stop, he said. You're not wearing anything.

I looked down at myself.

—Oh yeah.

I went back to the kitchen and pulled on my clothes. My jeans had ketchup on from where my boy squirted the bottle too hard at breakfast.

—Oh dear these aren't very clean. I'll just go and change them.

—No, said Jasper. If we're going we must go now.

*   *   *

The street was empty. Everyone was inside watching their tellies it was just me and Jasper Black out there. We got into his car. Like my husband said it was a lovely motor but I didn't really notice. I was thinking what I was going to make for tea when we all got safely back. Chicken nuggets probably. Jasper Black started the motor. It didn't sound like our Astra it sounded angry it made me tremble. We drove off fast. The tyres squeaked and we flew over all the speed bumps. It didn't matter on account of any other cars there were had pulled over to listen to their radios. We drove past Jesus Green and nobody was walking their dogs there. We turned onto Columbia Road and there was nobody shopping. No wasters drinking cider from cans and no yummie mummies pushing their babies in 3-wheel buggies.

—It was like this when Charles and Di got married.

—What on earth are you talking about? said Jasper Black.

—The empty streets. The Royal Wedding. I was only a little girl but I remember the streets were empty like this. Everyone was inside watching it on telly weren't they? I went out in the middle of it to get sweets and it was just like this. It was like the world had stopped. Then it was like this again when she died wasn't it? Everyone stayed inside. Nobody could believe it. We were all watching the news.

—Yes, said Jasper Black. Well listen it isn't Diana this time it's something quite else. I think you need to prepare yourself mentally. I really don't know if it's a good idea me taking you there like this. I don't know if it's the right thing for you.

—Don't worry about me. It can't be as bad as when Diana died. And we all got through that didn't we?

Jasper Black just looked at me.

—Why don't you take a few deep breaths? he said.

We were racing through Hoxton when I saw it. The tower of smoke ahead of us. It must of been miles away still but it was so tall. I followed it down from very high in the blue sky getting darker and darker as it got nearer the ground. Near the top it just seemed to drift but at the bottom before it disappeared behind the tower blocks you could see the black smoke boiling. It looked angry and urgent like it was late for something.

—Deep deep breaths, said Jasper. Just keep breathing for me there's a good girl.

We turned onto the New North Road. I watched the tower of smoke growing bigger dead ahead while Jasper Black drove us like crazy. When we got onto Canonbury Road there were cars and buses just stopped in the middle of the street. People had their doors open they were standing there listening to their radios and watching the smoke. Jasper Black swerved round all of them. The tyres screeched the motor roared and we kept going but it was getting tight. There were coppers at Highbury and Islington. They had the Holloway Road all closed off with cones and bikes with their lights going but we managed to get off up Highbury Crescent and into the backstreets.

The tower of smoke was bigger now. It was fat and horrible.

Great sheets of black were blowing off it and spreading all around us. It was starting to get dark. Jasper Black turned the headlights on and got the wipers going. He pressed some button on the dashboard to stop the outside air coming into the car but it was no good. I started coughing and so did he. He slowed down and we weaved through all these ambulances that were stopped on Bryantwood Road and then we had to stop too. We didn't have a choice. There was a girl lying in the road.

We'd sped up again just before I saw her. We were nearly on top of her. Stop stop stop I shouted. Jasper stamped on the brakes and turned the wheel hard. The brakes locked and we skidded sideways up the street. I was looking out of the window on my side. I was watching the girl coming closer and closer. Her eyes were open staring into the sky. She wasn't moving. She was wearing a Chelsea shirt. I remember thinking it would be a shame if we hit her. Even if she was only a Chelsea fan.

The next thing I remember was Jasper pulling me out of his motor. There was this huge crushing thing in the front seat with me. It was all pushed into my face and my tits and it was hurting me. I could hardly breathe.

—What's this big thing?

—It's the airbag, said Jasper. It saved your life I should think.

—Who are you?

—My name is Jasper Black, he said. We hardly know one another. We've had sex twice. I am very fond of you. I was driving you to a football ground that exploded.

—Oh. Yes I remember you now. You're very kind to me.

—Does anything hurt? he said. Do you think I can safely move you?

His voice was different. I looked at him. There was blood on his face and his nose wasn't quite where it ought to of been. I giggled I don't know why. He pulled me out of the motor. My legs were shaky but they held me up. I looked at the car. We'd gone into a parked van and everything was bent and broken.

—Oh no. Your beautiful motor. It's all spoiled. And your poor face.

I reached up to push his nose back into the right place but he wouldn't let me. He grabbed my wrist.

—It's okay, he said. It's been broken before it's no big deal.

—Oh my god. The girl.

—We missed her, said Jasper Black.

—Oh good. Where is she?

—She's over there, he said.

I looked where he was pointing and I saw her. She was still just lying there in her Chelsea shirt looking up into the smoke. I remember thinking that was pretty casual. I went over to her with Jasper Black holding me steady and I kneeled down beside her. I shook her and I asked if she was okay.

—She won't answer.

—That's because she's dead I'm afraid, said Jasper Black.

The girl was so pretty. She was an ASIAN STUNNER. She looked Chinese but she was too pale. She could of done with a bit of makeup. I stroked her face and her skin was very soft. Around us there was a terrible noise of sirens. All the car alarms in the whole street were going off and the hazard warning lights were flashing through the smoke and the darkness. It was a terrible noise but the girl just lay there. She looked ever so peaceful. She didn't look like someone whose side had been losing 1–nil. Then I noticed there was a red streak coming out from under her head and running away to the kerb. All the blood had gone out of her and into the storm drains it made me nervous. I stood up.

—Come on. Let's go and find my husband and my boy. Never mind your car. We can all get home on the bus.

I walked off up the road with the smoke hurting my lungs. I was coughing and dribbling I couldn't help it. It was getting darker. Jasper Black came with me. He was coughing too and there was blood pouring off his face. Now in the darkness I saw them. First just a few and then so many. Some wore red shirts some wore blue shirts and some had their shirts off so you couldn't tell. They were coming down the street towards us and they made no sound. Their eyes were wide and glassy and quite often they stumbled but they never blinked. There must of been hundreds of them shuffling out of the smoke. All of them with their eyes huge and wide like things pulled up from very deep in the sea.

A blond woman came towards us. She was wearing gold earrings and an Arsenal shirt and pink Kappa trackie bottoms. Her makeup was nice and her nails were done but she was screaming again and again and again. I wondered how come she was screaming when everyone else was so quiet. She went past us still screaming and I turned to watch her go past. Then I saw what it was. On her back she wasn't wearing anything at all. The Arsenal shirt and the Kappa trackies were all burned off her. There was just burned skin all the way up her legs and her back. You could see where her knickers had melted into her. The back of her head looked like something you take out of the oven. She disappeared into the smoke still screaming screaming screaming and I wondered why nobody was helping her. Then I remembered my husband and my boy and I forgot all about the woman.

I grabbed the next person that came past. He was a small man with a thin moustache about 50 years old I suppose. I grabbed him round the shoulders. He stopped and looked at me the way my boy used to look at strangers when he was 9 months old. All unsure.

—Have you seen my husband and my son? Have you seen them please? Think carefully my husband is a tall man 6 foot 1 very strong wearing an Arsenal shirt. My son is about this high he is quite strong too for his age he has ginger hair he would of been carrying a rabbit the rabbit is about so big he has purple paws and green ears his name is Mr. Rabbit.

The man stared at me.

—You're going the wrong way darling, he said.

—Please. Please think carefully.

The man broke free. He went away down the street. I started shouting.

—HAS ANYONE SEEN A LITTLE BOY? HAVEN'T ANY OF YOU SEEN A LITTLE BOY 4 YEARS AND 3 MONTHS OLD? HE MIGHT HAVE A RABBIT WITH HIM OR HE MIGHT NOT.

Nobody stopped. They were all pushing past me. They smelled of smoke and sweat and burned meat. I was crying again. Jasper Black was beside me.

—Come on, he said. Let's get you out of here. This is the wrong place for you.

He tried to turn me round but I shook him off.

—No. I'm going to find my chaps. You can come with me or not I don't care.

I went on up the street. It got darker and darker. My eyes hurt so bad I had to close them and I just carried on blindly bumping into people and motors. It was like going up a horrible river. I just made sure I kept on in the other direction from the people I bumped into. I was close to the stadium now. Whenever I opened my eyes there were coppers and firemen all mixed up with the people. The firemen had these masks on and tubes attached to big air tanks on their backs. They were going the same way I was. I held on to the back of one of the firemen and I walked along behind him for a while letting him make a way for me.

We came up under one of the huge entrances all metal and glass soaring up into the black sky. There were coppers there and press. The press were trying to get in. They were pushing into the police line and jumping all over the place flashing off their cameras into the smoke. The coppers wouldn't let them into the stadium and there was shoving and fights. I got down on my hands and knees and crawled in through the legs of the whole lot of them. I got kicked around and stamped on something terrible. I felt things break inside me but I kept on crawling. My elbows got torn ragged and I couldn't breathe. It hurt so bad but I didn't care. I was going to find my boy.

The ground started to get slippery under me. I was inside the stadium now. I could tell because the noise of car alarms was fading. All I could hear was shouts and police radios and people screaming. I was very weak. I knew there was stuff burst inside me because I looked under my T-shirt and my tummy was swelling up from the inside. I tried to stand but I fell over straight away. The ground was so wet and slippery and I was so messed up. I thought if I tried to crawl upwards I might get to dry ground. I found these steps and I started to go up them and this wet sticky stuff was running down and then I smelled it and I puked and puked. I was crawling to find my boy up a waterfall of blood and now it had my puke in it too.

I don't know how long I dragged myself through the smoke and the crackle of the police radios with the firemen's boots stamping down all around me. It was very hot and the blood hurt when it dried on my face. Someone stood on my hand. I heard it break. I heard the bones crunch past each other and I saw my thumb sticking out all funny but I couldn't feel it. I was thinking nothing much. I was thinking of those 3 kids turning slow circles on their bikes. Of me lying next to my husband and listening to him breathe.

I went up steps and down steps with dead bodies and bits of bodies lying all over them. The bodies were like islands in a river with the blood all piled up in sticky clots on their uphill sides. After a long time I felt grass under my hands and I knew I was on the pitch.

The floodlights were on. I could see them shimmering in the sky through the smoke. I crawled until I found the halfway line and then I followed that until I got to the centre circle. I suppose I had the idea I'd be able to see more from there. But in the centre circle there were just 2 men fighting. One of them was wearing a Chelsea shirt the other one was Arsenal. I crawled closer to them. I wanted to ask if they'd seen my boy.

The 2 men fighting weren't players they were supporters. They were both big lads with bellies. I suppose they were the YOBS THAT GIVE FOOTBALL A BAD NAME. The one in the Arsenal shirt was burned very bad you could see the bone showing through his arm.

The one in the Chelsea shirt had mostly lost an ear it was hanging off the side of his head upside down. The Arsenal man hit the Chelsea man in the face with his fist and he grabbed a big lump of something the Chelsea one had been carrying. The Chelsea one fell but he stood up again and he kicked the Arsenal man in the privates. Kicked him so hard he dropped the lump again and the Chelsea man grabbed it. Can't you see he's Arsenal you wanker? the Arsenal man shouted. He's one of ours. No shouted the Chelsea man I know who this is we paid 4 million for him last year. Bollocks you did the Arsenal man shouted and he hit the Chelsea man in the stomach and grabbed for the lump but he missed and it rolled across the turf towards me.

When I saw what they'd been fighting over I fell unconscious and I stayed that way for 3 days.

*   *   *

Well Osama I sometimes think we deserve whatever you do to us. Maybe you are right maybe we are infidels. Even when you blow us into chunks we don't stop fighting each other. I suppose you heard the details on the radio did you? It must of been strange for you sitting there in your cave with your Kalashnikov. I suppose you were sitting out on the rocks before dawn listening to the goat bells when one of your men came over to you. Did he say Hey boss turn on the radio we did it we blew up Arsenal's shiny new stadium? Did you smile? Did you hear the news breaking while you watched the sun rise over the mountains?

They stopped the Premiership but it was weeks before the score stopped rising. At first they said 700 dead but it went up and up. The survivors wouldn't stop dying you see. They had so many bits blown off them they couldn't really help themselves.

Did you wake up early each morning with the air very crisp and cold in your cave high up above the valley? Did you step outside and stretch and piss against a rock? Did you watch the shepherds driving the goats up the hillside? Did you sit in a high place where you could look down on the whole valley? Did you clean your Kalashnikov while you waited for the sun to come round the shoulder of the mountain and warm you up? Did you turn on the radio and listen to the death toll rise to 750 to 800 to 912?

912 was what it was at when I woke up in hospital. The sheets were very stiff and white. The radio was on in the ward. 912 dead it said. A nurse came in. She saw I was awake and she came over to me.

—Are you alright dear? she said.

—Do you have any news? Do you know if my husband and my boy are alright?

—Steady on dear. We don't even know who you are yet. In a while someone will be along to ask you some questions but for the moment you just try to get some rest.

—But I've got to know now. I've got to know where they are.

—Just get some rest dear, said the nurse. I'll send someone along.

I started screaming then. The nurse brought a doctor over and he gave me an injection. It was very nice I went straight back to sleep.

When I woke up again it was the next morning and the sun was blazing through the windows. They could of done with a clean. There was a BRAVE 82 YR OLD GRAN in the bed across from me. She'd lost both eyes at the stadium and she was singing 1 NIL TO THE ARSENAL again and again and again with her voice very high and crazy. The radio was still on in the ward. 966 dead it said. They kept calling it The Catastrophe. The BBC never did work out what to call the thing you'd blown up. After days of calling it the Emirates Stadium or Ashburton Grove or Gunners Park they gave up and started calling the whole thing May Day. Everyone did. Like you hadn't just blown up a football ground you'd blown a hole straight through our calendar.

I felt like I'd fallen through the hole. Day and night didn't mean anything it was all just buzzing neon. I was right at the back of the ward farthest from the windows with only fluorescent strips and green lino and the stink of disinfectant. I couldn't count the days all

I could count was the bodies. THE NUMBER OF CONFIRMED DEAD FROM THE MAY DAY ATTACK HAS RISEN TO 966 they said on the radio. WITH DOZENS MORE STILL MISSING OR IN CRITICAL CONDITION. The ward sister brought me a nice mug of tea.

Did one of your men bring you tea that morning Osama? In one of those little glasses? Did you look him in the eye and wonder if you could trust him? I suppose you must wonder that all the time. 966 is a lot of Gunners fans to blow up if you don't want it to come back to you one day. Did you drink your tea while you looked your man in the eye? Then did you walk out in the hot sun and breathe in the smell of dry goat shit and wild thyme? Did you turn on the radio and hear them say 966 dead? Did you turn to the east? Did you put your mat down over the rocks and kneel down to pray? Well I prayed that morning Osama. Maybe we were praying for the same thing. I was praying for the death toll to go up to 967. God forgive me but I was praying for the BRAVE 82 YR OLD GRAN across the ward from me to die and leave me in peace.

I marked the days off by scratching little lines in the guardrail of my bed like they do in the films. Each time the nurse came to give me my sedatives I reckoned it was a new day and I made a new mark although now I come to think of it the nurse might of come round twice a day. So maybe it was 16 days after May Day or maybe it was only 8 when the death toll finally reached 1,000. I think the whole country had been secretly hoping it would get there. It was like a relief when it happened. It felt like we'd got somewhere we'd all been headed for a long time.

I must of wished very hard because it was the singing granny who made it a clean 1,000 god bless her. I woke up very early one morning and it was all nice and quiet so I pushed myself up on the pillows and I looked across at her. It was obvious she was dead. The bandage had slipped off her eyes. There were just 2 holes there. The holes were packed with bloody gauze. The poor dear looked like a dirty old doll losing her stuffing. I was thinking YOU'RE NOT

SINGING ANY MORE. I started laughing I never knew I was so funny. The doctor came running. He shone a light into my eyes and suddenly I was back on the pitch with the floodlights shining down on me through the smoke. I started screaming again and the doctor gave me another injection.

When I woke up again the radio said 1,003 dead and they were playing a song Sir Elton John had just written called ENGLAND'S HEART IS BLEEDING that was going to be number 1 probably forever or at least until the sun and the stars burned out like cheap lightbulbs and the universe ended for good and it couldn't come soon enough if you asked me but nobody did.

The death toll didn't go up any more from 1,003. They started to work out what had happened. I listened to the BBC every morning. They reckon you sent 11 suicide bombers. I don't know if that was on purpose but you fielded a whole team. Nobody knew why you made them be Arsenal fans. Does Allah hate the Gunners even more than he hates the West in general or was it just a coincidence? Maybe you decided it on the toss of a coin the same way the 2 captains decide which team's going to kick off.

They reckoned what happened was that 11 of your men got into the ground with bombs under their Arsenal shirts. They had season tickets for seats in the East Stand. When van Persie took his shot on the volley everyone in the East Stand jumped up. The real Arsenal fans were shouting YES! but your men were shouting ALLAH AKBAR! The police played the TV pictures back frame by frame so they could read their lips.

Your men pulled the triggers on their bombs. 6 of them were wearing fragmentation bombs and the other 5 were wearing incendiaries. It had never been done before the experts said they were the most terrible suicide bombs ever used in the history of the world. They must of looked huge under those Arsenal shirts but nobody would of said anything except maybe oi you fatty guess who ate all the pies. There's a lot of beer bellies in the Gunners fan club you see. Well I suppose there's a lot less now.

They reckon maybe 200 people died straight away blown to bits by the fragmentation bombs. I hope my husband and my boy were part of that 200. That's a funny thing to say isn't it Osama? When I was growing up in the East End me and the other girls used to push our dolls around the streets in tiny little prams and pretend they were our real babies. I don't recall us ever wishing they would get blown to bits by fragmentation bombs. I don't think that was how the game ended ever. But that is what I hope. I hope my chaps died straight away. One second thinking YES! and the next second thinking nothing much. Because the 200 people who died straight away didn't have to suffer. 803 other poor sods didn't have it so easy.

After the first blast anyone who could still run did run. There was a stampede. People were legging it in all directions. Even the ones who had small bits blown off them like noses and hands and whatnot. There was phosphorus raining down all around. It set fire to the seats. To the stands. To the clothes and skin and fat of the fallen bodies. There was an inferno. They reckon maybe 500 people were crushed and burned to death while fire rained down on the East Stand. And that left 303 people still to die.

The hospital porters said that after the first ambulances started to arrive they had to borrow rubber boots from the operating block. They would swing open the ambulance doors and the blood would be an inch deep on the floor. They said some of the things that arrived on the ambulance stretchers didn't really look like anything.

Only 2 people died not at the ground or walking away from it or in the ambulances or in the hospitals. Quite near the stadium they found a couple of Chelsea fans hanging from a big old Victorian lamppost. They were strung up very high with electrical cord around their necks. You must of seen them Osama. They were in all the papers swinging very slow and peaceful in their blue shirts against the blue sky once the smoke had cleared. They stayed up there for the whole of that long sunny May evening. The authorities had to clear away all the abandoned motors before they could bring in the cherry-picker crane to take them down. While they were waiting for the crane to come the police sent a marksman to shoot the seagulls that wanted to eat the dead men's eyes. Nobody ever found out who strung those men up there.

*   *   *

It took a few weeks before it wasn't just May Day on the radio. Then some of the normal programmes came back but even the normal programmes weren't normal any more. Every day they put *The Archers* on in the ward but even *The Archers* kept banging on about May Day. It's funny Osama but the first time I realised May Day was actually real was when I heard Eddie Grundy sitting on his tractor and moaning about it.

By that time anyone who was going to die had died and now it was time for us that were left to get better. I had a broken knee and a broken hand but the doctors said it was my internal injuries meant I wasn't going anywhere for a while. So I lay there day after day watching the relatives coming on to the ward to visit their loved ones. Some of the relatives looked happy when they visited but some of them were heavy with sadness and you could tell their next visit was a grave. Then there was a third kind of visitor and they were the unhappiest of all because they weren't visiting anyone in particular. They were looking for a relative that was listed missing. They came like ghosts outside normal visiting hours and their eyes stared very hard at each of us ladies on the ward. You could see them patiently trying to turn our faces into the ones they were missing. Even through all the painkillers it made me cry Osama I would of given anything to look like their missing relative just for 1 second just to give us all a moment's hope.

The day they told me my husband and my boy were definitely dead was the day Prince William came to visit. The nurses were excited. They ran up and down the ward changing our sheets. Men in suits came with mirrors on sticks. They went along the whole ward looking under our beds for bombs. A photographer came and he put a gadget up to my face.

—What's that?

—It's a light meter madam, he said. You're too pale.

—My husband and my boy are missing. You'd be pale too.

The photographer ignored me.

—Please can you get this one some makeup? he said.

A leggy girl came over. She had a long plastic case like the box my husband used to keep his fishing tackle in. She put it down on my bed and opened it up. There was a whole makeup studio in there. She gave me some foundation and then she did my eyes and my lips.

—There, she said. You look lovely. Fit for a prince.

Now 2 men on ropes came down the outside of the building. They washed the windows so clean you couldn't tell they were there. A doctor wheeled in some big shiny medical contraptions with lots of flashing lights. He put one next to each of the beds on the ward. When he plugged in the machine next to my bed I propped myself up on my elbow to look at it. The doctor blinked at me.

—What does that do?

—It shows that the NHS is fully equipped for the 21st century, he said.

—Are you going to connect me to it?

—Not unless you're planning on having renal failure, he said. It's a kidney dialysis machine.

The doctor nodded at me and went off to install the next machine at the next bed. The nurses were frantic by now. They kept popping off to the night station to do their own makeup. They forgot to give us our painkillers. 4 coppers in uniform came on the ward. They stood by the doors. They had curly wires going into their ears. Their eyes were all over the place. Everyone went quiet. Now we were just waiting for Prince William. Then a woman came. She walked straight over to my bed with everyone's eyes following her. This woman wasn't a doctor or a nurse. She was wearing an ordinary tweed suit it made me nervous. She pulled the modesty curtain around my bed.

—Hello there, she said.

—What are you pulling that curtain for?

—Well, she said. I'm doing it because I have some news I'm afraid. I thought you might appreciate a little privacy.

—Is it my husband and my boy? Have you found which hospital they're in?

The woman shook her head. She was middle-aged. 50 maybe or 60. She looked like she hadn't slept in days.

—They're not in any hospital, she said.

—Well then. Just tell me where they are. I'm nearly better. I should think the doctors will let me go home soon. My boy'll be missing me and I bet he's not eating properly. I mean he's a good eater but you have to cook his greens just right or he won't touch them. Kids eh?

I laughed but the woman didn't. She just looked at the floor. She swallowed. She looked back up at me. Now she looked 500 or maybe 600 years old.

—I'm very sorry, she said. Your husband and your son are dead.

—No. No I'm sorry but you've made a mistake. They're just missing. If they were dead they would of told me so straight away.

The woman took a deep breath and spoke very softly.

—The identification process took a long time, she said. Because their bodies were so badly degraded.

—Degraded?

—Burned, she said. In the end we were able to establish their identities only by recourse to their dental records.

I lay there propped up in bed. I was looking at the green modesty curtain that hung all around us. It was nice in there. It was like being in our tent the one and only time my mum took me camping. The woman in the tweed suit squeezed my shoulder. I smiled at her.

—Dental records eh? That's funny. My boy used to love going to the dentist. He got all excited about the special chair. The dentist used to give him toothpaste to take home. You want to take care of your teeth the dentist said. You might need them one day.

I looked at the woman.

—And he was right wasn't he? The dentist I mean.

The woman looked at me.

—You're in shock, she said. It's going to take a while to sink in. What I'm going to do is I'm going to fetch a chair and bring it next to your bed. I'll sit right here with you and be with you and we'll talk it over.

—Alright. He always had such lovely teeth. My boy.

Then the woman reached up and pulled back the modesty curtain and there was Prince William stepping into the ward with the photographer walking backwards in front of him. There were a dozen people in suits walking all around him.

—Oh, said the woman in tweed.

She took a step back. I watched Prince William looking up and down the ward. So tall and handsome. We always liked the royals in my family Osama I don't care what people say about them. I wasn't thinking about anything much except maybe oh look there's Prince William. I grinned at him and he walked over to my bed. He stood over me. Doesn't he have his mother's eyes? I thought. He looked bigger than he seemed on telly but then we always did have quite a small telly.

—Hello there, he said.

He was smiling. He was RELAXED BUT SINCERE. Well that's what it said in the *Sun* the next day. In the caption underneath the photo the photographer was taking from the end of my bed.

—How are you feeling? said Prince William.

I looked up at him. Prince William had nice teeth very bright and even. I was remembering how I used to sit our boy on the edge of the basin to clean his teeth. They're only your milk teeth darling I always used to say. But we've got to get into the habit of brushing. Then when you're my age you'll have teeth like Mummy's. Zero cavities. Well we did get into the habit of brushing. It was fun. I never did imagine that teeth was all that would be left of him. I mean you don't imagine such things do you? I looked up at Prince William. I knew it was my turn to speak but I couldn't. I felt a huge misery welling up inside me. It was physical. Prince William frowned. Relaxed but sincere.

—How are you feeling? he asked again.

I leaned my head out of the bed and puked all over his shoes.

I puked again after Prince William had jumped back. It was like my whole life was coming out of my mouth and spattering on the green lino floor. When it was finished I felt so empty. Prince William stared at me while one of his men wiped my puke off his shoes. He had this strange expression on. It wasn't cross. It was far away and sad. You could see him thinking to himself well I suppose I am the prince of all this then. I am the prince of this poor blown-up kingdom and one day all these blown-up people will be my subjects and I'll be able to do nothing for them. I'll live in palaces pinning medals onto lawyers and architects while these people watch their tired faces get older each morning in dirty bathroom mirrors. It was that sort of an expression.

I stared back at Prince William. I felt so bad. The smell of my puke was rising from the floor. He smiled at me but you could still see him thinking I am the prince of puke and one day I shall be king of it.

—I'm so sorry your royal majesty.

—Please don't worry, he said. It's quite alright.

But we both knew it wasn't.

After Prince William was gone they unplugged all of the kidney dialysis machines and they wheeled them out but they left us where we were.

*   *   *

That woman in the tweed suit was a grief counsellor. All the time I stayed in hospital we met twice a week to talk through my loss. She honestly thought it would help. She'd never lost anything more serious than car keys. One day she said I might want to join a group of other mothers who lost their children on May Day but I said nah I mean I've never been much of a joiner.

In the end the view out of my window did me more good than talking. They moved me to a bed by the window where there was day and night again and I could look out on the whole city. The hospital I was in was Guy's. Maybe you know it Osama? Maybe you've studied just how to blow it up?

Guy's is tall and grubby and full of poorly people. You can see it from all over London if you ever need reminding you're going to get very poorly and die one day. From my window at the top of Guy's Hospital I could see everything from Canary Wharf to St. Paul's with the Thames cutting under it all like a fat slow wound.

London and me healed slowly. They worked on the city to make it stronger and they worked on me too. How they fixed me up was they put plaster casts on my broken hand and knee and stitched me up inside to stop the bleeding. I had 4 operations and then that was that. There was nothing to do except lie there and wait for myself to get better. For 6 weeks I just stared out of the window watching them fortify London.

Mena was my favourite nurse. She was a nice girl. She lived in Peckham but her family was from the East. Kazakhstan or Uzbekistan or one of those Stans anyway. She told me 2 or 3 times the name of the place but I never could recall it. I remember she said it was much nicer than Peckham but that doesn't rule out much of the world does it?

Mena's shift was earlies. She took my temperature at 5 a.m. every morning she always started with me because I was always awake. Then if the other ladies on the ward were still asleep she'd sit on the end of my bed and we'd watch the sun rising up over the docklands. First the towers glowed rosy pink. Then the sun rose huge and dirty orange like a soft warm egg yolk. It wobbled up through the haze getting smaller and harder and brighter until you couldn't look at it any more. Mena used to hold my hand while we looked out over the city. Her hand was small and hard like the sun.

—So many people down there, she used to say. So many people under this sunrise. So many people waking up right at this moment. And all those people want is to get through today.

She was like that was Mena. Philosophical. I'd definitely of killed myself if it hadn't of been for her.

Mena's philosophy started with Valium. Every morning she brought me 2 of them from the medical store. Little blue pills they were. I took 2 of those pills each day. One for my husband and one for my boy. Mena used to take a couple herself. That's how come she was always so calm. You can't blame her for that Osama you'd probably be the same if you had to live in Peckham.

The weeks went by like that without any fuss. 2 Valium to be taken with sunrise. The nicest prescription. Me and Mena watched each morning what they were doing to London. First they stopped boats using the river. All those boat buses and disco ships and sight-seeing barges. Well they just stopped them. They did it so you couldn't blow up the Houses of Parliament Osama. With some horrible floating disco full of Semtex and Dexys Midnight Runners. They drained the life out of the river till it was just an empty vein with police boats drifting up and down it like white blood cells.

Next they closed some of the bridges. I never did work out how that was meant to help. Maybe they thought it would demoralise your Clapham cell Osama if they had to go via the M25 to bomb Chelsea. Tower Bridge was the strangest. They raised it early one morning while me and Mena watched and they never lowered it again. It just stayed open after that. It looked like London was expecting something big to come up the river.

What really changed the view though was the barrage balloons. One night I went to sleep as normal and the next morning there they were. Me and Mena watched them shining silver in the rising sun. Bobbing on the ends of their cables. It gave me the shivers. It was like a dream. Mena gripped my hand and I could see the goose bumps on her arm.

—This is terrible, she said. This is grotesque. The world has gone crazy.

—I don't know about that darling. It all makes sense to me. I reckon it's to stop them flying planes into the tall buildings.

Mena looked at me. She had the nicest eyes Mena did. They were the colour of caramel creams.

—Listen, she said. I know this might sound awful considering what you've been through but we have to get things in perspective. After I finish on this ward I go down to the cancer ward. I'm telling you it is like going into hell. Do you know how many people die in this country each year of lung cancer?

—No.

—33 thousand, she said. 33 times more people than died on May Day die mainly avoidable deaths every single year. I watch them suffer with tubes jammed in every hole of their bodies. It takes them months to die. But does this country declare war on smoking? No it does not. Instead we turn London into a fortress. As if that could possibly stop the terror. As if they couldn't blow us up just as easily in Manchester or Pontypridd or the queue for the ice cream van on Brighton beach.

I could feel Mena's hand trembling. I watched a tear run down the side of her nose. It stopped on her upper lip. She had these very fine golden hairs there the way some Asian women do. I held her hand it was warm and strong.

—You're very young. You don't have any kids of your own do you Mena?

She shook her head. Another tear fell from the end of her nose. It fell glittering in the sunrise down through the barrage balloons and the disinfectant smell. It splashed down on the lino out of sight.

—If you had kids. Well. If you had kids I reckon you'd be all for anything they can do against the terrorists. It doesn't matter if it's logical or not when it's your own kids.

—It matters if you're Asian, said Mena.

—You what?

—Look, she said. My family is Muslim right. Do you have any idea what it's been like for us? I don't think you can imagine how it feels for me just to walk to work since May Day. To see the hate in people's eyes when they look at me. I have become the enemy number one. There's this one caff I walk past on my way here. The builders and the market traders go there. This morning I saw this old man in there. He must have been 80. He was reading the paper and the headline on the paper was THE CRUELTY OF ISLAM. He looked up when I walked past and he sneered at me. He actually curled his lips. That is the nature of this madness. It fills the sky with barrage balloons and people's eyes with hate.

We sat there very quiet me and Mena while we watched the streets waking up far below. London was a misty floating city with the thousand thick cables of the balloons lifting it into the sky. When it was time for Mena to go she turned to me. Her face was so young but the tears ran down it old and empty like the Thames. She took 4 little blue pills from her top pocket and popped 2 into her mouth and 2 into mine. She crunched her pills between her teeth. They worked faster that way.

—Merciful pills, said Mena. Now we'll forget about it all for another day. The hours will go by like a dream.

—Lovely.

—Yes, said Mena. My god isn't cruel. A cruel god wouldn't help us forget. This is why we say Allah Akbar. God is great.

I smiled at her and crunched my pills and felt the bitter taste spread across my tongue.

—Allah Akbar.

Mena gave me this lovely smile and touched her right hand to her heart.

—I must go, she said.

—Thank you darling. I'll see you tomorrow.

But I didn't see her tomorrow. In fact I never did see Mena again.

The next morning the sun turned up just like normal but Mena didn't. A new nurse came instead. She was Australian. She was blond and cheerful. You couldn't look at her without thinking 19 YEAR OLD PARTY GIRL SHARLENE IN HOSPITAL ROMP.

—Hello. What happened to Mena?

—They stopped her working didn't they? said the new nurse.

—Come again?

—Muslim wasn't she? said the new nurse. Security risk. They suspended all of them from working as of midnight. This country's finally starting to get it. Don't get me wrong. I'm sure 99 percent of the Muslims are fine but if you can't trust some of them you can't trust any of them can you?

—Well when's Mena going to come back? How long are they all suspended for?

—Who knows? said the new nurse. They say the suspension is indefinite but temporary.

—What does that mean?

—Who cares? said the new nurse. I'm not complaining. I need the work.

—Yeah but they can't just stop all the Muslims from working.

—Oh they haven't, said the new nurse. Only the ones who fly planes and work in hospitals and whatnot or have access to certain information.

—This is crazy. I'm going to write to my MP.

—You go girl, said the new nurse. I hope your MP's not Muslim.

I sank back into my pillow and I waited for the last of yesterday's Valium to wear off. The new nurse didn't hold my hand. She didn't watch the sunrise with me. She didn't bring me any more little blue pills to make my mind blank. By lunchtime my dead chaps had moved into the place where the pills had been. It felt like they died again every single second.

It always started the same way. I'd start to think of my boy fast asleep in his bed. He had this pair of tiger pyjamas. I don't know if I already told you that Osama. I would think of my boy asleep very peaceful in his tiger pyjamas and I would smile. I would be full of joy I couldn't help myself. And then it would hit me right in the guts that he was gone. Then all that joy was left behind like your stomach when you drive too fast over a bridge.

*   *   *

It hit me like that every minute for days and days. It was a torture. I couldn't sleep. Everything I ate came straight back up. They put me on a drip. Whenever I looked at the drip I heard the music from *Holby City*. It made me so nervous. I lay there watching tiny bubbles rise inside the plastic tube that went up from my arm to the drip bag. I watched the bubbles rise through the London skyline between the Gherkin Building and the NatWest tower and finish up in the drip bag that floated high above me.

At night I used to climb out of my bed and crawl around the ward. I dragged the drip stand after me. It didn't steer well. It had one lazy wheel like the trolleys in Asda. I dragged it behind me banging into beds and chairs and hoping the noise wouldn't wake the other ladies on the ward. I thieved pills off their bedside tables. I never did hold with thieving. I'm not proud of it. But I ate the other ladies' pills anyway. Red pills white pills long blue capsules I didn't care. Some of it made me sleepy but none of it made me forget for very long.

Then one evening Jasper Black came. I suppose I knew he would one day. It was visiting hours and I watched him come through the same door Prince William did. He walked up to my bed. He was smiling.

—Oh god not you. Go away for Christ's sake go away I can't even look at you.

He stopped. He looked surprised. He was holding yellow flowers and a carrier bag.

—I'm sorry, he said. I'll just go then.

I turned away and looked out the window. London was still there like a horrible memory and when I turned back so was Jasper Black.

He was watching me. I prickled inside I was sure he could see everything. Like I was the patient in that game Operation. The plastic person with the see-through skin and the giblets you can take out one by one. The plastic lungs then the plastic liver then the plastic heart. I was sure he could see right into the middle of me. I watched Jasper Black looking right inside me to that place where my emptiness was.

—Are you still there? I thought you said you were leaving.

—I still will if you really want me to.

—Well I do.

—Alright, he said.

But he didn't leave. He just stood there holding his hands together in front of him the posh twat.

—Why did you come?

He didn't say anything. He walked up to my bed and sat down. There was a brown plastic chair between my bed and the window and he sat on it. He put his flowers down on the floor with his carrier bag and looked out the window. London was huge and flat and brown in the evening light. He sat there very still for a minute or 2. I was watching the back of his neck and remembering how I held him there that first time in his flat. At first it was very nice. I could even feel my hands tingling. Then I started to see what his neck would look like with his head blown off it and the blood dripping like motor oil on the green lino floor. My hands went cold.

—Why did you come here Jasper Black?

He was still looking out the window.

—London's changed beyond all recognition, he said. And I've changed too.

He turned to look at me. He was older than I remembered.

—I so nearly went to that game, he said. I was all set to go. I had my hand on the door handle of my car when I saw you. I've still got the ticket in my wallet. I can't stop thinking about it. If I had gone to the match instead of. Well. You know. Then things would have turned out. Well. You know. I came to see if I could help you.

—Really? Well you weren't much help looking for my husband and my boy.

—You disappeared into the smoke. I searched and searched for you but you were nowhere.

—Really.

—Listen, he said. I understand it must be very painful for you to see me. It isn't my idea of a perfect night out either if you want to know the truth. I didn't want to come.

—So why did you?

Jasper Black looked out of the window and then back at me.

—I couldn't get you out of my head, he said. I kept seeing this picture of you with nobody to cook fish fingers for. It's a stupid picture but you're standing in front of the grill and suddenly you burst into tears.

—You're right it's a stupid picture.

—Yes, said Jasper Black. But I wanted to come and see if you were alright. It's interesting. Before May Day I shouldn't think I'd have given a shit.

He leaned closer to the bed and touched my shoulder. I smelled him then. Oh god that clean soapy smell of him. I closed my eyes and watched the East Stand explode into smoke and flesh. I screamed. The other ladies on the ward muttered and tutted. Jasper Black took me in his arms. I didn't want him to do that. I struggled but he held me while I screamed quieter and quieter until I was only sobbing. After a long time he whispered into my ear.

—Yesterday I couldn't stand it any more, he said. I was thinking what if she doesn't have anyone looking after her? What if she's all alone in that hospital with no visitors?

—What do you mean no visitors? I'm an East End girl I've got my gran and my mum and 14 aunts and 10 sisters and all the girls from the hairdresser's all rallying round to help. All saying Cor blimey apples and pears you'll get over it love now how about a nice cup of Rosie. I've got all the support I can handle.

—But you don't, said Jasper Black. Do you?

I sighed and looked at my feet making a lump at the far end of the bed under the bright green hospital blanket.

—Nah. I've got no one.

—Well you've got me, he said.

I pushed him away from me.

—You're worse than nothing Jasper Black. When you touch me all I can see is that bloody explosion. I don't know what I was thinking with you. I wish I'd never met you. I loved my husband and my boy but I waved them good-bye and I took you home and had sex with you on the bloody sofa didn't I. And then my life blew up. I didn't deserve my husband and my boy. I'm a slut. I'm a madwoman. You know what the hospital told me? They said there's nothing left of my chaps except their teeth. I could bury the pair of them in a flower pot. And here you are to remind me.

—Alright, said Jasper Black. Alright.

He held his hands up like he was surrendering. He pushed his chair back from the bed a little way. We watched each other for a long time not saying anything. The new Australian nurse came and changed the bag on my drip. Jasper Black watched her bum when she walked off.

—Pay attention 007, I said.

Jasper Black snapped his eyes back to look at me and then he laughed and shook his head.

—I don't get it, he said. You're funny. You're pretty. How is it possible that no one visits?

—Don't get me started about my family.

—What about friends? he said.

—I said don't get me started.

He shrugged and shut up for a bit. It's an incredible sight from the top of Guy's it's a shame you have to be half dead to get a good view in London. We both just looked out of the window down at the streetlights starting to come on.

—He never found out. My husband I mean.

—How do you know? said Jasper Black.

—He would of said something.

—Maybe he wouldn't have.

—Wouldn't you of?

—Well yes I probably would, said Jasper Black. But then maybe the life I have with Petra isn't worth saving. Maybe your husband knew but he kept his mouth shut because he didn't want to spoil the life you had.

—I wouldn't know would I?

—I think it was worth saving, said Jasper Black. That's the impression I get. The life you and your husband had was actually worth something.

I pushed myself up in the bed.

—What do you want?

He leaned closer to me again.

—What is it like? he said. To be a parent I mean.

I sighed.

—Once my boy drew me a picture of a dream he'd had. I couldn't see what the picture was of. I mean you never can tell with kids' pictures can you?

—I don't know, said Jasper Black. I've never been around kids.

—Well let me tell you then. If they do an orange squiggle it might be the Death Star blowing up or it might be a carrot. And god help you if you get it wrong. So you ask first don't you. I asked my boy what's that? And my boy said it's Tigger Mummy he's giving you a hug because you're so nice. He was such a lovely sweet boy. Of course he could be a right little horror too. I don't know how many nights I stayed up with him poorly. Or how many times I had to wash his crayon marks off the walls. If it wasn't one thing it was another from 6 a.m. till we finally got him off to sleep. I used to wish I had just a moment of time to myself. And now that I do have time to myself it's the last thing I want. It's silly really.

—No it isn't, said Jasper Black. I know just what you mean. I live with deadlines on the newspaper. I loathe them but I don't think I could operate without them any more. All structure would be lost.

—Oh really. Then you'd best hope nobody blows up your precious newspaper.

Jasper Black opened his eyes wide.

—Oh Jesus, he said what a prick I'm being.

—Yeah. But I suppose you're trying.

—It's just so difficult, he said. To know what to say I mean.

—That's alright. I'm glad you came really.

—I've brought something for you, he said.

—I can see. Nice flowers. I'll ask the nurse to put them in water if you can keep your peepers off her knockers for a second.

—It's not just the flowers, said Jasper Black. There's something else too. I'm not sure if I've done the right thing. I don't want to upset you.

—What is it?

—I have a lot of contacts, he said. It's my job really. I know people in the security services. After the explosion a large number of personal effects were recovered and not claimed. Jewellery and broken watches and so forth. I got them to let me look through it all. I was looking for something in particular. I heard you talking about it and I thought I would try to find it for you because I thought it might. Well. You know. Help. Anyway I finally found it and I have it here. If you don't want it then I am most terribly sorry and I'll take it away again.

—What is it?

Although of course I'd already guessed by now. Jasper Black took Mr. Rabbit out of the carrier bag and gave him to me. It's funny but you never see the big things first do you? You see the small things. The things you know just how to fix. I took Mr. Rabbit out of Jasper Black's hand and I thought oh hello Mr. Rabbit well you have been in the wars haven't you? Look you've lost your paw. I know just what we'll do about that. We'll take a needle and thread and we'll sew that paw back up for you and you'll be right as rain just with that arm a little shorter eh. And after that we'll give you a spin in the washing machine. I know you don't like the washing machine do you Mr. Rabbit but I'm afraid there's nothing else for it. We'll pop you in on a boil wash and that should get most of these nasty black stains off you. There's a brave bunny.

Jasper Black was staring at me.

—Are you alright? he said.

I looked up at him. I realised I'd been grinning at Mr. Rabbit. I took a deep breath I could feel the emptiness inside me growing again.

—I don't understand. How come he isn't burned?

—It isn't nice to say, said Jasper Black. But a lot of things survived because they were trapped under bodies.

—Oh. Do you think these black stains are my boy's blood then?

—It's impossible to say, he said. I think you should try not to think about such things.

I hugged poor broken Mr. Rabbit. I was crying again.

—How can I not think about it? Please tell me how I can stop thinking about it because that's all I can think of. I can't think about anything else not for one second it's horrible horrible horrible. And I'm so scared all the time. I look at people and I see them blown to bits. Every teaspoon that drops sounds like bombs. I'm too scared to carry on even one more day. How can anyone carry on living in a world like this?

Jasper Black sighed.

—People keep themselves busy don't they? he said.

He turned to look out over London.

—Look at all that, he said. Under each lightbulb is somebody keeping themselves busy. Exfoliating and applying the anti-wrinkle cream. Writing long sales reports people will only ever read the last page of. Agonising whether their cock is shrinking or the condoms are getting bigger. What you see down there is the real front line in the war against terror. That's how people go on. Staying just busy enough so they can't feel nervous. And do you know what they're mostly busy doing? DIY. For a whole week after May Day the airports stayed closed and the DIY stores stayed open. It's pathetic.

People are laying their fears to rest under patio slabs. They're grouting against terror.

I looked away from the city and back at Jasper Black.

—You don't think much of people do you?

He shrugged.

—I'm a journalist, he said.

—Well I'm a person. Pleased to meet you. My flat smells of chips. I do very ordinary things like go down the shops and get my family blown to bits. I don't think you'd know the first thing about it. I really don't know what you want with me Jasper Black. I suppose you get a thrill out of slumming it do you? Do you want us to have sex again is that it? Maybe you haven't noticed I'm half dead with tubes sticking out of me. Or maybe you really do just want to help. Well if so then you can start by showing some respect for ordinary people because I am one.

—I don't think you're being quite fair, said Jasper Black.

—Oh really. Look me in the eye and tell me you just came here to help. I don't think you know the meaning of it. I don't think you have an unselfish bone in your body. I WISH YOU'D BEEN AT THAT GAME I WISH YOU'D GOT BLOWN UP INSTEAD OF MY HUSBAND AND MY BOY.

Jasper Black stood up and stared at me. He stood there very tall and pale with the lights of London glittering below and the sky all red from the sunset.

—Fine then, he said. Fine.

He turned and walked away down the ward. I couldn't bear it. The emptiness went mad inside me. I could feel its teeth biting at my stomach and its hands scratching against the inside of my skin. I shouted at him.

—Stop. Oh please don't go. Don't leave me here alone. I'm so sorry Jasper. Don't leave me here I have nobody. Nothing. NOBODY.

Jasper Black stopped but he didn't turn. He just stood there very still. I stopped shouting and I watched his back and I wondered what he was going to do. All the ladies on the ward and their visitors were gawping at us. You could see their sick eyes going between me and him. Their heads swung back and forth like in the crowd shots you get of Wimbledon. And it was your kind of Wimbledon Osama. The crowd was mostly dying and there weren't any strawberries.

Jasper Black took one slow step forward and then another one and there were tears streaming in my eyes by then so I didn't see him walk out of the ward I just heard his footsteps on the lino slow at first and then getting quicker and then I heard the big safety-glass door of the ward open and swing shut behind him. After that it was very quiet for a bit and then a horrible sound began it was the sound of the ladies on the ward ooohing to each other at the scandal of it all in their sick little whispers. I put my hands on my ears to block the vicious cows out but I could still hear them so I started screaming to shut them all up and that's when a doctor came and gave me a shot of something. After that I just lay very still and looked at the red glow on the inside of my eyelids.

*   *   *

Jasper came again the next night. I didn't think he would. I smiled so wide I thought my face would snap in half. He brought fancy chocolates and we sat there for a while not saying anything just eating those chocolates and looking out at the view.

—I'm sorry Jasper. I shouldn't of made a scene.

—Forget it, he said. I was condescending.

—I felt bad because I cheated on my husband. I still do.

He made a face.

—Oh please. You loved your husband and your boy. That was never in question and what you did with me had nothing to do with it. You were scared. You just needed a little human contact. We all get scared.

—Not you Jasper.

—Especially me Jasper, he said.

—What of? What does someone like you have to be afraid of?

—Same thing as anyone, he said. Being alone.

—What about your girlfriend?

—Petra? said Jasper Black. Let me tell you a story about Petra. After you and I got separated I looked for you but then I gave up and I drove in to the paper. The front end of the car was a mess but it still went. All the way to work I was thinking why doesn't Petra ring? As far as Petra knew I was at that match. So I was wondering why she didn't call my phone to see if I was okay. I called her but all I got was the busy signal. I thought maybe the network was saturated. So. I arrived at the paper and the place was absolutely chaotic. I mean the last thing a Sunday newspaper wants is actual news to happen. Right? On any day of the week really but on Saturday afternoon especially. And when the news is that big. Well. The place was going nuts. They decided to spike the whole paper and go to press with just 4 pages. Anyone who'd made it in to the office was set to work. I was one of the last to arrive. There were roadblocks everywhere by this time. The tube was out. People couldn't get around. So we had junior court reporters knocking up profiles of the possible terror suspects. The football editor was doing 15 hundred words on I SAW HELL. They had bloody 16-year-old interns for Christ's sake pulling together REACTION FROM AROUND THE WORLD. There were 3 hours till deadline. The chief sub had a heart attack. He actually fell down dead on his keyboard. It was insane. You should have seen it.

—Nah. You're alright. It doesn't sound like my cup of tea.

—Nor mine, said Jasper. I just wanted to grab Petra and get us out of there as soon as humanly possible. But Petra wasn't in her office. I asked around and nobody knew where she was. I started to worry. I was beside myself. I thought maybe something had happened to her in all the panic. And it had. Of course. Petra being Petra.

—Was she alright?

—More than alright, said Jasper. I found her in the editor's office writing the leader. She was the only person in the building not running around like a headless chicken. I saw her through the glass wall. She was sitting there very calm and composed drinking a Diet Coke and writing 500 words on A NATION UNITED IN HORROR. I watched her nails clicking on the keyboard. Petra has lovely nails. I tapped on the glass and she looked up at me. That's when it hit me. She looked at me as though I were a complete stranger. There was just this look of absolute blank incomprehension on her face. Then slowly I watched it change. I could see the precise moment when she recognised me. Me. Her partner of 6 years. Then I saw her raise one of those lovely manicured hands to her mouth and gasp. And I knew. She wasn't gasping because I looked a mess with my broken nose and blood on my jacket. She wasn't gasping from relief that I'd survived. She was gasping because this was the first moment since it had happened that she had even remembered my existence in the world. And she knew that I saw this.

Jasper wasn't looking at me any more. He was looking out of the window. He was talking quietly.

—So I stepped in to the editor's office. Petra took her hands off the keyboard but she held them hovering just above it. As if I were interrupting her for fuck's sake. We didn't say anything. We just stared at each other for a minute and then I walked out. I walked all the way home 5 miles through the chaos. My face was swelling up and people were saying things to me that I couldn't hear. It was like watching fishes in an aquarium. I just walked home and sat there very quietly on the sofa and when it got dark I just sat in the dark. Thinking. Petra turned up around 10 p.m. and switched the lights on. Look she said I'm sorry okay. I'm sorry I didn't call. I'm glad you're fine. I'm not fine I said to her. I can't believe you would go to work before you even thought about me. Oh god Jas said Petra. I've said I'm sorry. But they let me write the leader. The leader Jas. Don't you understand? They ran my leader word for word. This is just the hugest thing for me.

Jasper sighed. He looked pale green in the fluorescents on the ward.

—I just looked at her, he said. I don't think I've ever felt so low. I looked at Petra and I thought god you are so pretty and so clever and so much fun and such a total fucking cold heartless bitch. And I could see her looking at me and thinking don't do this to me you prick don't make me feel guilty when I know damn well you've been playing away from home. She knows you see. She knows about you and me. God knows how but she knows. Maybe she just saw it in my eyes. So there we were. Looking at each other and hating each other but not saying anything. And that's when I started to feel afraid. I looked at Petra and suddenly I realised it wasn't just her. Everyone I know is cold and heartless. Nobody rang me that night to see if I was okay. And you know why? Because I am a fucking cold heartless cunt too. Why would anyone ring me?

Jasper Black shrugged.

—I think you put it rather more delicately, he said. When you said I didn't have a selfless bone in my body. But it amounts to the same thing. My life is pointless. I have the kind of friends who aren't that curious whether or not I have been destroyed by suicide bombers. Still. There's always cocaine.

I looked at Jasper's face pale and sick under the striplights. Behind him in the night a million other lights flashed like cheap jewellery. I sighed. Bloody London. Jasper stood up from the chair and kneeled down by the bed. He laid his head on the covers by my knee.

—This world is all fucked up, he said.

—Yeah but we were born here so what can you do.

I couldn't move. I just watched him lying there. We stayed like that till visiting hours were over and then Jasper went off to spend the night with Petra Sutherland.

*   *   *

I slept even less after that. You burned up sleep Osama when you burned up my husband and my boy so I just used to sit in the brown plastic chair looking out over London. Jasper came back a couple of times and he brought me vitamins and things from my flat. I didn't need all those things half as much as I needed him to lay his head on my bed again but I never could seem to tell him.

One night I sat looking out. Jasper was meant to of visited that evening but he never turned up. It was full moon and the barrage balloons shone very still in the sky. It was Friday night but the streets were empty. There was a curfew on and it was just the police vans drifting up and down. They had numbers on their roofs and they were driving round in a pattern. I counted them coming round again and again but I still wasn't sleepy. They say to count sheep when you can't sleep Osama well I hope they work better than police vans. Where you are you probably have sheep or goats or little dead hostages to count I bet you sleep like a baby.

I lay awake and I listened to the ladies on the ward coughing and snoring and moaning for the nurse. I was so miserable that night Osama. I had no one. I looked down at the lights of London switching off one by one. I never knew there was so much light to go out. About 3 a.m. I couldn't stand it any more. Normally I would of put the telly on to take my mind off it but there wasn't any telly on the ward only Radio 4 so I decided to kill myself.

It isn't easy to kill yourself in Guy's Hospital. I suppose they make it that way on purpose I mean I probably wasn't the first girl who'd had enough. For starters the nurses don't leave anything sharp lying about. I wanted to cut my wrists but the nearest thing I could find to a knife was the edge of a plastic food tray. I snapped it in half and sawed away at my veins with the broken edge. I don't know if you've ever tried to cut your wrists with a hospital tray Osama well I wouldn't waste your time if I were you. It's more itchy than anything and after about 10 mins your wrists will be a bit red and sore but that's it.

I looked around the ward for something else to try. I'm a simple girl Osama there isn't much to me. Once I get an idea in my head I don't think about it any more. So now I'd decided to kill myself it was making me nervous that I was still alive. I decided to poison myself and quick sharp. I crawled up the ward collecting all the other ladies' pills and I ground them up into powder under the wheel of my IV stand. There must of been 20 pills at least in all shapes and colours. They made a nasty grey powder. I pricked a little hole in the top of my drip bag and I poured the powder in and gave it a good shake. The powder swirled around and the nice clean liquid in my drip bag went all mucky and vicious-looking. I was very pleased with it and I lay back down on my bed and looked out of the window and waited to die.

I was never scared. Not for one second. While I was dying there was just me and the streetlights below and this orange glow over-head like I was all alone between heaven and central London. It was very peaceful and it gave you shivers like being in church. I started thinking about my boy and whether I was going to see him in heaven when I was dead. Funny really because I never did believe in heaven. I believed in my chaps and my chaps believed in Arsenal football club and I don't know what the Gunners believed in. That's where the trail goes cold.

I closed my eyes and I saw my boy smiling at me. My boy had this extra special smile he did when he wanted to show you all of his teeth at once. He threw his head back and his mouth went wider than his whole face so he looked like one of those monster fish you see in the aquarium. Remembering my boy doing his monster smile I started laughing and then I opened my eyes and I saw the tall tow-ers of the City standing out all solemn against the orange light. I smiled because it was pretty. Then I started to wonder what I was smiling for when I was supposed to be dying. And that made me laugh. I was feeling so good all of a sudden. I looked up at the drip bag with all those crushed-up pills trickling into my arm. That's when I realised the stupid thing wasn't killing me at all it was mak-ing me feel brilliant.

Then I started feeling angry that I was feeling so brilliant. None of this was getting me dead. I decided to stop mucking about and throw myself out of the window. Like I say Osama once I get an idea in my head I stop thinking about the whys and wherefores. I suppose you could find plenty of work for people like me. So anyway I got out of bed and crawled over to the window and pulled myself up on the frame. I turned the handle and swung the window wide open. Cold air came in and I shivered.

It's funny because when it comes to the moment you don't think right okay here I go then and plummet 30 floors to your death. You think oooh isn't it chilly out? Cold is a funny one. It's impossible to remember it until you actually feel it. I don't know if you've ever jumped into freezing cold water Osama? Well it's easier to imagine yourself doing it than actually to do it. Don't you find? Once you're standing there on the edge of the mountain lake shivering in your Kalashnikov and Speedos I mean.

So I stood there for the longest time holding myself up on the window frame and shivering in my hospital nightie. Another thing. You don't notice it getting lighter do you? You just suddenly realise you can see certain things. Now I could see the outlines of the towers at Canary Wharf with the sky all milky behind them. I just stood there with the drip bag dribbling the last of those powdered pills into me and feeling better and better. Soon the sun came up. Flashing through all the brand-new concrete and glass. The dawn crept up on me and I was still alive. And that's when I saw it all. Everything.

London is a city built on the wreckage of itself Osama. It's had more comebacks than *The Evil Dead*. It's been flattened by storms and flooded out and rotted with plague. Londoners just took a deep breath and put the kettle on. Then the whole thing burned down. Every last stick of it. I remember my mum took me to see the Monument to the Great Fire. London burned WITH INCREDIBLE NOISE AND FURY is what the monument has written on it. People thought it was the end of the world. But the Londoners got up the next day and the world hadn't ended so they rebuilt the city in 3 years stronger and taller. Even Hitler couldn't finish us though he set the whole of the East End on fire. Bethnal Green was like hell my grandma said. Just one endless sea of flames. But we got through it. We built on the rubble. We built tower blocks and the NHS and we kept on coming like zombies.

You've hurt London Osama but you haven't finished it you never will. London's like me it's too piss poor and ignorant to know when it's finished. That morning when I looked down at the sun rising through the docklands I knew it for sure. I am London Osama I am the whole world. Murder me with bombs you poor lonely sod I will only build myself again and stronger. I am too stupid to know better I am a woman built on the wreckage of myself.

I looked down on the whole of London spread out under me that morning and I knew it was time for me to go back down into it.

*   *   *

I was walking with a crutch. A grubby aluminium stick with a green plastic handle. Clack clack it went on the pavement. Its soft rubber foot was all worn away. It was just the bare metal end clacking down between the old black blobs of chewing gum and the thin white streaks of pigeon shit. I hoped it wouldn't slip because then I would slip too. Clack clack clack I walked away from Guy's Hospital along St. Thomas Street.

My body was mostly healed. I was carrying Mr. Rabbit and 2 bottles of Valium in an Asda carrier bag. It was not warm and not cold. There was no wind and the sky was very low and grey but it wasn't raining. It was like they'd completely run out of weather. I was wearing my white Adidas trackie bottoms. White Pumas. Red Nike T-shirt with the big white tick. I could of been anyone. It was a great comfort. Jasper brought the clothes to me in hospital. I'd asked him to. I'd given him the spare keys to the flat. Clack clack clack.

It was an effort walking with the crutch. I was tired and out of breath. I'd lain 8 weeks in bed after all. I sat down at a bus stop on an orange plastic bench. It made me dizzy to watch the people rushing all around. I took deep breaths. I just watched my Pumas on the

pavement. My crutch had a label on it held on with Sellotape. PROP-
ERTY OF GUY'S HOSPITAL it said NOT TO BE TAKEN AWAY. Well I
peeled that label off. I was on my way to see a copper after all and
there was no point in taking chances. I scrunched the label into a
ball. I looked around for a rubbish bin but there weren't any. They'd
taken them away in case anyone tampered with them. There were
no rubbish bins any more and no Muslims with jobs. We were all
much safer.

I dropped the scrunched-up label on the ground. There was an old
dear on the bench next to me. Like I say it wasn't cold but she was
wearing a big fur coat. The kind of coat that might of cost 10 thousand quid at Harrods or a fiver at Barnardo's you couldn't tell. She
hissed like a cat when I dropped that ball of paper and Sellotape. She
had purple lippie on.

—Do you mind? she said.

I looked at her and I saw just what she would look like with her
guts blown out and her cheeks burned off till you could see her false
teeth clattering loose in her gob. Clack clack clack.

—Sorry.

I picked up my litter and I put it in my pocket.

—Good girl, said the old dear. That's the spirit. Are you waiting
for the 705?

—I don't know. I'm just resting. I'm ever so tired.

—Where are you trying to get to love? said the old dear.

—Scotland Yard. I'm going to see a copper.

—Oooh dear, she said. I hope you're not in some kind of trouble.

She shuffled away from me on the bench like she was afraid of
catching something off me.

—No. I'm not in trouble. I'm going to see a copper who works
there. He used to be my husband's super. Because my husband and
my boy are both dead you see they were blown up and all they found
was their teeth and Mr. Rabbit. Would you like to see Mr. Rabbit?

—No thanks darling, said the old dear. You're alright.

The old dear looked at me for the longest time without saying anything. The traffic roared past us. She had these small thick glasses on and her eyes looked like cheap sweets behind them.

—Well love, she said. If you're going to Scotland Yard then you need the 705. Take it till just after Waterloo then you might as well walk over Westminster Bridge. After that you want Victoria Street don't you.

She didn't say anything else. We waited for the 705 and when it came I sat near the front and the old dear went upstairs. Even though she was old and there were lots of empty seats on the bottom deck. I was crying a bit. I put my hand inside the carrier bag where I could stroke Mr. Rabbit in secret while London went past outside the bus windows keeping itself busy. I got off too early. I mean you always do on a new bus don't you? I got off at Waterloo Station and I should of waited until a couple of stops later. At Waterloo Station was where it happened. I was getting off the bus all wobbly on my crutch and I saw my boy.

My boy was holding some woman's hand. The woman was taking him into a newsagent's. It was my boy alright. It was his beautiful ginger hair and his cheeky little smile. He was pointing at something in the window of the shop and you could tell he really wanted it. It was Skips probably. He always did love Skips I mean kids do don't they? They fizzibly melt you see Osama. In one second all the emptiness in me was gone. They'd made a mistake. My boy was alive. It was so wonderful.

I went straight across the road with my crutch. A cab nearly killed me. The cabbie screeched his brakes and he called me a stupid slapper. I couldn't of cared less. I went in the newsagent's and I saw my boy straight away. He had his back to me. He was on his own looking up at the drinks fridge. The woman was at the counter buying ciggies. I went straight up to my boy. I dropped my crutch and the carrier bag. I turned my boy round I kissed his face. I picked him up and I gave him a huge hug and I buried my face in his neck.

—Oh my boy my brave boy my lovely boy.

My boy was shouting and kicking against me. He didn't smell

right either. I suppose it wasn't surprising. The woman probably hadn't been feeding him right. My boy always was fussy you see. He would eat his vegetables but you had to cook them just right for him. Did I say that already?

—Oh you poor brave boy. Mummy's here now. Mummy's back and she'll never let you out of her sight again. I bet you miss Mr. Rabbit so much well he's been missing you too. We came all the way across town to find you. Me and Mr. Rabbit. We did have an adventure! We took the 705!

Then it all went wrong. My boy got pulled away from me. One second he was in my arms and the next second the woman was holding him. She was screaming and screaming at me. My boy was screaming too. Both of them were bright red and screaming.

—Give me back my boy.

—E int your boy, screamed the woman. Git chore ands off im yer crazy car.

—Give me back my boy. Hand him over.

—But e int yours! Carn choo see? Look at im fer Christ's sake! Ave a good look at im!

The boy was sobbing. The woman was holding him right up to my face and shaking him like my eyes couldn't focus on him if he wasn't moving.

—See? she said. E's mine. Ain cher Conan?

There was snot running down the boy's face. His nose didn't look right and his eyes were the wrong colour. Suddenly he wasn't my boy any more. Suddenly he didn't look anything like my boy. I couldn't work it out.

—Oh god. Oh god oh god I don't know what I'm doing I'm so sorry.

Then the woman started ranting at me with the boy sobbing in her arms. She just went on and on. I could see her mouth moving but the words didn't make any sense. I was hypnotised just watching that mouth moving moving moving in her angry red face. She looked like one of those live crabs on the market with their pincers done up in rubber bands and their mean little mouths moving moving moving.

I turned round and I picked up my crutch and my carrier bag and I walked out of the newsagent's clack clack clack with the woman still screaming effing blue murder behind me.

You'd think it would of got better after that but actually it got worse. There I was walking down Lower Marsh Street with my heart thumping and now my poor sweet boy was everywhere. I saw him getting onto buses and going into shops and walking away down the street. It was always the back of him I saw and there was always some woman holding his hand taking him away from me. He was every little boy in London.

I don't know how you did it Osama but you didn't just blow my boy to bits you put him back together again a million times. Every single minute ever afterwards I watched my boy walk off with Sloaney mums and traffic wardens and office girls out on a shopping break and I never thought any of them looked like they could of made his tea the way he liked it. Choc-chip ice cream! I wanted to shout at them. I wanted to tell them he loved choc-chip almost as much as he loved his dad but there's no point telling people things when you're stark raving mad is there? They won't listen.

I walked across Westminster Bridge watching the empty river sliding past underneath. I shivered. It should of been nice and quiet on the bridge because it was closed to traffic but there were 2 helicopters hovering low above the Houses of Parliament. The noise was horrible. They were shocking vicious things those helicopters. They were like fat black wasps looking outwards through their glittering eyes.

There were 2 Japanese walking in front of me. Their T-shirts said 23 BECKHAM and OXFORD UNIVERSITY. They started to video the helicopters. A copper walked up to them very fast. You could tell he was trained to walk not run. He made the Japanese stop filming and he took their cameras off them. The Japanese were going nuts and mouthing off at the copper in foreign. The copper just stood there very patient and calm. He was wearing a thick bulletproof vest and a thin black moustache. I walked past the 3 of them. The copper smelled of nylon. He had a radio clipped to his jacket and there was a voice coming out of it like a bossy child shouting through a hurricane. TANGO TANGO NINER it said PROCEED TO SECTOR SIERRA 6 AND STAND BY. It did make me nervous.

Parliament Square was closed to traffic too so I walked straight down the middle of the road past Churchill and Smuts and all those other bronze chaps. The traffic started again on Victoria Street. I didn't have far to go. New Scotland Yard had a row of coppers stopping anyone from parking or loitering in front of all the metal and glass and that silly spinning triangle on a stick that always looks like it could do with a clean. One of the coppers tried to move me on when I stopped there but I wouldn't leave.

—I'm here to see Superintendent Terence Butcher.

—I'm sure you are madam, said the copper. Now move along please if you would.

He looked down at me with my crutch and my Asda bag. It's true I didn't look quite right.

—Please constable. My husband was blown up on May Day. Terence Butcher used to be his boss.

—What did your husband do? said the copper.

I told him and I gave my husband's warrant number.

—Open the bag if you would please madam, said the copper.

I showed him what was in the bag.

—Alright madam, he said. Wait there just a moment if you would.

He turned away and he spoke into his radio.

I won't tell you the questions they asked me Osama. I won't tell you how I got in to see Terence Butcher. I'm not going to give you anything you could use to blow up Scotland Yard. A lot of my husband's old mates still work there. I won't tell you where Terence Butcher's office was. I won't even tell you his real name. Terence Butcher will do it's close enough anyway. I mean all those coppers have meat-chopping names don't they? Like Peter Slaughter. Francis Carver. Steven Cleaver. All the coppers in there had names you could take a grindstone to.

Scotland Yard was just like you'd expect inside. All nerves and notice boards. A constable took me down god knows how many grey painted corridors. The whole place smelled of sweat and Dettol on the lower floors and coffee and Dettol on the upper ones. Terence Butcher's office was high up I won't tell you how high exactly. The pale green gloss paint on his door was chipped and grubby but the metal sign was bright and new. CHIEF SUPERINTENDENT TERENCE BUTCHER it said. I don't know anything about police ranks but the constable who was taking me was so worked up he could hardly knock. ENTER said a voice and we did.

The office smelled of new paint. There were bare shelves all over the walls and cardboard boxes all over the floor. Terence Butcher was sitting against the window behind a long wide metal desk. There were 3 phones on the desk and a photo of a wife and kids. I supposed they were his. I mean it'd be wrong for any man to have a photo of someone else's wife and kids on his desk but especially for a copper. Terence Butcher was wearing a white shirt with black shoulder tabs with silver crowns on them. No tie. He was talking into one of the phones.

—No, he said. It's very simple. I'll tell you again. I told them to go to sector Sierra 6 and wait for orders. I did not tell them to start arresting the Japs. The Japs are not the enemy Inspector. They are a welcome fillip to our capital's tourist economy. You want to get your officers under control.

He slammed the phone down. He kept his hand on the receiver and dropped his head till it was nearly on the desk. Then he took a deep breath and as he breathed in he straightened up so it looked like he was being pumped up with air from the phone. He was very tall when he stood up and he had big grey eyes that looked at me.

—Sir, said the constable. This is the lady.

—Yes, said Terence Butcher. I can see that. Good lad. Off you go.

—Thank you sir, said the constable.

I walked into the middle of Terence Butcher's office and I held my metal crutch in front of me to stop my hands shaking. Terence Butcher stood up. Behind him I could see the black helicopters hovering in the grey sky over Westminster Abbey. They made no sound. The window was double glazed. Bombproof. Terence Butcher came half out from behind his desk and then he stopped and looked like he wanted to go back behind it. You could tell he didn't know what to do with himself I shouldn't think he was used to people who weren't there to take orders or dish them out. In the end he just sat there on the corner of his desk and twisted his fingers together. That's what I do with my hands mostly but it looked strange on a big man.

—I'm so very sorry for your loss, he said.

—Don't say sorry if it isn't your fault. This life's hard enough.

Terence Butcher shrugged and looked at his phones like he was hoping one of them would ring.

—I came in case you could tell me anything about my husband and my boy.

—I'd like to help, said Terence Butcher. But I didn't work with your husband on a day-to-day basis. If you'd like to speak with someone who knew him better I can arrange a meeting with his direct supervisor or one of his colleagues.

—Nah you're alright. I know all about what he was like alive. I came to find out how he died. I'd be happier to know my husband and my boy were blown to bits rather than trampled or burned to death you see.

—Christ, he said. Look. You'd be better off talking to the officer in charge of the May Day incident room. If you really think it would help then I'll instruct him to take you through the details.

—Yeah but I wanted to see you didn't I? I'm in a state at the moment I don't need to be talking with a complete stranger.

Terence Butcher narrowed his eyes and looked at me like I was the smallest row of letters at the optician's.

—Do I know you? he said.

—Do you not remember?

Terence Butcher looked at me for a long time.

—I'm sorry, he said. I meet so many people in this job.

—And you buy them all a G&T do you? You tell them all they're much too pretty to be a copper's squaw?

—Mmm? he said.

—Bomb squad fancy dress disco? 2 Christmases ago? You were dressed as Russell Crowe in *Gladiator*.

—Oh no, he said. You weren't the little Red Indian girl?

—Pocahontas actually.

—Christ. I don't know what to say.

—Nothing to say. Nothing happened did it.

—Didn't it?

—Nah. I'd of remembered.

Neither of us said anything for a while. It was so quiet you could hear the air-conditioning blowing the smell of hangovers and paperwork round the building.

—Are you seeing a grief counsellor? said Terence Butcher.

—Nah.

—You probably should. We could arrange it if you like.

—Nah. You're alright. There was one at the hospital and she didn't do any good.

—How do you know?

—Cause I tried to kill myself last night didn't I? I'll probably try again.

Terence Butcher stood up from the corner of his desk but he didn't take his eyes off mine.

—Don't give me that, he said. I'm a pretty good judge of character. If you wanted to kill yourself. Really wanted to I mean. Then you would have done it by now.

—I was in hospital. It isn't easy. I would of jumped out the window only it was ever so cold.

Terence Butcher sighed.

—I see, he said. Then let's make it easy for you shall we?

He reached down and opened a drawer in his desk. He took out a pistol. It was sharp and black and vicious-looking. It was bigger than they are on TV. It was about the same size as the entire universe. He held the pistol out to me still looking in my eyes. He held it by the barrel so the handle was pointing at me. At least I think it's called the handle. I'm no good with guns. The end you hold anyway.

Terence Butcher's hand was as steady as his eyes. He held the pistol there and my hand moved towards it. I don't know why. I never wanted to touch the thing but his eyes made me do it. My hand closed around the handle. It was cold and shiny and the thing was too big for me. I watched myself holding it like a girl trying to lift something made for grown-ups. Terence Butcher let go of the barrel and my arm fell down with the weight of the gun. I tried to point it at myself. I tried and tried but I couldn't lift it with one hand and I couldn't use both hands without dropping the crutch and falling over.

I burst into tears and sat down on the floor. I let the crutch fall onto the cardboard boxes. I looked at Terence Butcher through the tears in my eyes and I put both hands on the handle of the pistol with my fingers laced round the back of the handle and my thumbs around that metal bit that goes round the trigger. I lifted the gun up and put the barrel in my mouth.

The expression on Terence Butcher's face changed. I don't think he expected me to do it. He looked very sad and calm now. The gun felt so strange in my mouth. It was metal but it wasn't a knife or a fork or a spoon so my mouth couldn't work out what to do with it. It's funny but you can't think about killing yourself. When there's something in your mouth your body thinks it ought to be food. My tongue licked round the end of the barrel. It tasted of oil. The taste was sour and my body pulled the gun out of my mouth. I made a face. I couldn't help myself. I sat there on the floor in the middle of all the cardboard boxes and I stopped crying. I was thinking nothing much.

—See? said Terence Butcher. You don't really want to kill yourself.

—What if I'd pulled the trigger?

Terence Butcher grinned. He got up from behind his desk and stepped through the mess of boxes on the floor and knelt down next to me. He took a Marlboro Red out of a pack in his shirt pocket and put it in his mouth. Then he took the gun out of my hands and lit his ciggie with it. He pulled the trigger and the gun went click and a little yellow flame came out of the end of the barrel. I looked up at him.

—If you'd pulled the trigger you'd have suffered a serious case of hot mouth, he said.

—Oh.

—Yes. Welcome back to the land of the living. Now let that be the last I hear of any silliness. I've got a whole bloody city to look after. Don't want to add you to my worries.

Terence Butcher reached down and gave me his hand. I grabbed it and he pulled me up like I weighed less than a polystyrene cup. My face came close to his chest and I breathed in his smell of fabric conditioner and cigarette smoke. I held on to his hand longer than I should of. I was trembling and he felt it.

—You've got the shakes, he said.

—Yeah.

—You and me both, he said. Ever since May Day.

—Yeah?

—Yes, he said. Ordinarily I would have been at that game too. I haven't missed the Arsenal against Chelsea since. Well. Since ever.

—Yeah well you wouldn't would you.

He looked at me very steady.

—Come on, he said. Let's get you sat down.

He helped me across the room to his chair. It was the only one in the office.

—I'm sorry about the mess, he said. I just moved in here yesterday. I haven't unpacked.

—I suppose you got promoted did you?

—Yes, he said.

—Nice one.

—Thanks.

He wasn't looking at me he was looking over my shoulder out the window. I just sat behind his desk and waited. His chair was too high for me so I sat with my white Pumas swinging just above the floor. I looked at Terence Butcher's 3 phones and the photo of his wife and kids. His wife looked alright. She had a nice smile. The photo was of her and 2 kids sitting on a lawn. She looked very comfortable sitting there. She looked like the sort of girl who'd always been around lawns. It was sunny in the photo and she had a summer dress on with a blue flower print. The dress was pretty ordinary but she might of had nice legs under it you couldn't really tell. Her ankles were alright but she was wearing Dunlop Green Flash. The laces were done up with a double bow. I was making myself notice these little things because I couldn't let myself look at her kids.

I looked at her face and I wondered what it would feel like to pick up one of those 3 telephones and call her. I imagined what it would be like to hear her voice say hello darling. To hear the 2 kids squabbling in the background. Fighting over lego. Everything very normal and everyday. I imagined what it would be like to look straight at her pretty face in the photo and say I won't be back till very late tonight darling. Something's come up at work.

Terence Butcher looked down at me and smiled.

—The wife, he said.

—You love her do you?

—Of course, he said. What sort of a question is that?

—It's the sort of question you ask a bloke who buys you a G&T dressed as Russell Crowe.

Terence Butcher coughed.

—Yes, he said. Well. Please don't take it personally.

—Yeah well I wouldn't take it personally if it'd been anyone else.

—Look, he said. I've already told you I'm sorry. It's the job. Okay? This job is a bastard and so sometimes you have a few drinks and you let your hair down.

—Tell me about your job.

—Why?

—Because my husband never would.

—He was right, said Terence Butcher. You don't want to know.

—I'll be the judge of that.

Terence Butcher sighed then and it was more like a blowout than a slow puncture.

—Well if you have to know it's bloody simple, he said. Counter-terrorism is the worst job in the world. You watch Londoners going about their business. You see them getting onto buses. Taking their kids to school. Drinking half a lager at lunchtime. And all the time you're getting this information. From phone taps. E-mails. Tip-offs. It's not like it is in the films. You never know what the bastards are planning. You only get these peaks of activity. You know something's going to happen. You don't know what and you don't know when. But you think it might be today. So you get jumpy. When a siren starts up you hit the roof. If a car backfires you have to stop yourself diving for the pavement. There's a million volts of electricity churning round in your guts. That's why you can't sleep. You get nervous.

Terence Butcher stopped talking. There was sweat on his forehead.

—I know just what you mean.

—You do? he said.

—Yeah. I get very nervous too.

Terence Butcher swallowed.

—I shouldn't be telling you this, he said. You just lost your husband and your boy. I doubt you've slept in days and here I am telling you my life is hard.

I caught the first flash of it then. I saw what Terence Butcher would look like with my arms around his neck. My arms so thin and white against his skin.

—I don't mind. Talk if it makes you feel better. Get it all out.

—You're a remarkable woman, said Terence Butcher. Listen. Can I get you something? A coffee or a tea?

I looked up at Terence Butcher and I saw what he'd look like with his fingers pushing under the waistband of my white Adidas trackies, with those big hands around my bum pulling me down on him and both of us moaning and the windows exploding inwards in a bright white flash and his office filled with flying glass cutting us into small pieces his cheating flesh all mixed up with mine so they'd have to bury us together.

—Tea please.

He walked up to the desk he picked up one of the phones I forget which.

—2 teas, he said. Biscuits.

He held the phone and I watched the muscles in his back through his shirt while he ordered us tea. It felt nice to have this big man do something small for me. It gave me the shivers. I wondered if Jasper Black would bring me tea and biscuits if I turned up at his office. It's funny Osama the way you start to think when you're a widow.

I reached down into my Asda bag. I got out one of my bottles of Valium and held it out to Terence Butcher on the palm of my hand. My hand was shaking so hard the pills were rattling. I blushed.

—Here. They're tranquillisers. I got 2 bottles so you might as well have one of them if you're having trouble sleeping.

He reached out his hand. He held the bottle so it stopped rattling but he didn't take it out of my hand. He looked into my eyes.

—The wife doesn't approve of these things, he said. Says they disrupt the body's natural equilibrium.

—Yeah? Well so do bombs.

Terence Butcher was quiet for a moment and then he closed his hand around the bottle. I felt the tips of his fingers against my palm as he took the pills.

—Thanks, he said.

—You're alright.

The tea came. It was just how you'd expect police tea to be Osama all lukewarm and milky. Terence Butcher put the bottle of pills in his trouser pocket.

—Listen, he said. A favour deserves a favour. I wouldn't bother drinking the tea around here. It's disgusting. I pour it into the plant pots.

He grinned and I grinned too. It felt nice. I hadn't smiled much since they stopped that nurse Mena from coming. Then one of the phones on his desk rang. He looked at it for a moment before he picked it up.

—No Inspector, he said. Sector *Sierra* 6. I'd spell Sierra for you if Sierra wasn't already a letter of the phonetic alphabet.

He slammed the phone down.

—Poor bastard's had even less sleep than me probably, he said. We should start a club. Insomniacs against Islam.

He smiled again but I didn't. I was thinking of Mena. How she used to pop those blue pills into my mouth at the hospital. The mercy of her god that she stole from a jar for me so I could crunch it between my teeth and forget about things for one more day. Allah Akbar we used to say. Now I remembered that bitter taste of love.

—You really think it was Islam that killed my husband and my boy?

Terence Butcher stopped smiling.

—Well, he said. It wasn't the Easter Bunny.

—I knew a Muslim. She was a nurse in the hospital. She was the gentlest woman I ever met. Her god wasn't a bombing god.

—Yeah, said Terence Butcher, well it isn't their god that bothers me. It's the devils that sell them the Semtex.

—They're not all like that.

—No, said Terence Butcher. And not every kid kicking a ball about in the park will get to play for Arsenal. Doesn't mean they wouldn't all love a go.

—You'll just make it worse talking like that. You want to try to understand them.

—I'm not paid to understand, said Terence Butcher. I'm paid to prevent.

—Yeah well you didn't prevent May Day did you?

He looked at the floor.

—No, he said.

—So maybe you're going about it wrong. I don't see how you can stop the bombers if you don't understand them.

Terence Butcher came round to my side of the desk. He stood behind the chair and put his hand on my shoulder.

—Look, he said. The Arabs are different from us. Don't fool yourself you can understand them. In the Iran-Iraq war they sent children to walk across the minefields. To clear a path so the grown-ups could go and gas each other. They gave each kid a little metal key to paradise. The kids hung those keys around their necks. The grown-up Arabs told the little Arab children that there weren't enough landmines to send all the kids to paradise. So the little children actually ran. Can you picture what an antipersonnel mine does to a human child? If you saw it I dare say you wouldn't think it was getting anyone closer to god. But that's what's in Johnny Arab's mind. He can't get to heaven without sending you to hell.

—That's not right.

—Isn't it? he said. Can you think of another name for what you're living through?

I looked up at him. He was all blurry with tears on account of I was thinking about my boy with his ginger hair flying in the wind running ahead to be the first boy in paradise. He'd of been the first to go. He was a bright boy but kids will believe anything you tell them Osama I suppose you don't need me to tell you that.

—You need to get this straight in your mind, Terence Butcher said. It's us against them. War against terror. Fighting fire with fire.

—But you can't.

—Yes we can, said Terence Butcher. It's an ugly war and there's no honour in it. But we will win because we have to. It's a war we win by ditching our principles. By interning people who are high risk. By listening to private phone calls. And it's a boring war too. A workaday war. We win by persuading the Brits to have balls. To stand up on the Circle Line and ask Does this bag belong to anyone? We win by following up on every single lead. However insignificant. We win by phoning our wife and saying Sorry darling. I'm not going to make it back till very late again. Give the kids a kiss for me.

He was looking at the photo of his wife and kids. His hand was still on my shoulder. I held on to his desk.

—Alright then. I want to fight.

—What? he said.

—You heard. If it's a war then I want to fight. Give me a job and I'll do it I don't care how dangerous it is I'll do it. I'll do whatever you want. Just give me a job where I can do something to help.

—No, he said. Let's not go there. Trust me you don't want to get involved in this.

—But there's nothing else I can do is there? My husband and my boy are gone. All I want is to stop another May Day from ever happening again. So no mother ever has to feel how I feel now.

—I admire what you're saying, he said. You're a good girl. But you don't need a job right now. I'm sorry but what you need is counselling.

His hand was heavy on my shoulder. I looked at him and I felt myself go tight inside. It was pitiful all that emptiness whimpering for something to fill it. I made myself sit still but my body was only half tame I could feel it pulling against its rope. I know what you're thinking Osama but don't you dare judge me you goat-watching bastard. You wouldn't know the first thing about it you're not a woman.

—No. I'm fine. I don't need counselling. I'm completely back to normal. I've seen counsellors I've seen grief therapists I've even seen Prince William he's taller than he looks on telly. It's all useless I just feel empty it doesn't get better it only gets worse. Please. You couldn't possibly know what it feels like. I'll do anything. I could be a spy or I could just do the cleaning or whatever. I could make a better cup of tea than you get around here. I'll do anything at all. Just please give me a job to do. If I have to go back and just sit in the flat alone I know I really will top myself.

Terence Butcher stared at me and I felt his hand slide on my shoulder. His fingers were beginning to sweat. I felt his breath on my cheek. Then one of the phones went. His hand was shaking when he picked it up.

—Yes? he said. Right. No you just stay there and get Anwar and Janet on a conference line. I'll be right down.

He hung up.

—There's something I have to do, he said. I'll be ten minutes. Will you be okay to wait here till I get back?

—Alright.

—Don't leave this room will you? he said. I'm not supposed to leave you here alone. But you're on our side apparently. Aren't you?

I smiled.

—Apparently.

When he left the room I turned round in his chair. It was one of those adjustable chairs with levers all over it. I swear that chair was more complicated than me. There isn't all that much to me Osama and certainly nothing you could adjust. I'm sorry but I'm far too stubborn. I felt like doing something to cheer myself up so I pulled up my legs and spun round and round and round in Terence Butcher's chair. I was singing La la la la Wonder Woman I always liked to do that ever since I was a girl.

I waited for a while. I don't know how long because I lost my watch on May Day. I looked out over London and it was starting to rain and there were 2 grey pigeons on the window ledge doing the nasty. The one underneath was thin and sick-looking. Her wing was scrunched up against the glass and you could see the feathers all bent. The one on top was pecking at her neck and flapping his wings to stay there. His feet were just raw pink lumps all the toes had gone off them. He finished his business and slung his hook. She just sat there for a minute not even looking where he'd gone and then she flew off too in the direction of Westminster Abbey. I sat there for a minute getting nervous and then I started to tidy up. I couldn't help myself.

Most of the cardboard boxes were full of files. I took them out one by one and stacked them on the shelves. There must of been 40 or 50 of them. They were big box files with their names written on their sides in magic marker. They had brilliant names all those files. They were code names. My boy would of loved them. They were called COUGAR and RED SKY and OPERATION THUNDER RESPONSE you know what coppers are like Osama. I took all those files out of their boxes on the floor and I put them on the shelves that ran along the sides of the office. I put them in alphabetical order it was a great comfort. I wish I could put the whole world in alphabetical order Osama there would be Deserts and Forests and Oceans between you and my boy.

When all the files were arranged I took the cardboard boxes they'd come out of and I broke them down flat and stood them against the wall. It felt so nice making everything neat and clean I wanted it to go on forever.

I'm that sort of person Osama you could give me any sort of mess and I'd straighten it out for you. I'd be happy to. Let's say you'd had a party and your flat was a state. Well I could come round in the morning and put all your glam rock CDs back in their right boxes and take the ciggie butts out of your plant pots and clean up the sick that had missed the toilet bowl. I'd be fine with it. Or let's say your kitchen was on the small side and you couldn't find anywhere to put anything. Let's say all your cupboards were stuffed so that saucepan lids fell out when you opened the doors and all your work surfaces were covered with bomb parts and tins of beard wax so there wasn't anywhere to stack the dirty dishes. Well I could come round and sort it all out with you. I'd go through your drawers and hold things up one at a time and ask if you really needed them. And what I'd do is I'd put all the things you hardly ever used into a box and put the box under your bed and that would leave you with space in the cupboards to put away everything you actually used. See?

When I'd finished arranging all Terence Butcher's files I started taking the rest of his stuff out of the boxes. Some of it could just go straight into the desk drawers. Things like pens and Post-it notes. Then there was a box of magazines. I thought maybe I shouldn't look inside in case they were glamour mags but I couldn't stop myself so I opened the box. Actually the mags were only *Caravan Club Magazine*. There must of been 6 dozen of them. It was quite sweet really. It was nice to think of Terence Butcher driving his family down into Essex in a big blue Vauxhall Cavalier. Getting farther and farther from his city full of bombs. The kids needing to stop for a wee and his wife wearing Dunlop Green Flash and him peering in those big mirrors you strap onto the side of the car so you can see round the back of the caravan.

I put Terence Butcher's magazines up on the shelves and I emptied the last of the boxes as best I could. It was just coffee mugs and football shields and stuff. The sort of things you'd expect. When everything was tidied away and all the cardboard boxes were flat up against the wall I sat back down on Terence Butcher's chair and took 2 of the Valiums washed down with the cold police tea.

When Terence Butcher came back in he looked at his office all unpacked and he just started laughing.

—Wow, he said. I don't know what to say.

—Don't mention it. I'm used to tidying up after boys.

He stopped smiling then.

—Listen, he said. If you're serious about coming to work here I think I could find something useful for you. You've just shown me you can be handy around an office. How are you with paperwork?

—I don't know. I can read and write if that's what you mean. I'm not thick or anything just don't ask me where the commas go.

Terence Butcher smiled again.

—No problem, he said. You might need to type up incident reports from time to time. They read like SUSPECT WAS APPRE-HENDED AT 0630 WIELDING A SHARPENED SPOON. That stuff needs commas like Covent Garden needs a gardener. Anyway we're not writing literature here. We're trying to stop people bombing people.

I saw how Terence Butcher would look with his forearms blown off and tumbling across the turf at Ashburton Grove.

—I like you, said Terence Butcher. I like your spirit. I want people on my team who have a reason to care about the work. I want people I can trust. There's a lot of highly sensitive information floating around this place.

—You can trust me I'll keep my mouth shut it's not as if I've got anyone to tell anyway is it?

Terence Butcher looked out of the window for a while and then back at me.

—I could offer you a job on my administrative staff, he said. You wouldn't be a police officer. You'd be assisting the officers. Taking on some of their administrative burden. Freeing them up to perform their duties. It's an essential role and you'd know you were doing something for the effort.

—Right. When do I start?

—Whoa, he said. Steady. I can't just appoint you like that. This is the Met. We've got procedure. First you have to get approved by Personnel. And before we let you anywhere near Personnel we need to get you a haircut and the kind of clothes that have their labels on the inside.

I looked down at my red Nike T-shirt and my white Adidas track-ies and my white Pumas. He was right. I mean I didn't look like someone you'd give an administrative burden to if you didn't want it dropped.

—Alright. What do the girls dress like round here?

—Blouses, said Terence Butcher. Black skirts. Thick stockings. Sensible shoes. Short hair. Think *Prisoner: Cell Block H*. Come here tomorrow afternoon looking the part and I'll get you in.

—Oh god. I'm going to look like a 3-wheel trike.

Terence Butcher grinned.

—It's like I was saying, he said. This is a war we win by ditching our principles.

*   *   *

Terence Butcher lent me 200 quid so I got the Victoria Line to Oxford Street and bought my *Cell Block H* clothes in H&M. I kept them on to get the feel and went looking for a place to get my hair cut. All I could find was one of those trendy places in Soho. My boy wouldn't of liked it. For him a good hairdresser's was where they let you put on the nylon capes backwards and run around shouting DINNER DINNER DINNER DINNER BATMAN. This place wasn't like that at all it was a fashion hairdresser's which is much more serious. It was all skinny girls and smoked glass in there and they were playing a club remix of ENGLAND'S HEART IS BLEEDING.

One of the girls came up to me when I walked in with my crutch and she asked would I like a drink.

—You don't mean a G&T do you?

—Sorry, said the girl. I can offer you tea or coffee.

—Tea please then. 3 sugars.

The girl looked hard at me. There was no fat on her at all I reckon 3 sugars would of finished her off. She told me to sit down in one of the basin seats. I drank the tea they brought me and they washed my hair it was lovely. When they asked me how I wanted my hair done I said like Lady Di.

Afterwards I took the Central Line home to Bethnal Green. I couldn't face walking down Bethnal Green Road at first. I needed something to take the edge off it all so I stopped in at The Green

Man which was a mistake on account of The Green Man is one of those pubs that never quite stops smelling of puke. It isn't the nicest pub in the world in fact I needed a couple of drinks just to take the edge off The Green Man. In the end it was last orders before I got out of there.

It felt amazing having short hair. The wind was cold on my neck and my ears. Everything felt very fresh it was like I'd just been born.

I don't know if you've ever walked with a crutch through the gangs of kids down Bethnal Green Road on your way from the tube station at 11:30 on a weeknight Osama. I should hope so. I mean we're the kind of people you're bombing so I would of hoped you'd of chosen us personally.

Anyway if you have ever walked through Bethnal Green at night you'll know why it's best to do it wearing a red Nike T-shirt with white Adidas trackies and white Pumas. You want to sort of blend in don't you? But I was carrying all that clobber in my Asda carrier bag along with Mr. Rabbit and the bottle of Valium. What I was wearing was a white blouse and a dark-brown skirt from H&M and 40 denier hold-ups from Pretty Polly and Clarks black leather shoes. It wasn't easy trying to look natural in that getup I don't mind telling you. I had makeup on too. Dark-red lippie and black mascara. I felt like a tranny on her first trip outside as a woman. My new Diana hair had so much lacquer on it I swear a single spark would of left a crater where the East End used to be.

There were posters up everywhere telling you not to break curfew. They had a nice family on the posters. The kids were tucked up safe in bed and the parents were smiling and watching telly. SAFELY INSIDE AFTER MIDNIGHT the posters said. WE'RE DO-ING OUR BIT.

The Valium was mixing funny with the G&T. I kept seeing my boy in the lit windows above the shop fronts. I'd catch a glimpse of him and I'd think oh naughty monkey it's well past your bedtime young man go back to sleep. Then I'd look again and the window would be empty so all you could see was the cold light from a bare bulb and the dirty flock wallpaper on the inside of the walls. If you could of looked in my eyes you'd of seen the same thing I shouldn't wonder.

I turned right onto Barnet Grove. It felt weird being back on my street. It felt like coming back from a long holiday only I hadn't been anywhere nice had I? When I reached our estate it was all quiet and dead. The light was on in our flat. I must of left it on when I rushed out. I tried not to think of the electric bill. I was feeling very tired and alone. I should of liked to pop in and say hello to Jasper Black before I went back to my flat. I wanted to tell him I was out of hospital and maybe he'd of let me stay with him for an hour or 2 if Petra wasn't around. Not to do anything I mean. We could of just watched the telly for a bit. I looked across the street at his house but there weren't any lights on so I turned round and went into our estate.

I went through the swing doors to the stairwell. Oh god that smell. It was like my life had been quietly waiting there for me all along. Old chip fat. That's what my life smelled of. And BK onion rings and ciggies and hash and sweaty trainers and nappies. The smell wrapped itself around me till I was choking and I sat down on the stairs and cried and cried and cried. My crying echoed in the stairwell and outside I could hear the police cars going up and down with their loudspeakers squawking at the last stragglers to get inside for curfew.

After a while I stopped noticing the smell. I was back in my life I didn't need any more reminding. I stood up and climbed the stairs to our flat. We were only on the third floor so it wasn't far to climb. I stopped outside our front door. I could hear noise from inside. It sounded like the telly was on. That's funny I thought. I could of sworn I turned the telly off before we left. It made me feel a bit poorly thinking what a lightbulb and the telly left on for 2 months was going to look like on a red electricity bill. I found my keys and I opened the front door and went inside.

There were 2 people's coats hanging off the pegs in the hallway and they weren't anything to do with my family. One was a man's

Barbour jacket. You wouldn't of caught my husband dead in one of those. The other was a woman's coat. It was wool and dark pink with a purple silk lining it looked like it cost more than our flat. I put my carrier bag down quietly. I didn't know what was going on. It wasn't burglars was it? I mean burglars don't usually come in posh coats. At least not in Bethnal Green they don't. I tiptoed down the hallway. The lounge door was open. I sort of wish it hadn't been and then I wouldn't of seen what I saw next.

Jasper Black was on my sofa with a woman. The woman was wearing pink stilettos and nothing else and she was on her hands and knees and Jasper had his thing up her. The woman was shouting. Ow yeah she was shouting. Fuck me you posh bugger I deserve it it's all I'm good for. Jasper was whacking her with the back of his hand. Her arse was all red you could see the bruises starting. The woman had one hand up underneath her she was playing with herself. I watched them going at it. I felt so confused with the pills and the booze I thought maybe I was imagining the whole thing. So I stepped back into the hallway and I went up to the coats. I touched them with my hands. I put the silk lining of the woman's coat up against my cheek. It felt so soft and cool. I thought about putting the coat on and walking out in the night all the way to the Thames and drowning myself like a kitten in a priceless sack. I probably would of done it as well. If it hadn't been for the curfew I mean.

I tiptoed back to the lounge and I watched them for a long time through the gap in the door. My lounge smelled of sex. The telly was showing *Murder Detectives* but neither of them was watching. There was a lot more shouting. Jasper was calling the woman a DIRTY WORKING-CLASS SLUT. Then they both just went uh uh uh. When it was finished they collapsed facedown on my sofa. Jasper was panting and the woman was giggling. She reached down for a bottle of champagne that was open on the floor. I never did like champagne. She took a long drink of it and passed it to Jasper. She giggled again. It was a horrible sound like a hacksaw going through pipes. Jesus Christ Jasper she said you are a sick bastard that was fucking unbelievable.

—Oh hello Jasper I didn't recognise you from behind.

They both spun round then and saw me and the woman screamed. She pulled a cushion up to cover her tits which seemed a bit silly considering I'd practically seen her insides. Jasper jumped up and he put his hands over his bits. He stared at me. He couldn't work out who I was.

—It's me Jasper. I've got a new job. This is my new look. Do you like it?

I watched his eyes go even wider.

—Oh god, he said. Oh god oh god oh god. I thought you were in hospital.

—Well I was. But I'm back now aren't I? I'm pleased you found a use for my spare keys. Make yourself at home there's fish fingers in the freezer if you're hungry. Don't mind me I'll just be tidying a few things up. This is the first time I've been home you see since my husband and my boy got blown up and burned to death and I ought to start putting their things into boxes.

The woman stared at me then she looked at Jasper.

—Oh Jasper you absolute cunt, she said.

She burst into tears and I turned around and went into the kitchen. It was nice and tidy in there just the way I'd left it. There was the bottle of vodka in the freezer where it always lived. I took down a glass and I poured myself a shot. The vodka was cold and lazy. It poured slowly like water in a dream. I let about an inch go into the glass and I drank it straight down. I took out 2 more of the Valiums and I put them in my mouth. They lay there hard under my tongue like I was an oyster and these were my pearls. I poured more vodka into the glass and drank down the pills. I didn't give a monkey's any more. I just sat at the kitchen table waiting for the pills to work. I was looking at my boy's drawings on the wall. I wished I'd remembered to write on them what they were meant to be. After the longest time the woman came into the kitchen. I heard her walk in and stand behind my chair but I didn't turn around.

—Look, she said. I really don't know what to say.

Her voice was amazing. It was comedy posh. It was the sort of voice corgis would obey without question. I laughed I couldn't help myself.

—No please, said the woman. I think perhaps I owe you an apology.

I still didn't turn around. I was so empty there were tears running down my face but I didn't feel anything.

—It's alright. I'm sure you're very sorry and everything I don't blame you I don't even care really so why don't you just fuck off?

—Um, said the woman. Well I'm afraid we can't just fuck off. Much as we'd love to. There's the curfew. It's gone midnight. I realise these are absolutely appalling circumstances but I'm afraid you're stuck with Jasper and me for the night.

I turned round then and I looked at her. I couldn't help gasping. The woman looked just like me. She was wearing my pink bathrobe and her pink stilettos. She was about my height and she had my figure. Long legs. Small tits. Big eyes. Thin neck. Maybe a few pounds lighter. Her hair was the same colour blond as mine except it was cut very long and pretty and it shone like in the adverts. Like each hair had been individually polished by tiny angels. God knows what she used on it and it must of cost a packet. But it was her eyes that made me gasp. They were my eyes it was as simple as that. Her cheeks were pink from the sex and the champagne. She looked back at me and I could tell she could see the same thing. Even though I must of looked a state with my Lady Di hair and my mascara running. It was obvious. The woman shrugged.

—Oh dear, she said. I suppose we must be Jasper's type. I'm Petra Sutherland by the way. I've heard so much about you.

—Yeah? Well. There isn't much to say about me really.

She leaned back and put her elbows on the work surface behind her.

—I'm sure you're right, she said. But I wish you'd tell Jasper that. The silly boy is obsessed by you. He's in your bathroom crying his eyes out. He's absolutely devastated. He won't stop gibbering on about how he's hurt you.

I looked at her. I didn't feel hurt. In fact I didn't feel anything. The vodka and the Valium were starting to work.

—Petra. Fancy that eh? I never thought I'd meet his girlfriend.

She sighed and looked at me like I was a ciggie she'd of liked to knock the ash off.

—Girlfriend is such a neat little word, she said.

—Yeah well what are you then?

—I am someone who is having a surreal day, she said. This afternoon I had a light lunch with Salman Rushdie. We drank Côte de Léchet. We discussed V. S. Naipaul and long hair on men.

A police helicopter flew low above the street. It was looking along the footpaths of the estate with a spotlight. The beam flashed across the window for a second. The light on Petra's face went cold and bright as white cotton pants in the Persil ads. Suddenly I felt angry.

—You people can't ever just say you're sorry can you?

Her nostrils flared and that voice of hers changed. It still sounded of money but now it was dirty money. Money people carry in Reebok holdalls in nightclub car parks.

—Why should I be sorry you poor cow? she said. I don't see why I should have to apologise to you. Am I the one who started this? No. You are. You fucked Jasper. And you a married woman. While your husband and your son lay dying you were right there on your awful Ikea sofa fucking my man. So don't you dare make me feel ashamed.

I looked at her. I couldn't see straight. My head was exploding from the pills and the booze. I felt like a plane crash and not one of the especially bright ones. Petra grabbed the vodka bottle out of my hand.

—Give me that, she said.

She took a long drink from the bottle and slammed it back down on the table and spat on my kitchen floor.

—There, she said. That's what I think of bitches like you.

She turned round and bumped straight into Jasper who was just coming into the kitchen. He was wearing my husband's black bathrobe. He was chewing his lip. He sniffed. Petra slapped him round the face so hard spit came out of his mouth and splatted on the fridge.

—And you can fuck off too, she said. You think I'd have played your stupid game if I'd known this was part of it?

—It wasn't, said Jasper. I thought she was still in hospital. I promise.

—Car salesmen promise Jasper, said Petra. Estate agents promise. Men in my life are supposed to fucking deliver.

She slapped his face again and screamed at him and the upstairs neighbours started banging on the ceiling. I tried to stand up but I'd forgotten my crutch so I just fell down in a heap on the lino. I watched Petra's stilettos slamming past my face as she stormed out of the kitchen. Then I rolled on my back and lay there looking up at the striplight on the ceiling. Jasper's face was looking down at me. His face was wobbling all over the place and going in and out of focus like something you find on the videotape when you thought the camera was turned off but actually you left it running.

—Are you alright? he said.

—Do I look alright?

He knelt down beside me and put his hand on my cheek. His hand was all cold and trembly.

—Oh Christ, he said. I can't believe what we've done to you.

—Yeah. You and Osama bin Laden.

—No, he said. I meant me and Petra.

—Oh. Well. Never mind eh.

He opened his mouth to say something but then he closed it again I suppose there wasn't much to say.

—Listen do you think you could take me to bed?

—Oh god, he said. I don't know if that's a good idea. I mean Petra's right here in the flat.

—I don't mean do you think you could have sex with me you twat I mean do you think you could just take me to my bed please I can't seem to move my legs you see.

—Oh, he said. God. Sorry. Yes.

He picked me up off the lino. I didn't weigh much any more you see Osama on account of you don't have the same appetite once all your favourite food just reminds you of bombs. Jasper carried me through to the bedroom and laid me down on the bed. He put me down on my husband's side I didn't have the strength to tell him to move me to the other. So I just lay there staring at my husband's water glass. All the water in it had evaporated there was just this thin white crust left on the sides of the glass. It's funny what's left behind once what you had is all dried away. It's funny how it never made the water cloudy.

—Jasper. Stay with me. Just a few minutes.

—I don't think that's a good idea, he said.

He moved his face very close to mine I could feel his breath on my face. He opened his mouth to say something but just then Petra shouted from the lounge JASPER WHAT ARE YOU DOING IN THERE? GET IN HERE NOW.

Jasper stroked my hair back off my face.

—I have to go, he said.

—Just 5 minutes. Please.

—I can't, said Jasper. I couldn't explain it to Petra. You saw how jealous she is.

—2 minutes.

Petra shouted from the lounge again JASPER IT'S HER OR ME CHOOSE WHO YOU LIKE BUT CHOOSE RIGHT NOW.

Jasper stood up and shrugged.

—I'm sorry, he said. You know if I stayed it would just make it worse.

—For you or for me?

Jasper looked at me for a long time.

—I'm sorry, he said.

Then there was just his back walking away into the lounge. After that I cried a bit and then I lay awake listening to Petra and Jasper arguing with each other in whispers. It was a horrible noise very vicious and quiet like 2 insects fighting in a jar. It didn't sound like love to me Osama but then what would you or me know I mean we're half deaf from the bombs already.

After a long time I couldn't hear Petra and Jasper arguing any more. The pills and the booze made me sleep for a bit but then in the middle of the night I woke up. It was the noise that woke me. I got up and went over to the window and held on to the frame of it to steady myself. I looked up at the helicopters circling overhead and flashing light out in all directions. It was like a free police disco and about as much fun. I mean I don't know if you've ever been to a police disco Osama but I have so you can take it from me. The DJs are always coppers themselves and if you don't think they play the theme tune from *The Bill* near the end then you think wrong.

I couldn't face lying down and waiting for my boy's voice to start babbling round my head again so when I got sick of watching the helicopters I went into the lounge on my tiptoes. I shuffled along the walls to hold myself up. Petra was asleep on the sofa and Jasper was on the floor by the telly. They both had their coats over them. I went down on my hands and knees and crawled over to Petra very quiet and slow. She was curled up on her side to fit onto the sofa and there was just her head and neck sticking out from underneath her coat. I knelt and watched her for a bit I suppose I was trying to remember what it was like to be able to sleep like that.

Petra's face was soft and still and yellow in the light that came in from the street lamps. Whenever a helicopter came overhead the windows rattled and Petra frowned in her sleep and in the white searchlights you could see this little pulse fluttering away in her throat. I watched her pulse and I listened to my boy's voice starting up again in my head very distant at first and then nearer and nearer like the radio tuning in on a station m m mum mum mummy mummy MUMMY! I tried to tune it out I tried to concentrate on that vein banging away on Petra's neck. On and on that pulse went because it never stops does it? Your heart bangs away like a stuck record and the streetlights on Barnet Grove switch on again and off again and the tide sloshes up and down in the Thames and it's life whether you can sleep or not.

Summer

Dear Osama everything I've written so far happened in the spring and it never stopped for one second. It was dirty and sad and anyone who wasn't blown up and burned was doing the nasty with each other like they might never get another chance. It was just like being in nature. I mean I'm a London girl Osama but I know what goes on in the countryside. I watch the telly like anyone else. Spring is when everything is fighting and killing and mating and London was no different after you went at it with bombs. It was like we all became animals again. You could look at people on the bus and you'd almost see the fur bristling under their nice clean clothes. After May Day everyone was nervous. It wasn't just me any more.

But then summer came and the weather got hot and people slowed down. If you hadn't had your husband and your boy blown up then I suppose May Day started to feel like a long time ago. People stopped thinking about how short their life was and they started thinking about motors again.

—Would you look at that? said Terence Butcher. They've given tow car of the year to a bloody Volkswagen.

We were in his office and *Caravan Club Magazine* had just come in the post along with a bunch of memos about terror suspects. He'd opened the magazine first. That did surprise me a bit Osama on account of in my opinion he had the sort of job where you ought to have a good old go at defeating the global jihad before you get on to hobbies but what would I know. Terence Butcher stood behind his desk and held up the magazine so I could see the article.

—That's nice sir.

—Nice? he said. What do you mean nice? It's a Kraut abomination. Give me a Vauxhall Cavalier any day. Plenty of poke when you need it on the uphills. Don't have to send off to Dresden every time you need a spare distributor cap.

—Well I wouldn't know about that sir. My husband always saw to our motors.

—Then take it from me, he said. You wouldn't catch me dead in a Volkswagen. I've a good mind to write a letter to the editor. Do I have a ten-minute window this morning?

—No sir I've got you pencilled in to fight Islamic terror all day. Your tea alright is it?

Terence Butcher looked down into his mug and he nodded.

—Yes, he said. It bloody well is. I don't know how I drank that slop the last girl made.

—You didn't drink it did you? You used to pour it into the pot plants and they got sick and died sir.

Terence Butcher smiled at me and I smiled back. The look went on too long.

—Listen, he said. How long have you been with us now?

—2 months sir.

—And you're enjoying it? Right?

—Oh yes sir I like it here I'm glad to be doing something useful it takes my mind off it all you know.

—Yes, said Terence Butcher. You never seem to stop for a second. You're a force of nature. There isn't one minute of my day you haven't organised. I'd be surprised if you'd left a single sheet of paper out of place in the entire building.

—No sir well I can't stop can I? The doctor won't give me any more Valium.

—Oh, he said. Well how do you cope in the evenings?

—Don't worry about me I cope fine thanks sir.

Actually Osama how I coped in the evenings was I used to come in through the back entrance to the estate and sneak into our flat and keep very quiet with the telly and all the lights off so Jasper Black wouldn't see I was home and come knocking.

Our flat was hot in those summer evenings so I left the windows open for a bit of air and sometimes if you were lucky there was a breeze. It wasn't any of your fresh mountain air Osama it smelled of summer in the East End which is mainly hash and car exhaust but a breeze is a breeze my husband always used to say. The breeze lifted the net curtains in the lounge and the shadows moved on the walls and in those shadows if you weren't looking straight at them you could see my boy mucking around with his toys. It was better if you half closed your eyes. I used to watch him playing for hours it was better than the telly ever was anyway.

—Coping fine eh? said Terence Butcher.

—Oh yes sir.

—Very good.

Terence Butcher was looking out of the window. He took a sip of his tea. It was still the same view of London out of his window only like I say it was summer now. The air was grubby and shimmering. The 2 helicopters hovering over the Houses of Parliament weren't black any more. They'd painted them red white and blue and the Japs were allowed to film them.

There were still the barrage balloons hanging over the city only they weren't bright silver any more. Each balloon had the face of one of the May Day victims painted on it. They'd winched them down one at a time and sent them back up. Each one with its smiling face. Of course they weren't called barrage balloons any more. They were called the Shield of Hope. My chaps were up there doing their bit Terence Butcher had seen to that. My husband was defending the Oval Cricket Ground and my boy was attached to the roof of Great Ormond Street Hospital. When the wind blew it screamed in the balloons' cables and the noise made the hairs stand up on your neck. That was my boy's only voice now Osama. That was my only sky.

Terence Butcher turned back to me and put his tea down on the desk. He put it down too hard so some of the tea slopped out.

—You know what the best thing is about caravans? he said.

—No sir.

I looked down at his hand resting on the desktop beside his tea. His big hand brown from the early summer sun with its tendons strong as cables. I followed the line of his arm up to his elbow where his shirtsleeve was rolled. I imagined my small hand slipping inside that shirtsleeve and sliding up to the warm curve of his bicep. Sometimes in those days Osama I got a flash of a life where I didn't have to sneak around hiding from Jasper Black. It was just the quickest flash of someone standing beside me again. Someone strong enough to start all over with. I looked at Terence Butcher's hand and I thought yeah. You'd do.

—The best thing about caravans is that they're always exactly the same, said Terence Butcher. You can tow your caravan to Brighton or Bournemouth or Bognor. Doesn't make the blindest bit of difference. When you close the door behind you at the end of the day you're home. You can rely on it. When I close my eyes at night I always think about closing the caravan door. It doesn't matter what kind of a day I've had. Whatever awful things I've had to worry about are left outside.

He stopped and looked down at his shoes. Then he looked up at me again.

—But now that feeling is gone, he said. Ever since May Day. I've had to make some hard decisions. I've done things I'm not sure about. I don't sleep. It's as if I can't close the caravan door any more. I can't leave the horrors outside. That's what those Arab bastards have done. They've got inside my caravan.

I looked at Terence Butcher. He was in a state alright. His eyes were red around the edges and that hand on the desk was white around the fingertips where he was pressing down too hard.

—Anything else I can do for you sir?

He blinked.

—Oh, he said. I'm sorry. Christ. Listen to me going off on one.

—That's alright it's not your fault I mean you're a bundle of nerves aren't you sir. With all due respect you're an accident waiting to happen you're ready to blow a gasket you're an effing liability to yourself and others. Sir.

Terence Butcher rocked backwards on his feet.

—Oh dear I'm sorry I shouldn't of said all that. It's my big mouth I can't help it I'm a bundle of nerves myself I suppose you'll have to sack me now.

He sucked his teeth and shook his head slowly and turned to the window. Down below in the street a procession was going past. It was some sort of dress rehearsal for the Gay Pride Parade but you couldn't hear the music on account of the bombproof glass and it didn't look like much of a show. There was so much security down there it looked like a procession of police with a light gay escort. Terence Butcher looked down at it all and sighed.

—I don't know what to do with you, he said. I can't sack you because you're absolutely right of course. I can't promote you because frankly I'd be bloody surprised if you weren't the least-qualified woman on the force. And we can't carry on as we are because you're starting to get right under my skin.

Terence Butcher turned back from the window.

—I hired you to make the tea, he said. That's all.

—Yes sir I'll just make the tea from now on. I'll keep my big trap shut.

—No, he said. Don't. I don't have anyone else I can talk to.

—What about your wife sir?

—What about her? he said.

—Can't you talk to her?

—Wives are different, he said.

—Different how?

—Different like this. The difference is I can talk to you about her but I can't talk to her about you.

—Why would you? There's nothing to say about me.

—Yes there is, he said.

—What's that supposed to mean?

—What do you think it's supposed to mean? he said.

—I think it means you think too much.

Terence Butcher sat down on the edge of his desk and lit a Marlboro Red. He blew the smoke out and it drifted up towards the air-conditioning holes in the ceiling. His eyes looked up at the disappearing smoke.

—Listen Terence sir I know what you need I used to have a husband myself you know. You need to take your mind off things. Let's go down the boozer tonight. Me and you. Let's drink ourselves silly. We won't go to a coppers' pub we'll go somewhere nobody knows who we are so we can make tits of ourselves.

Terence Butcher frowned.

—No, he said. You've seen how I get when I'm drunk.

—Yeah and so what? Nothing happened did it.

Terence smiled and shook his head.

—Tessa still wouldn't like it.

—Yeah sir well is Tessa going to know?

He looked across at the photo of his wife and kids. He stared for the longest time and when he looked back at me he looked old and tired and sick of himself.

*   *   *

We left from Scotland Yard at 8 that evening. We went in the back of a riot van with wire mesh over the windows and a rubber skirt so you couldn't throw petrol bombs under it. It had a white-noise siren and a tear gas cannon. It was the perfect way to get through London traffic Osama I don't suppose you've had the pleasure. Me and Terence Butcher rattled around in the back like spare parts. We were headed for the Approach Tavern just off Victoria Park. One of the lads from the motor pool was driving and he got us there in 20 minutes flat. It must of been some kind of a record. The outrider was a great help. He rode in front of us in tight leather trousers and his big

BMW motorbike was all painted up in yellow and purple squares. He looked like Darth Vader riding a Battenberg cake.

The van stopped before we got to the Approach and we walked the last 100 yards on account of Terence Butcher said if you turn up at the pub in a riot van people do start to ask daft questions about why they bother paying their taxes. I chose the Approach because it was near enough my neck of the woods to get home easily afterwards but far enough away not to be the sort of pub where coppers stumble out covered in blood. Anyway blokes like the Approach on account of they do a perfect pint of Guinness. My husband used to like the place. My husband always thought a pub ought to be busy and loud. You probably think a pub ought to be firebombed and turned into a mosque Osama well that's the difference between my husband and you. I bet he could of drunk you under the table.

Terence Butcher was wearing civvies but he wasn't fooling anyone. He had these blue jeans on with a lime-green polo shirt tucked into them and light-brown Timberlands. He wore his mobile clipped to his belt in a little leather pouch the way only coppers do or your dad. I was wearing my brown skirt and white blouse and Clarks shoes. When we got inside the place was pretty quiet. There was half a crowd in there but it was nothing like what a Friday night would of been before the curfew. The barman winked at us and said Good evening officers.

Go on laugh if you want Osama but I've seen photos of you and it's not as if you're god's gift to fashion. Baggy white trousers cammo jacket digital watch and a fussy beard. You're a right state aren't you? You're ever so Hoxton.

We chose a table in the corner and I sat down while Terence Butcher went to the bar. He took his time on account of he was getting a Guinness. They pour them in 2 parts you see which is something you'd know Osama if you got out a bit more. While I was waiting for Terence Butcher to get back I sat there and thought about my boy. I was thinking of the way he waved good-bye to me with his nose pressed up against the back window of the Astra. I was looking down at the floor and I suppose I must of been in a world of my own because when Terence Butcher came back with the drinks he had to snap his fingers to get me to look up.

—Cheer up love, he said. It might never happen.

He sat down across the table from me. He sat his Guinness down in front of him and he pushed my drink towards me.

—There you go, he said. Chin chin. Here's to brighter days.

I smiled then but it was a nervous smile. If that smile had been a kid it would of been one of those kids you see on telly on the kidney machine with the tubes coming out of them. COURAGE OF BRAVE KELLY, 5. Terence Butcher watched me and took a sip of his pint.

—How's your drink sir?

He sat back in his chair and put his hands down around his pint. He frowned.

—Listen, he said. Don't ever call me sir again when we're off duty. If you do then I'll have you transferred to the British Transport Police. You will spend the next five years telling fat children not to drop crisp packets on the Docklands Light Railway. If you prove to be especially effective in that capacity you will be promoted to the District and Circle Lines. After fifteen to twenty years if you perform well you will be taken off the night shift and you might even be permitted occasionally to see the light of day in such prestigious surface stations as Gunnersbury and Chiswick Park.

I downed my G&T and it exploded in my tummy.

—Doomed to the underworld. Is that what happened to the last girl you had an affair with?

He didn't answer straight away. He drained his Guinness first. His eyes watched me over the top of his glass while he drank. He put his pint down very careful and wiped the white Guinness foam off his top lip. He lit a ciggie.

—Is that what this is? he said. An affair?

—Not yet. Not properly.

I slid my hands across the table so that the tips of my fingers were touching the tips of his. Terence Butcher looked around to see if anyone was watching. He let his head drop almost to the table then he lifted it up again and looked at me.

—Would you like it to be? he said.

I didn't answer I just pushed my hands forward so my fingers laced in with his. He didn't move his hands back but he didn't fold them round mine like he could of.

—Well? he said.

—Oh god do you have to be such a copper about everything?

—What? he said. What do you mean?

—Everything has to be black and white with you doesn't it? In your world we're either having an affair or we aren't.

—That's right, he said. I want to know where we stand. Life's hard enough without making it complicated.

—I do like you Terence Butcher. I get so lonely and I think you're a good man and I think you understand me.

He grinned.

—Great, he said. We're having an affair.

I shrugged. He was such a little boy sometimes.

—Alright then. Yes. Oh actually no. Come to think of it no. No it would never work you see. Trust me you don't want anything to do with me Terence you don't know what a state I'm in.

He shook his head.

—You're fine, he said. There's nothing wrong with you a couple of drinks won't fix.

I held on tight to my glass and tried to block out my boy's voice singing COUPLE OF DRINKS! COUPLE OF DRINKS! NOTHING WRONG WITH MUMMY.

—Yeah you're right. I'm fine.

—That's my girl, said Terence Butcher.

He leaned over the table and he stroked my face with both his hands. He pushed the hair off my face and he hooked it behind my ears just exactly the way my mum used to. I don't suppose he knew how sweet he was being when he did that. I looked up from my G&T and I smiled at him I couldn't help myself. Tears started up in my eyes. He smiled back. He moved his face closer to mine and he smudged the tears off my cheeks with his thumbs.

—There, he said. You're too pretty for tears.

I leaned forward and kissed him on the lips there was nothing else for it. I held his top lip between my teeth very gentle and I breathed in his smell of ciggies and Guinness. He didn't move a muscle. I sat back and looked at him.

—Same again?

—Mmm? he said.

—Guinness?

—Oh, he said. Yes. Yes please.

I smiled at him and I took our empties up to the bar and I nearly died of shock. Jasper Black was sitting up there on his own drinking a glass of red wine. He was looking the other way and I thought he might not of seen me but I had to stand quite close to him on account of there wasn't much space at the bar. I asked the barman for another Guinness and another G&T and I made myself small but it was no good. Jasper Black winked and got down from his stool and came over to me. He looked better than I remembered. He looked like he'd had his blood drained out and sunshine pumped in instead. He was grinning and bouncing up and down full of beans but when he came close there were stains on his jacket and his eyes looked sore. He puffed out his chest and leaned his elbows back on the bar and I looked down at his feet and he was wearing black slip-on shoes and no socks.

—Hi, he said. No disrespect but I have to tell you you're looking fantastic tonight.

—Jasper. What are you doing here?

—Me? he said. I'm drinking possibly the most disgusting Merlot it's ever been my misfortune to be served. I'm guessing the bottle was opened several days ago and stored on a radiator.

—Well. You know. It's a beer pub. If it's Merlot you were after you'd of been best off going to a Merlot pub.

—Merlot pubs, he said. There's a thought. Do they have them these days?

—Well I wouldn't effing well know would I? I wouldn't know Merlot from Tizer.

—Probably safest that way, he said. Anyway. I didn't come in for the wine. I came in to see if you were alright.

—How'd you know I was here?

—I didn't. I was walking past on my way home and I saw you coming in here with that man.

Jasper flicked his head back in Terence Butcher's direction. Jasper Black's hair was a right state. He'd had one of those haircuts where you don't know if you should say that's nice or sorry.

—I thought I'd pop in and stand by, he said. In case some misfortune was befalling you.

—Misfortune?

—I thought you might be in trouble, he said.

—Why?

—Your man is wearing a green polo shirt, he said. A lime-green polo shirt. I may not be blessed with Petra's fashion acuity but I know a plonker when I see one. Your man is wearing beige Timberlands for Christ's sake. A respectable man would not allow a chasm of such proportions to open up between himself and fashion. I was worried about you.

—You can talk. What the hell have you done to your hair?

—Oh do you like it? he said. I thought I'd treat myself to one of those Shoreditch hairdos. It's great isn't it? It's like 7 haircuts in one. It depends what angle you look at it from.

—It looks a mess.

Jasper Black sniffed.

—Correction, he said. It looks destructured.

—Yeah right.

He flicked his head back at Terence Butcher again.

—I suppose Mr. Timberlands is your new boyfriend? he said.

I looked at the landlord. He'd half-filled the Guinness and it was sitting there waiting to settle. The creamy foam was swirling through the dark stuff. It was fighting to rise free it made me nervous. I looked back at Jasper.

—That's Terence Butcher. He's my boss.

—I was watching you together, said Jasper Black. Forgive me if I note that your relationship gives all outward appearances of having transcended the purely professional.

—Come again?

—Are you fucking him? he said.

—Don't use that word.

—Well are you?

—Mind your own business.

—I miss you, he said. If you *were* fucking someone I'd very much rather it was me.

He grinned at me. His teeth weren't very clean and his fingers were drumming on the bar. I looked over at Terence Butcher. He was watching me talking to Jasper Black and he didn't look too pleased about it.

—Listen Jasper. My husband and my boy were torn to bits by rusty nails and bolts flying through the air at supersonic speed and then what was left of them was burned to cinders. All of it happened while I was *fucking* you so don't blame me if it's put me off.

Jasper Black leaned back on his bar stool and made a face like he'd just mistaken a dog turd for a KitKat Chunky.

—Jesus Christ woman, he said. I was only trying to be nice. Nothing personal but if you want my advice you need psychiatric help.

I stared at him.

—Yeah well I don't see why I should take brain advice off a man with 7 haircuts.

I turned away from him. It's funny how quick people can turn on you. The Guinness was finally ready and the landlord slid it across to me along with my G&T. I paid and picked up the drinks and started back to our table.

—Crazy fucking bitch, said Jasper Black.

He was off his head and he said it too loud. The whole pub stopped talking. Terence Butcher stood up. I stopped halfway back to our table holding the drinks. I was shaking. There was Guinness slopping everywhere. The smoke from everyone's cigarettes was making me think of May Day and my legs started to wobble. Terence Butcher stepped up to me and put his arm around my shoulders. He was staring over the top of my head at Jasper Black.

—Who's that bloke? he said.

—No one. Just some plonker trying it on. Please just leave it okay?

I went over to our table and I put the drinks down.

—Sit down. Please Terence. Let's just sit down and forget it.

He looked from me to Jasper and back.

—You sure? he said. Think carefully before you answer. I'm a very senior police officer. I have the resources of the entire Metropolitan Police Force at my disposal. I'm reasonably confident I could make this the worst night of that man's life.

—No Terence. Please leave it.

I put my hand on his chest and I pushed him down into his chair. He let himself be pushed. He could be as good as gold that man.

We didn't speak for the longest time after that. We just looked at each other and drank our drinks. I could feel the G&T starting to work. It was nice being out. Pubs were the best places for me really. I mean all the smoke made me nervous but I never actually saw my boy in pubs. They don't serve the dead or anyone under 18.

When our drinks were finished Terence went up to the bar for another round. He stood right next to Jasper Black so their elbows were touching. They were both tall men and they didn't say a word to each other and I couldn't look it made me nervous. After a while Terence Butcher came back with 3 drinks. He'd got himself a whisky chaser with his Guinness and my G&T was a double. He slid mine over to me and sat down.

—Alright? he said.

—Yeah. Terence?

—Yes?

—Thanks for being good to me.

—It's more than that, he said. I really like you. In fact I think I'm—

—Stop. Don't say it.

He smiled.

—Sorry, he said.

He drank his whisky and put the glass down loudly on the table.

—Right, he said. So tell me what do we do now then. I'm a copper. I need rules. I haven't done this before.

—Oh. Well I have god help me. It's quite simple really and there are rules so you'll be right at home. You start by telling me how you don't have sex with your wife any more. That's the hard bit for you. That isn't something you ever ought to tell another girl so once you've said that then we're both in it together. Then we have sex until your wife finds out and takes your kids to live at her mum's place.

—You're the perfect little optimist aren't you? he said.

—Well. That's just the way it works. I'm only saying.

Terence Butcher looked down into his pint. He made little circles with his finger in the creamy foam of his Guinness. I watched a thin line of blood start down his arm from under the lime-green sleeve of his polo shirt. The blood ran down the back of his hand and along his finger. Drip drip drip. It made bloody red craters in the creamy white head of his Guinness. He sighed and looked up at me.

—Tessa, he said. That's my wife's name. Loves the theatre does Tessa. We have to go once a fortnight. You like the theatre do you?

—Nah.

—Good, he said. The whole thing goes right over my head. Tessa must have dragged me along to a thousand plays by now and I still couldn't tell you the difference between *The Cherry Orchard* and the magic forest from *The Wizard of Oz*. More drinks?

—Yeah go on.

Terence went to the bar and came back with the same again. Jasper Black followed him back to our table with his eyes. I gave Jasper a look and he looked back at me for a long time before he dropped his eyes. Terence sat down.

—Everything alright? he said.

—Mmm? Oh yeah. Fine thanks.

I picked up my new G&T and rattled the ice in it. Terence Butcher lit another ciggie and I took one too on account of I was drunk enough.

—We got married too fast, he said. Me and Tessa. In those days people still waited till they were married. It made you want to get on with it. We were married 3 months and 3 days after our first date. It's all a bit of a blur. I remember standing at the altar and saying I do. I remember kissing the bride. And then I turned round and looked at everyone in the church. That's when I noticed I was out of my depth. On my side of the congregation there were all my mates from the force plus all their wives and girlfriends. They were a nice enough bunch but you could tell the suits were on hire if you know what I mean. Whereas on Tessa's side. The bride's side I mean. There were lawyers. Stockbrokers. An unbelievable number of ladies in hats. Their own hats I'm reasonably sure.

—You poor bugger.

—I noticed it all in a flash, he said. Us coppers are known for our powers of observation.

He swallowed half his Guinness and banged the glass down and laughed.

—Christ, he said. It looked less like a congregation and more like the two sides lining up for the English Civil War. I looked back at Tessa and I saw her looking out over the church too. She was trying to be brave but I could tell she'd just seen the same thing I'd seen.

There it was. All laid out before us. Tessa looked at me and from that moment I don't think we were under any illusion. I don't think you could really say it was love after that. The theatre. Child rearing. United front. But not really love.

—Sex?

—Yes, he said. Every now and then until the mid-90s. I can't say I was sorry when it stopped. Tessa had this way of making me feel like I was walking across her carpet with muddy boots on. She used to lie very still and not make a sound. I'd look into her eyes when we were making love. It was like looking through church windows from the outside.

—Poor you.

—Don't mind me, he said. I'm fine. I just get like this when I've had a drink or two.

—I reckon a bloke like you deserves more from a marriage.

—What I have with Tessa is not a marriage, he said. It's a nuclear class war.

He gripped his pint so hard I was scared it was going to break. I put my hand on his wrist and he looked up at me.

—Know what's different about you? he said. Warmth. That's what I get with you that I don't get with Tessa. Basic human warmth. Can I tell you something?

—Go on.

Terence Butcher blushed.

—I sometimes imagine you and me in bed together, he said. But not having sex. Just talking. It's the morning and we're away somewhere in my caravan and the sun's coming through the windows. We're miles from London. You can see the specks of dust glowing in the air above us. Everything's very quiet and still. And we're chatting away and suddenly you turn towards me and you ruffle my hair. That's all. You ruffle my hair and we smile because we understand one another.

I smiled at him and put my hand on his face.

—That's nice.

He leaned towards me.

—Would you do it? he said. Would you come away with me for a weekend? We'd take the caravan down to the coast. Brighton maybe. Or Worthing. What do you say?

—I'm not sure.

—I'm not sure either, he said. They've got better facilities at Worthing but it's quite dear so maybe Brighton would be a better bet.

—I mean I'm not sure whether we should go at all. What about your wife?

—I don't think we'd take her, he said. It's quite a small caravan you see and Tessa comes with rather a lot of baggage. Breeding. Family money. The people who have it aren't like you and me. They'll be polite enough to you. But try to get too close and they'll put back that distance. Try to step inside their circle and they'll close ranks. Us and them are not the same species. Don't make the same mistake I made. Don't ever get involved with the upper classes.

—Shall we have another drink?

Terence Butcher stood up.

—Alright, he said. Stay there. I'll go.

He took our empties back to the bar and I sat there thinking about Jasper Black and Petra Sutherland. Terence was 100 percent right god help me I never should of got involved but I couldn't think about that now on account of I was having trouble balancing on my seat and I needed a wee. I got up from our table and I picked up my handbag and walked over to the Ladies. I wasn't too steady on my pins.

There were 2 cubicles in there and wouldn't you know it I picked the one with no lock on the door. It's sod's law only you probably call it something different down your neck of the woods Osama like THE DIVINE WILL OF THE PROPHET but my point is there were 2 cubicles and I chose the one with no lock on the door and I was so desperate for a wee that I didn't care so I just pulled my knickers down and sat on the seat and did my wee while I held the toilet door closed with my foot.

I was doing my wee and thinking about what Terence Butcher said. I thought about ruffling his hair in the caravan with the sun coming in very bright through the windows and my boy laughing and doing somersaults on the long grass outside. My boy was giggling. He was ever so happy. He had his yellow wellies on. When he'd had enough of somersaulting we'd go for a walk. Him and me and Terence Butcher. We'd laugh and play 1–2–3 Whoops! and find some puddles for the boy to splash in.

I was so happy. Suddenly I really could see myself with Terence Butcher. I started whispering to my husband don't worry love I'll never forget you but you know how it is. You'd of wanted me to find someone wouldn't you? You wouldn't of wanted me to drift and blow away all alone like some old carrier bag. I smiled it was like all the emptiness was draining out of me with my wee. I sat there on the toilet for a little while after my wee was finished. I closed my eyes and hugged myself because for the first time in I don't know how long I wasn't feeling nervous. I was smiling because just for the moment I didn't see flames and I didn't hear screaming. I was smiling because my life wasn't empty any more it was ready to be filled. There's a difference you see Osama and that difference is called HOPE.

But when I opened my eyes I stopped smiling straight away because Jasper Black was standing in the door of the cubicle. I pulled my legs together and hugged my arms round my knees so he couldn't see anything.

—What the hell do you think you're doing?

—You left the door open, said Jasper Black. I thought you wanted company.

He came into the cubicle and closed the door behind him and leaned back on it. He stood there for the longest time just looking down at me with his 7 haircuts and his stupid grin. He looked a bit unsteady on his pins too. I should think he was more drunk than I was.

—Who were you talking to? he said.

—No one.

—Yeah right, he said.

He took a wrap of paper out of his jacket pocket and unfolded it.

—Cocaine, he said. Want some?

—No. Listen you'd better get out before my boyfriend comes to see why I'm taking so long. He's a big chap. If he finds you in here with me you'll be dead meat.

Jasper lifted his powder up to his nose and sniffed it right off the wrap. He stood there watching me. I think I knew what was coming but I didn't even have time to scream. He moved so fast. He came forward and pushed his hand over my mouth before I could open it. I tried to get up but he sat on me. His weight crushed my bum into the toilet seat and his crutch was pushed against my tummy. It was hard to breathe. I was slapping at his face with my hands and scratching him but it didn't seem to bother him. He was just laughing. With the hand that wasn't covering my mouth he started fingering my neck and my tits. The way his hand scratched at my tits it reminded me of this programme I saw on the telly where an armadillo tries to dig into an anthill.

There wasn't anything I could do. He pinned me down on that toilet seat. I thought he was going to rape me but he didn't. He moved his face right up to mine and he started kissing me on the cheeks and the eyes and the nose. His breath had that horrible sweet smell that comes in the evening from starting to drink in the afternoon and not stopping. He kept kissing me it went on and on. Like he was putting off what had to come next.

There were cuts on his face from shaving. It looked like he must of been drunk before he even left his place. There was dandruff on his shoulders. The T-shirt he was wearing could of done with a wash. Maybe it was all the G&T but I suddenly felt so sad for me and for him. You've got to be pretty far gone before you pull a stunt like he just had. I mean the list of your crimes is pretty long Osama but I don't think anyone's accusing you of following girls into the khazi.

This wasn't like Jasper Black. I looked in his eyes and I could see it now. He wanted to stop but it was out of control. His life was skidding into mine and it was happening in slow motion like a car crash. He shoved one hand down between us and he pushed his thumb up inside me and it hurt because I wasn't ready and all the emptiness flooded back in with it.

I gave up struggling. There was no point any more and I didn't want him to hurt me any worse than he had to. It was very quiet then in the cubicle with just the hiss of his sick sweet breath on my face. He stopped kissing me when I stopped fighting. I could tell he was surprised. His eyes went narrow and he stopped pushing so hard with his hand on my mouth. He just held me there for the longest time with his thumb pushed inside me. I could feel the blood pulsing in it very quick.

Tears ran down my cheeks onto his hand. Jasper stared at me in the green glow of the toilet striplights. I watched the flesh scoured off his face by white-hot flying shrapnel and spattered on the wall of the toilet cubicle until all the lonely dykes' graffiti was drowned and dripping with blood. Jasper's thumb made small nervous twitches inside me and my guts began to twist. I listened to his breath hiss and a tap drip drip in the washbasin outside. Then I heard the door to the Ladies open and swing closed again. There were 2 footsteps. Then silence. Terence Butcher's voice came from the other side of the cubicle door.

—Hello? he said. Look I'm sorry about this but you've been in there for ages. I just wondered if everything was alright?

Jasper was staring at me. I saw the pupils of his eyes go twice the size and I felt his hand tighten on my mouth. He looked over his shoulder to the cubicle door and then he looked back at me. Both his hands were trembling. I could feel his panic on both sides of my skin.

—Hello? said Terence. Look if you're poorly it's alright. Come on out of there. I'll help you clean up. We'll go for a coffee somewhere.

Jasper's eyes went wild. He was looking all around the cubicle for another way out. Maybe one of those small high windows they always have in films. But there wasn't one.

—Listen, said Terence. Just tell me you're alright and I'll wait for you outside. Otherwise I'm going to have to come in.

Jasper made the tiniest sound then. It was the smallest start of a cry. Just a sad little squeak right in the back of his throat. It was the exact same sound my boy used to make the instant after he'd fallen over and banged himself a nasty knock. Just before his face crumpled up with misery and the tears started.

Now you wouldn't understand this Osama because you're not a mother. That's my whole point I suppose. But when I heard that sad little squeak I went on autopilot. I still had my hands free and I moved one of them up to Jasper's cheek. I stroked his face very gentle. Then I took my other hand and I pulled down on the wrist of the hand he was holding over my mouth. He fought against me for just the tiniest part of a second and then he looked in my eyes and he let his hand fall away from my mouth onto my shoulder. Suddenly he was as good as gold. He was waiting to see what I was going to do. I looked right into his eyes and I felt his thumb trembling inside me. I opened my mouth.

—Terence? I'm alright. Sorry about this. I've just had a little bit too much to drink I'll be right as rain in 2 ticks. I'm a bit embarrassed so go on and have your drink and I'll be out in a minute.

—Sure? said Terence Butcher.

—Sure.

I stroked Jasper's hair. Terence Butcher went away then and Jasper breathed out.

—Oh Jesus, he said. Thanks.

He let his forehead drop onto my shoulder he was still shaking. I stroked his hair and I reached down with my other hand and I took his wrist and I pushed his hand down very gently so his thumb came out of me. I pulled his head in closer to my neck and I whispered in his ear.

—There you go. You're a good boy really. You've just been very lonely haven't you?

Jasper didn't say anything. His breathing was shallow and fast in my ear and then very slowly it turned into sobs. He didn't make any fuss he just sobbed very quietly and it didn't die down for a long time. I sat there just letting him get it all out. You'd think all that sadness inside us would of been deafening but actually it made less noise than the slow drip drip of the tap in the basin outside the cubicle door.

*   *   *

When I got back to our table I smiled at Terence Butcher and the drink he'd lined up for me.

—Ah. Gin & Terence. Lovely.

—You sure? he said. I thought you might've had enough.

—Yeah well that was 10 minutes ago. This is now.

—Alright, he said. But on your own headache be it.

Terence Butcher stood up and I went up to him and put my arm round his waist. I leaned in to him and put my head against his chest. I closed my eyes and the flames and the shrapnel were gone again. There was just my boy playing on the long grass outside the caravan. I opened my eyes and looked up at Terence Butcher.

—You're alright Terence Butcher. You know that?

We drank our drinks and I went up to the bar with Terence to get 2 more in but just then the landlord called time. Terence told him to give us a lock in.

—I don't think so, said the landlord. The police are pretty strict at the moment.

—Listen, said Terence. The police are pretty drunk at the moment. We've had a hard week trying to stop you lot getting blown up. If we're not allowed to get properly drunk now then we won't let off enough steam. Which means we'll be all wound up at work next week. Which means we won't be able to do our jobs properly. Which means every single one of you will die. So I tell you what. I'll give you a signed order to stay open another 10 minutes for security reasons.

The landlord smiled.

—Very good sir, he said. Always pleased to do my bit for national security.

—Good man, said Terence Butcher.

He wrote the landlord an official order in biro on the back of a beer mat and the landlord gave us 2 free drinks.

We rolled out of the Approach about half 11 and it was chaos out there. Everyone was trying to get home before curfew. There was a line of choppers flying low over Approach Road heading into town. They battered away into the darkness making a noise like death and nobody wanted reminding about dying so everyone was out the front of the pub giving them the finger. The choppers made a dirty twisting wind that raised up all the rubbish from the side streets. It was going everywhere. All the Burger King wrappers and the fag butts and the used condoms were blowing against the car windscreens like a poorly blizzard.

We were lucky to get a black cab. Terence flagged one down and told the cabbie Barnet Grove and when the cabbie said no Terence showed him his police ID and asked if he wanted to keep his licence. So we got in and Terence slammed the cab door. The helicopters and the rubbish were left outside and it was all quiet apart from the cabbie effing and blinding to himself about weren't we just his typical bloody luck.

—Thank Christ for that, said Terence.

He slid back into the seat. He was sitting closer than he needed to. His leg was touching mine. I felt his weight pressing against me when we turned right onto Old Ford Road.

—God I feel better for that, he said. You were right you know. A night out was just what the doctor ordered.

I just looked out the window. I didn't feel like answering. I must of had 8 G&Ts inside me. It felt like I wasn't going anywhere but London was racing past me. Actually it looked like London was trying to get to the khazi before it puked. It was one of those nights you get sometimes in London where every last bastard is drunk. It was one of those nights where City toffs in Hackett shirts jump out in front of your cab waving their hands and shouting TARXI! TARXI! so the cabbie has to swerve round them and shout can't you see I'm taken you silly little cunt excuse my French. It was one of those nights where the day can't come soon enough.

Terence Butcher put his hand on my knee. My tights were ripped and I felt his skin on my skin. I looked at him and I smiled.

—Not here Terence. There'll be time for all that.

I turned and looked out of the window. We'd just turned down Cambridge Heath Road and the traffic was all jammed up. People were running to catch the last buses and there were coppers with megaphones bawling at them to get a move on.

I closed my eyes and I felt something on the back of my neck. It might of been his lips. Or it might of been my husband's lips or Jasper's lips I had 8 G&Ts inside me telling me it made no difference. Terence's hand moved on my thigh. I gasped and it moved up my leg. I felt his hand push under the elastic of my knickers. Oh god I thought here I go again. I felt his fingers combing through my pubes and I felt the white van behind us blow up and I felt our cab flying eighty feet up in the air high above Bethnal Green tube. I felt the red blood gushing out of me while our cab spun black in the night under the smiling faces of the Shield of Hope. I felt his weight on mine as we lay burning in the wreckage. Oh god it was so bloody nice not to die alone.

The rush of booze got stronger. I opened my eyes and we were turning right onto Bethnal Green Road and we hadn't been blown up after all. I felt sweet saliva in my mouth.

—Oh dear I think I need to get out.

The cabbie stamped on the brakes and pulled the cab over quick sharp. They know from the tone of your voice when you're serious. I got out and puked on the double yellows while Terence Butcher held my shoulders. My puke was pure gin you could of cleaned brass with it. When we got back in the cab I felt much better. I smiled at Terence.

—Sorry.

—Don't apologise, he said. There but for the grace of god and all that.

We were driving past the KFC and the sari shops now we were only 2 mins from my flat.

—Oh look I'm nearly home.

—Are you sure you're going to be alright? said Terence.

The driver turned onto Barnet Grove.

—Let me come in with you, said Terence.

—It's almost curfew. You realise if you come in you'll be stuck with me for the night.

—Yes, he said. That was the general idea.

—What about your wife?

—I'll call her, he said. I'll tell her I'm overnighting at the office.

I held on to his hand. My skin was tingling and my stomach was jumping. The emptiness inside me was howling like the wind round tall buildings. The driver slowed up for the speed bumps on Barnet Grove. My street was all grey and dismal with Tesco bags blowing down it like the ghosts of value shopping.

—Anywhere in particular? said the cabbie.

—Anywhere here.

The cab stopped and I squeezed Terence Butcher's hand.

—Terence. I like you. Let's not spoil this. Go home to your wife tonight. Get up tomorrow morning and feel good. Look after your kids. Believe me you don't know how important it is. And then think about it and if you want me then you can have me. Only let's not do it like this. Please let's do it so your wife and kids don't ever find out.

Terence blinked at me. He looked so sad. I wanted him so badly I could feel the emptiness inside me shouting NO NO NO but I did it anyway. I squeezed Terence's hand one last time then I let it go and I opened the cab door. I got out and grabbed the door handle and slammed Terence Butcher safely back inside his life and his kids and his wife in her Dunlop Green Flash. I waved good-bye and watched his tired face pressed up against the window glass.

I stared up at the dead faces of the Shield of Hope floating in the orange sky. I stared for a long time and then I went inside and up to my flat and I got Mr. Rabbit and I curled up with him on the floor of my boy's room. I slept and I dreamed of my husband and my boy. They were setting off for heaven in our old blue Astra and their Arsenal away strip. They were ever so excited to be going. I'd made them packed lunches in case it was a long journey. My husband smiled at me. He was tall and handsome and he was all in one piece. I smiled back at him. We'll be off now love he said. You come after us as soon as you like. I waved them good-bye. My boy was smiling and waving with his nose stuck up against the back window. I watched them drive off up Barnet Grove and into the rising sun.

When I woke up my boy's room was rosy pink from the new day coming in through the curtains. And me? Me I was still smiling.

*   *   *

Later that morning I took my hangover into the shower. I say the shower Osama but actually I was standing in the bath. Our shower was one of those rubber hose efforts you stick on to the bath taps. My boy used to love it. He used to take it off the taps and make you hold the rubber ends to your ears so he could talk to you through the showerhead like it was a microphone. What he used to say was COME OUT WITH YOUR HANDS UP I suppose it was my husband taught him that.

The boy loved that game it used to take hours to actually wash his hair. Still you saved me that chore didn't you Osama. So it was just my own hair I was washing when the doorbell went. I was washing it for the third time. I never could get the smell of smoke out of it since May Day.

I wrapped a towel round my head and I put on my pink bathrobe and went to the front door. I put the chain on the door and opened it a crack and looked out. It was Petra Sutherland standing there.

She was wearing maroon stiletto boots silky flower-print skirt pink cashmere rolltop sweater and her hair was long and straight and shiny. She stood there looking at me. Her face was very white there was no blood in it.

—What must I do to get rid of you? she said.

I tried to shut the front door but Petra jammed one of her boots into the gap. Both of us started pushing at the door but she couldn't open it on account of the chain and I couldn't close it on account of her foot.

—What do you want?

—I want you to stop chasing after Jasper, she said.

—I never chased after him.

—Liar, said Petra. Trollop.

She pushed her face right up into the gap of the door and sneered at me.

—He came home reeking of you last night, she said. I know your smell. You smell of this place. I spent a whole night in it.

—You don't understand.

—Oh I understand perfectly well, she said. He wouldn't look me in the eye. Let me in.

—Nah I don't think so.

—People don't tell me no, she said. Let me in. We're going to have this out once and for all.

—Please. I'm not feeling well. Can't you and Jasper both just leave me alone?

—Us leave you alone? said Petra. Oh that's funny. That's a good one.

—Please. You don't know the situation. It's Jasper you want to have a word with. Not me.

—No, she said. Let me in. I'm prepared to stay here all day if that's what it takes.

—Suit yourself.

I went back and finished my shower. It wasn't the sort of shower you see on the Timotei adverts with a Swedish girl in a waterfall.

The water was a bit brown from the rust in the pipes and I could hear Petra banging on the front door the whole time and screaming at me to OPEN THIS DAMN DOOR. By the time I got out and started drying my hair she was trying something different she was yelling THERE IS A PAEDOPHILE IN THIS FLAT. I suppose she thought an angry mob would appear out of nowhere like they do in the *Daily Mail* and help her storm in but she still had a lot to learn about the Wellington Estate. Round here they wouldn't piss on themselves if they were on fire let alone the neighbours.

I went into the bedroom and put on a white T-shirt and white trackie bottoms. I lay on the bed just minding my own till the banging and the shouting went quiet and then I went back to the front door. Petra was sitting on the floor with her back against the wall and her foot still jammed in the door. Her head was down on her knees.

—You finished are you? Got it all out of your system?

Petra looked up at me her eyes were red and puffy and there were streaks of black mascara down her face. It was a bit of a shock I hadn't put her down for the sort of girl who has feelings. The timer ran out on the stairway lights and the landing went dark behind her. We just stared at each other for a long time through the gap in the door. Petra sniffed.

—You'd better come in.

I took the chain off the door and opened it wide and Petra snapped her head up to look at me.

—Come on get up before I change my mind.

Petra started to put her hands down on the floor to push herself up but the floor was all mucky and she had a good look at it and held her hand out to me instead. I took hold of her hand and pulled her up. When she was up we let go of each other's hands as quick as we could.

—I need to clean up, said Petra.

—Yeah. Well. You know where the bathroom is don't you?

I went into the kitchen and I didn't know what to do with myself so I took all the mugs out of the cupboard and then I put them back in with their colours in the same order as the rainbow from right to left and all of their handles pointing outwards except for the one mug that had a handle on each side. I didn't know what to do with it and I was still holding it in my hands when Petra came into the kitchen. She'd washed all that streaky mascara off and her face looked very white and new without makeup. I held the mug up.

—Coffee?

Petra looked at the jar of instant sitting on the worktop.

—I think I'd rather have vodka, she said. Do you still have some?

—Yeah. Only I didn't have you down as a morning drinker.

—It isn't the morning yet, said Petra. I haven't slept.

I poured Petra a vodka from the freezer. I felt poorly just looking at it but Petra knocked it straight back and passed me the empty glass.

—Ouch, she said. Again.

I poured her another and we went into the lounge and sat down at different ends of the sofa. Petra looked out at Barnet Grove through the net curtains. Those 3 kids were out there on their bikes again turning slow circles just like they were on May Day it made me nervous.

—The really stupid thing, said Petra. Is that I never really cared about Jasper. Until I realised he was slipping away from me.

I didn't say anything.

—It's awful of course, she said. Not really to feel anything about someone until one's faced with losing them. I suppose you think that's awfully selfish.

—Nah. I don't think. I mean I don't really have the imagination do I?

Petra smiled. She was still looking out the window.

—You can be terribly dry can't you? she said.

I just gave her a small shrug she couldn't see on account of her back was turned. I sat there hugging one of the sofa cushions I was getting another wave of my hangover and it was best not to move around too much.

—It hasn't been the same between Jasper and me since May Day, said Petra. I don't know whether to blame you or Osama bin Laden. I don't know which of you is worse.

—Yeah. Well. Have you talked to Jasper about it?

—Jasper's not in a good place right now, said Petra. He's been overdoing it. He's not easy to talk to.

—You'd better give it a go though eh?

Petra was still looking out the window. You could see her back going all stiff and angry and when she spoke her voice was shaking.

—How dare you? she said. How dare you tell me what I better had and better hadn't do? You're the one that's got my Jasper into this state. You're the one chasing after him with your cute little tush and your sweet little sob story.

Petra stood up and spun round to face me.

—You parasite, she said. Just because your sad little life is over doesn't give you the right to come after mine.

—You're having a laugh aren't you? I've seen how you live and I'd rather die.

—Hah, said Petra. Look at me and tell me you weren't with Jasper yesterday evening.

—That's not what I'm saying.

—Slut, whispered Petra.

She slapped me round the face it was hard and vicious. I didn't see her hand coming and it caught me half round the chin and half in the throat it snapped my head back so I heard the bones in my neck click. I fell back on the sofa I was holding my face but it didn't hurt I was just thinking how strange this is how very bloody strange. How strange to of been around so many blokes in my life and some of them real mischievous pieces of work at that and would you believe it the very first person to slap me about is the Lifestyle editor of the *Sunday* effing *Telegraph*. Well I couldn't help it Osama

I just started laughing I mean you'd probably be the same yourself if after everything you've been through the first person to get past all your bodyguards and storm into your high mountain cave was wearing maroon stiletto boots and lipstick. I took my hand away from my face and there was blood on it. I suppose I was cut from the rings on Petra's fingers. I just lay back on the sofa and laughed with the blood dripping off my face and onto my white T-shirt.

—You really are a lunatic aren't you? said Petra. You think this is funny?

—Listen Petra you've said your piece now why don't you just clear off.

—I am not budging, said Petra. Not until you promise never to have anything to do with Jasper again.

—Petra. Just listen for once will you? Jasper's the one chasing me. I hide from him. I sneak home and stay here with the lights off and when he comes knocking I keep the door shut.

Petra shook her head and frowned.

—What I don't understand, she said, is what on earth Jasper sees in you.

She spread her arms out.

—I mean look at this place. This horrendous little place. Is it the squalor he gets off on? Because I could do squalor. Or is it the drudgery? Would he become besotted with me if I gave up one of the best jobs in British media and started doing. I don't know. Whatever the hell it is you do?

—Tea. I make the tea and I do a bit of filing.

—Super, said Petra. How thrilling for both of you. The conversations you must have.

—Give it a rest will you?

—Or is it simply you? said Petra. Is it your nice little tits and your sad little eyes and your darling Lady Di hair? Because I can do the tits and I can do the eyes and I can do the hair. I can do it all. You think I'm joking? You want to see me do the hair?

Petra ran out of the lounge and into the kitchen. I heard her smashing about in the drawers and when she came back in she was carrying the kitchen scissors. She held them up to her lovely long shiny hair.

—No. Petra. Please. That's enough now.

Petra started cutting away at her hair thwack thwack thwack. There was gold hair falling all over the carpet and Petra was shouting THERE! THERE! THAT'S HOW HE LIKES IT IS IT? THERE! I couldn't stop her she was in a rage and I wasn't going to go near her while she had those scissors. So I just did like they do in the nature films when they get some wild animal going off like that. They just hop up on the roof of the Land Rover and stay up there till it's safe again. I just went round the back of the sofa and let Petra get on with it and when she was finished she let the scissors fall down on the carpet and she stood there trembling and looking like the things you want to forget about the 1980s. Actually I suppose what I mean Osama is the things we want to forget like Duran Duran and the Thompson Twins not the things you want to forget like the Soviet occupation of Afghanistan. Anyway my point is I was safe round the back of the sofa.

Petra started grabbing things and throwing them at me. She picked up my husband's football trophy from the time his lot beat the Flying Squad and she slung it and I ducked and it smashed against the wall behind me. The next thing she grabbed was an ashtray and she threw that too and it caught me on the arm and rolled off into the kitchen. I was getting scared on account of I was still weak from the hospital and it didn't look like Petra was going to stop till she'd done for me. She was just grabbing up any old thing she could find and slinging it at me and shouting HARLOT FLOOZY JEZEBEL BITCH and then suddenly she stopped very still on account of she'd picked up Mr. Rabbit.

She stopped with her arm raised up ready to throw him and then she saw what she had in her hand and she just froze. There was something about Mr. Rabbit you see Osama. You wouldn't of had the heart to chuck him. Anyone could tell he'd suffered enough.

Like I say he was stained black with my boy's blood and one of his paws was blown off and you could see the scars on him where his skin had burned through and his stuffing had roasted brown and hard as crackling. When Petra saw what she had in her hand she let out this little scream. Just a tiny surprised scream like the blip the scanner makes at the supermarket when it sees the bar code on your beans. Petra let her arm drop very slow and careful. She sank down on her knees and she laid Mr. Rabbit down on the floor in front of her very gentle in the middle of all her cut-off hair and then she just knelt there looking at him like she was in a daze.

I came round from the back of the sofa and I knelt down next to her and I put my arm round her shoulders. Petra was burning hot I could feel it through her jumper it must of been the vodka.

—This is all real isn't it? said Petra. This is all really happening.

—Yeah.

—We can't go back, she said. We can't go back.

—Nah.

Petra raised her head up and looked around the lounge.

—Shit, she said. I'm sorry about the mess.

—You're alright.

She looked at me.

—Your poor face, she said.

—Yeah well I'm going to wash it.

I went into the bathroom and filled the basin. It took a long time to get the blood off. After a bit Petra came and stood behind me and she stared at her new haircut in the mirror. She couldn't work it out.

—It's appalling, she said. No. No. It's sexy and audacious. Um. No. Tell me honestly. It's horrid isn't it?

—It just needs neatening up. Do you want me to do it? I used to do both my chaps' hair there's not much to it.

—Do you really think you can fix it? she said.

—Do you really think I can make it worse?

Petra sniffed and went off to fetch the scissors and I sat her down on the edge of the bath and neatened her up a bit. I stuck my tongue out I always do that when I concentrate. It was nice cutting her hair it felt nice to have something to do. When it was done I stepped back and had a good look.

—There. That'll get you as far as the hairdresser's anyway.

—Thank you, said Petra.

She stood up to look in the mirror but she stood up too quickly and I had to grab her to stop her falling. She leaned on the basin.

—Oh dear, she said. I think I'd better lie down.

I held on to her arm and took her into the bedroom. She wasn't too steady and the vodka on her breath was dragging my hangover back up from my stomach. The wardrobe was open in the bedroom and Petra's mouth went wide when she saw inside. She lurched over and held herself up on the wardrobe door.

—Oh good god, she said. Why do you torture yourself like this? You ought to take all of this to a charity shop.

—Oh no. I couldn't give my husband's clothes away. They're all I've got left of him.

—I didn't mean his clothes, said Petra. I meant yours.

She started grabbing stuff out of the wardrobe and chucking it on the floor.

—Oh for goodness sake, she said. You're a grown-up woman. Puma no. Kappa absolutely no. Nike. Gap. Reebok. NEXT. No. No. No. NO. Adidas a tentative yes but only for actually running in. Do you actually run in these?

—Nah. I don't have the energy for running. I couldn't run a bath.

—Right then, said Petra. Adidas no.

She threw my Adidas trackies on the floor with the rest of my stuff. Then she had a look at what was left on my side of the wardrobe. She held up my brown H&M skirt and wrinkled her nose.

—Alright, she said. I'll let you keep this for schooldays so long as you never tell a living soul I said you could.

I smiled.

—Look at you, she said. You'd scrub up just fine if you took a little more care over what you wore.

—Yeah well when you have kids you give up on wearing anything smart don't you? I mean not if you don't want choc-chip sprayed all up it.

Petra took my wrist and put her other hand on my cheek and swayed so her face came very close to mine.

—Yes, she said. But you don't have kids do you?

—That's enough. Let's get you lying down.

I shoved her towards the bed and she fell down face first on it with those stiletto boots sticking out over the end. She closed her eyes and groaned and her voice came out very slow.

—I'm not tired, she said. I just need a moment.

—That's alright you just have a little rest you'll be right as rain.

—What happened with Jasper last night? she said.

—Why don't you ask him?

—Why don't you tell me?

I just shrugged I was looking out the window. I was watching these nice white clouds blowing high above the balloons in the bright blue sky. There was a whole pack of them headed east out towards Stratford way and it looked like they were going to drift on and on all day. Not a care in the world those old clouds. I thought of them drifting till the city disappeared and then just floating on over the mooing cows and the buttercups. And when they saw the estuary mud underneath all speckled with gulls I supposed they'd just carry on drifting out over the flat grey sea.

When I turned back from the window Petra was asleep. She had her hands under her face palms down. I took off her boots for her and she mumbled something in her sleep it sounded like I thought I told you no anchovies in the salad. I rubbed my eyes. My hangover was pulling me down like the concrete lump they tie on when they want your body to sink. I lay on the bed next to Petra and watched her sleeping for a bit with her face all scrunched up on her hands. Then I fell asleep too and in my dream I was drifting over the estuary and out to sea. When I woke up the clouds were thicker out the window and Petra was still asleep and her hand was holding on to my wrist very gentle. I stayed still so as not to wake her and I must of drifted off because when I opened my eyes again the sky was overcast and the bed was empty beside me.

*   *   *

It rained for 6 whole days. London was a city on a lukewarm rinse cycle there was water everywhere. The Central Line flooded and Bethnal Green Road ran brown as the Thames and the pigeons sat down in doorways all sulky and wet and they didn't even bother flying off any more when you went near them. It was summer Osama what can I say?

I went to work in the rain and I came home in the rain. I did it again and again all week. Every day was the same except Wednesday there was thunder and Thursday it just rained harder instead. The wallpaper peeled in the flat and I couldn't be bothered to go down the shops so I just ate what was in the freezer and when the freezer was empty I started on the Cup-a-Soup.

On the Friday I went down the pub again with Terence Butcher but it wasn't the same. The crowd in the Approach was moody as the pigeons. I had so much Cup-a-Soup in my system the G&T tasted like minestrone. Terence was just banging on and on about caravans so I told him can't you give it a bloody rest? We had words and I smashed my glass on the table and walked home through the rain with my clothes wet through and sticking to me. Back home I lay in the lounge in my bra and pants with the telly off just listening to the rain.

I was still on the couch when I woke up. There was this shocking bright light shining through the window I couldn't remember anything like it. After a bit I worked out it was the sun. I stood up and opened the window and looked at Barnet Grove drying out with the steam coming off it and all the motors sparkling like new.

I had a shower and got dressed and the doorbell went. It was Petra and this time she was smiling.

—Isn't it a gorgeous day? she said.

I shrugged.

—Are you going to ask me in? said Petra.

—Depends. Are you going to start throwing things?

Her face fell.

—I was completely out of line last week, she said. Jasper told me what he did to you in the pub.

—Yeah?

I turned and went into the kitchen. Petra shut the front door behind her and followed me.

—Another woman might have called the police, she said.

I was looking out the window with my back to her. I shrugged.

—Jasper doesn't need the police does he? He needs to pull himself together.

—You could have made life quite difficult for us, said Petra. I owe you one.

I turned towards her.

—You don't owe me anything and I don't owe you. Forget it. Are you finished?

Petra stood there fiddling with her hands.

—Don't be like that, she said. I came to make a peace offering.

—Listen Petra I don't need a peace offering I just need peace and quiet.

I started the water running in the sink. Petra sat down on the corner of the kitchen table and watched me.

—You're quite something aren't you? she said. You just get on with things.

—Yeah well what would you do?

Petra thought about it for a bit.

—Me? she said. If I were feeling blue? Shopping.

—Yeah well there's nothing I need is there.

—You could do with something nice to wear, said Petra. Go on. Let me take you shopping today.

The sink was full. I turned the taps off and started scrubbing dried minestrone off the insides of the mugs.

—I'm fine with the clothes I've got.

—No you're not, said Petra. Trust me. You're a pretty girl but the way you dress all you're missing is the hairnet and you could be working in an abattoir. Your life isn't going anywhere. You need a bit of luck but nothing good is going to happen to you till you can walk out of that front door dressed for it to happen.

—You reckon.

—Darling, said Petra. I don't reckon. I know. If there's one thing I've learned from ten years in fashion it's that good luck adores good shoes. So come on. We're going to the shops.

I sighed.

—What if I've got something planned today?

—Well do you?

Well I thought about that one Osama and the truth was I didn't have anything planned for the whole of the rest of my life that was the whole problem. I shook my head.

—Nah.

—Super, said Petra.

She flipped open her mobile and ordered a black cab before I could say it was stupid to waste my bus pass. The cab arrived quicker than I could change my mind so I just put on my Pumas and left the washing-up in the sink. Outside on the street the tarmac was still steaming and my hair was drying in the sun.

—Listen Petra does my hair smell of smoke to you?

I moved closer to her and she took my hair and pulled it into her face. She breathed in slowly and breathed out. I felt her breath cool on my cheek.

—No, she said. Your hair smells delicious.

She brushed her fingers down the side of my face and I shivered. Then she let her hand drop. I watched it fall onto the pavement. Her arm was severed below the elbow and the naked bone peeped out of the ripped flesh. Her pretty pale fingers twitched. I had to close my eyes and open them again before things came back right.

We got in the cab and I saw the cabbie looking at us in the mirror. He did a double take and I don't blame him. We must of looked like one of those science experiments. You know. Where one twin gets the money and the other twin just gets in a state. I didn't really know what I was doing out with Petra. All I knew is it was better than staying in the flat all day.

—Where to? said the cabbie.

—Harvey Nichols, said Petra.

—You're having a laugh aren't you? I haven't got the money to shop at Harvey Nichols I'm an Asda girl.

—It's not a problem, said Petra. I have money. It'll be my treat.

—No Petra you can't buy my clothes for me.

—Then we'll just have to add it to my list of can'ts, said Petra. Can't throw tantrums. Can't let one's boyfriend sexually assault the competition. Can't slap said competition and vandalise her flat. Next to all that I would have thought treating you to a frock or two should count as a minor misdemeanour wouldn't you say?

—I wouldn't know I mean you lost me there.

—Then think of it this way, she said. I am Petra Sutherland. I can do whatever the hell I please.

Petra giggled. The cabbie sighed.

—Listen ladies, he said. If you've quite finished. Is it Harvey Nichols or isn't it?

—It is, said Petra. It always is.

It was a long ride to Knightsbridge and so it should be. I mean it's a different world isn't it? It doesn't seem right that you can get from Bethnal Green to Knightsbridge in a cab you should have to go via space or something. Petra kept moaning at the cabbie for taking so long but it wasn't his fault. All the roads we needed were closed off. It looked like the authorities were determined not to let your men get anywhere near the fashion shops Osama. So I suppose you'll have to stick with the cammo look for now. Even if it is a bit late 90s. As for me and Petra we had to take a big diversion.

—Good god driver, said Petra. Why don't you see if you can go a bit farther north? I think I saw icebergs over there but I'd like to make sure.

—Alright sweetheart, said the cabbie. Don't get your knickers in a twist.

When the cab dropped us outside Harvey Nichols Petra paid what it said on the meter. I'd never seen a meter go past 50 before. It made me feel a bit poorly. Petra didn't seem bothered. While she paid I stood on the pavement trying not to get in anyone's way. The streets were almost dry now it was a lovely sunny morning. Sloanes were bursting out all over Knightsbridge like desert flowers after the rain. I stuck out like a sore thumb Osama. I was thinking you would of done too. Even if you weren't wearing the beard and the AK47 I mean you'd still of been the only chap not wearing brogues and a Hermès jumper.

And then I started thinking maybe that was your secret after all. Maybe everyone was looking for you in the wrong place. Maybe you were sitting on Knightsbridge right now drinking a Frappuccino outside Starbucks in a check Barbour shirt and light-tan chinos smoking a Marlboro Light. Maybe the girl at the table next to yours was saying Good lord I suppose you get this all the time but you look just like Osama bin Laden without the beard. And maybe you were laughing and saying yes it can be a frightful bore listen do you know where a bloke can get hold of a decent-sized lump of Semtex round here?

Petra was saying something. She looked cross with me. I'd been off in my own world I suppose.

—Come on, said Petra. We haven't got all day. These clothes aren't going to cleverly select themselves.

I followed her into Harvey Nichols. An old man in a grey tailcoat and top hat held the door for us.

—Thank you Tom darling, said Petra.

—Always a pleasure madam, said Tom.

He looked at my clothes and frowned. We went inside and the traffic noise closed behind us. It didn't smell posh in Harvey Nichols it smelled of all the different perfumes in the world very strong and mixed up together. It felt like having your throat scraped. I took my boy into John Lewis once and it smelled just like that in the perfume section. Yuk Mummy he said. It smells nice and nasty all at once. It smells of angels' feet.

I kept my head down and followed Petra. We walked right through the first floor without stopping. It was all just perfume and BE PREPARED sort of stuff anyway. Louis Vuitton crisis bags and gas masks by Kenzo with matching headscarves. On the up escalator Petra turned and looked down at me.

—Right then, said Petra. Here we are in Harvey Nick's. I'd better talk you through it. Floors 1 and 2 are ours. Forget the third floor it's ghastly. The first floor is the designer stuff. Alexander McQueen Bottega Veneta Dries Van Noten. Nobody actually wears that stuff but it is essential that it exist because it adds a sense of mystery to existence. It's a bit like Mummy's makeup. It's just for looking at it's not for touching. The clothes one actually wears are on the second floor. And here we are now.

We stepped off the escalator.

—Let's have some fun, said Petra. Choose anything you want.

I followed Petra around the floor. She looked so happy stroking her hand across this and that. Stopping to go ooh at some of the clothes like she was a gardener and she was so pleased with how her flowers had come up. I was a bit lost. The problem with Harvey Nichols was that you couldn't work out what any of their clothes were for. Nothing was the shape of actual clothes. There was nothing you could look at and say Ooh look that's a nice pair of trousers. Don't get me wrong it was lovely stuff but it was all lovely silky fluttery stuff with lace tabs and things you had to know how to fasten around you before the stuff became clothes. The labels weren't any help either. The brands were called things like PHILOSOPHY and THEORY and IMITATION OF CHRIST. They didn't sound like clothes they sounded like the things I failed my GCSEs because of. Petra grinned at me.

—Do cheer up, she said. Why wear a long face when you could be wearing Helmut Lang?

I kept moving. I was terrified in case Petra made me try something on and I didn't know how to. Give me a Kappa T-shirt any day Osama at least you don't need a degree to know which hole your head goes through.

I gave up looking at the clothes. It was more interesting looking at the other shoppers. They were the kind of women that wouldn't be seen dead without their Prada handbag and Chanel sunglasses. You're a bit of a Knightsbridge girl yourself at heart Osama. We never see you without your AK47 and matching bullet belt I suppose Allah is big on accessories.

All those classy Knightsbridge women were making me nervous. The only accessory I had was Mr. Rabbit in my pocket. He came with me everywhere. I put my hand on Petra's arm and she stopped and turned.

—Listen Petra. I don't know what I'm looking for here. The last place I went clothes shopping was H&M. You're going to have to help me out.

Petra laughed.

—Oh no, she said. Aren't you something? Alright. I'm looking at you and I'm thinking white slacks from Helmut Lang and a pretty tunic top. Maybe Celine. And some nice strappy heels oh and a decent bag. Here. Follow me.

Petra was away. She was dashing between the racks grabbing clothes off the rails and throwing them over her arms. She knew just what she was doing she never stopped till her arms were full. She was all out of breath.

—Right, she said. Let's see what these look like on.

We went to the changing rooms. The attendant just smiled and found us a cubicle. Apparently she wasn't worried I was going to sneak out wearing Hermès slacks under my trackie bottoms. I suppose they don't get much of my sort at Harvey Nick's. It was a big changing cubicle and me and Petra went in together. There was plenty of room. Petra locked the door behind us.

—Right, she said. We'll start with the trousers.

I just looked at her.

—What is it? she said.

—You want me to take my trousers off? Here? With you watching?

Petra rolled her eyes.

—Oh good god, she said.

She pushed me down so I was sitting on the bench and she knelt to pull my Pumas off. Then she pulled my trousers down like a busy mum getting her kid ready for swimming lessons. When she saw my old grey knickers she stopped. She dropped her chin onto her neck and sighed out of her nose.

—Oh dear, she said. I'll be right back.

When she was gone I stood up in the changing cubicle and watched myself in the mirror. It felt strange on account of I wasn't used to staring at myself. I never had the time I suppose. And now here I was seeing myself right after watching all those classy ladies and it was a bit of a shock. I looked like something you find at the back of the cupboard. I was ashamed. It's funny what a bomb can do Osama I never used to care how I looked but now I blushed. I stared down at the carpet tiles.

In a little while Petra came back into the cubicle with a bunch of fancy undies and she locked the door behind her again.

—Right, she said. Choose what you like and put it on. Bra and panties. You'll notice that everything is white and simple. Lesson one. The artist begins with a blank canvas.

We looked at each other.

—Alright. But don't watch.

—Cross my heart and hope to die, said Petra.

She turned round and put her hands over her eyes. I took my knickers off and I felt the cool air against me. My tummy jumped. It felt like I was falling. I took off my Nike top and my bra and I let them drop on the carpet tiles. I got goose bumps. It was very quiet in the cubicle. You could hear Petra breathing and you could hear the little bright spotlights buzzing. I stood there for a moment. I was thinking nothing much. Then I put on a pair of the white knickers and one of the bras. I don't know if they matched I didn't care. I swallowed. My heart was going.

—Alright you can turn round now.

Petra turned round and her eyes went up and down me.

—Mmm, she said.

I blushed. I folded my arms over my tummy and I pressed my knees together.

—Relax, said Petra. Deep breaths. You're doing fine.

I liked the first pair of trousers Petra handed me. They were bright white and silky. They felt lovely against my skin it was like swimming in cold milk. Petra grinned when she saw them on me.

—Good god, she said. I knew you were a diamond in the rough. We'll be fighting the boys off with a stick.

The next thing we tried on was the strappy heels. The pair we chose was Fendi. They made me a foot taller I swear. The top half wasn't so easy. We tried 4 tunic tops before we found one Petra liked. It was Hermès and I could of kept my boy in food and clothes for 2 years for what it cost I'm not joking. I showed Petra the price tag.

—Look they've made a mistake.

—No, said Petra. They've made about 100 million pounds this year. And you know why? Because clothes are like magic. It's a small price to pay.

—Yeah right.

I was laughing at Petra but then I turned to look at myself in the mirror and I gasped. It was crazy. I could of been on the cover of a magazine. I was tall and beautiful and all I could think was HA! I'd like to see you banging on about caravans when you get an eyeful of THIS Terence Butcher. I looked at myself I just stared and stared I was so happy I started to cry. I watched the tears run down my face I was thinking Oh dear god it really could happen couldn't it my luck really could change.

—I look alright don't I?

Petra came up close behind me and she put her chin on my shoulder and her hands on my waist. She was grinning at me in the mirror.

—Here's to turning a new page, she said.

We both just stood there for ages watching the new me. I smiled back at Petra in the mirror. She was so like me especially now we were both dressed classy. It was like we were sisters but you couldn't really tell till we were dressed the same. Petra had thick pink gloss on her lips. It was nice and shiny like the back of a beetle.

The flames started in the ends of Petra's hair and they moved along it like a fuse. They spread to her face quite quickly. Her hair burned yellowy blue like a gas fire. The lacquer on her lips started to go brown and blister. Her lips started moving but it wasn't Petra's voice that came out it was my boy's. Mummy her lips said help Mummy my hair's on fire it hurts it hurts.

I turned round and I pushed Petra to the floor of the cubicle. I rolled her across the blue carpet tiles trying to put the fire out. She was screaming and kicking and swearing blue murder at me. The flames were spreading up my arms too. My whole front was on fire I could feel the wire of the new bra red hot and sizzling into the soft skin under my tits. It hurt so bad I don't have the words. The skin was peeling off my hands but I kept trying to put the flames out. I grabbed all the clothes we'd been trying on and I pushed them down all over Petra's body. I was trying to smother the flames but all the clothes caught fire instead. It all went up in flames the Katherine Hamnett and Armani and Diane von Furstenberg it all looked the same when it was burning.

I started to scream there was nothing else I could do my hands were burned down to stumps. I closed my eyes. I could still hear my boy's voice screaming out of Petra's mouth MUMMY MUMMY

WHY DON'T YOU HELP ME? I put my arms over my ears and screamed into the smoke and the dark.

* * *

The first thing I heard was Petra's voice. It's okay she was saying. It's okay it's over it's okay. I opened my eyes. I was sitting on the floor of the cubicle and there were clothes lying all around me. Nothing was on fire. Nothing hurt. A first aider was in the cubicle with us and she was dabbing at a scratch on my face with witch hazel. It stung but I always did love the smell of witch hazel. Petra was holding my head and stroking the hair back off my face. Deep breaths she was saying. Deep breaths. Could someone please fetch us a glass of water?

I looked up. There were security guards outside the cubicle watching us. One of them nipped off and came back with a plastic cup of water. It was half full and warm. The water tasted of blood I suppose I must of bit my tongue.

—Is your friend going to be alright? said the first aider.

Petra looked at me. Her hair was all messed up and her eye makeup was running it was obvious she'd been crying. She smiled at me.

—Of course she's going to be alright, said Petra. Can you get up?

—I think so.

I stood up with the first aider helping me. My head felt light. Like it might just up sticks any moment and float off into the Shield of Hope. After a while the first aider and the security guards left us alone. I watched myself in the mirror. I was very pale in my bright new clothes. I looked at Petra.

—I'm so sorry.

She hugged me for a long time. I was shaking. We stood there in the cubicle and it was very quiet again with just our breathing and the sound of the spotlights buzzing.

We left my old clothes behind in the cubicle. The only thing I took out of there was Mr. Rabbit. Petra paid for the clothes I was wearing. It came to more than our old Astra.

When we got outside it was lunchtime. The weather was lovely. Hyde Park was right in front of us on the other side of Knightsbridge.

—Let's keep you out in the fresh air for a while, said Petra. We'll go on the Serpentine. We'll bob around on a boat.

—I don't like boats they make me nervous.

—No they don't, said Petra. And if we get bored we'll step ashore and seduce the park wardens.

I was in a bit of a daze still. Petra had to get hold of my wrist and lead me. We went into a take-away place I don't remember which. Petra bought sushi and 2 bottles of cold white wine and we walked into the park as far as the Serpentine.

There was a long queue to hire a rowing boat so Petra stuck her fingers in her mouth and whistled. She hailed this young couple who were already in one of the boats like they were a cab. She gave them 50 quid to turn the thing over to us she was that kind of girl. I was very wobbly getting into the rowing boat I don't think they were meant for heels. We had a go with the paddles but we couldn't work out how to make the boat go straight so we just let it drift.

We lay back in the bottom of the boat. It was less wobbly that way. You'd of thought it'd be nice out there on the water but it wasn't particularly. The sky was blue but you couldn't see much of it what with all the balloons in the Shield of Hope. They hadn't chosen very nice people for the balloons round Hyde Park anyway. The faces were mostly fat blokes who looked like they could tuck the pints away. They were the sort of blokes who'd call each other by nicknames like oi Baz and oi Todger and you could imagine them pinching your bum at a New Year's Eve party. Saying How about it darling? It was funny seeing those dead fat blokes 500 feet up in the air saving us from kamikazes. It might of been the first decent thing they'd done in their lives most of them.

There were helicopters buzzing around between the balloons. One of them was doing a circuit and it kept coming down low over the park. You could see the pilots in their big helmets just like my boy's lego men. I waved at them but they didn't wave back. I suppose it isn't easy when your arms don't bend at the elbow. As if the chopper wasn't enough there was a police boat on the water. It was only a small rubber boat with 2 coppers in short-sleeve shirts. I don't know what they were in aid of. I suppose if you had been planning a raid on the ice cream van on the north shore of the Serpentine Osama then you'd of had to call it off. When the police boat went past it made our little boat rock.

It wasn't very relaxing out there but everyone was making the best of it. That's the British way after all. The Serpentine is half full and all that. We started drinking the wine out of plastic cups. It was hot in the sun and the wine was cold and it went straight to my head. Petra sighed. She was trailing her hand in the water making little ripples.

—How do you feel now? she said.

—Better. I still don't feel right though. I'm trying not to panic.

—I know what you mean, said Petra. Listen. I just want you to know that I'm here for you. However long it takes for you to get better in your mind.

—Thanks.

—You're welcome, said Petra. Anyway I'd much rather spend a nice sunny day with you than with bloody Jasper. Frankly he's turning into a bit of a bore. He used to be such an extraordinary boy. There was nothing he wasn't interested in. He could talk for hours about pop music or plutonium or chicken pox it didn't matter. It was always fascinating because he was always fascinated. All that's finished now. Ever since May Day he's been depressed. He's been seeing quite a bit of Charlie at weekends and it puts him in a mood all week.

—Charlie?

—Coke, said Petra. Cocaine. The pale mistress. How is a girl to compete?

—I wouldn't know. The worst my husband ever took was 2 Alka-Seltzer in a small glass of water.

Petra laughed and poured us more wine into the plastic cups.

—Coke's not the big deal, she said. Not in itself. I know lots of perfectly glamorous people who seem able to dispatch tons of the stuff without feeling compelled to follow girls into the lavatory.

Petra let her head fall back against the wooden side of the boat. Thump. The helicopter went over again very low. The wind it made sent dark little waves rushing outwards from the middle of the Serpentine and it ruffled our Lady Di hairdos.

—You shouldn't of done that to your hair. It was nicer before.

Petra's head was still resting against the side of the boat. She closed her eyes.

—True, she said. Still. Jasper likes it.

—Does he?

Petra opened an eye and squinted at me.

—Yes, she said. We have better sex when I look like you.

—Oh.

—Yes, said Petra. It's so ironic. You'd think I could come up with some other look to turn him on. Considering my job is to inform millions of people how to render themselves more attractive to the gender of their choice. Considering I'm Lifestyle Editor of the *Sunday Telegraph* and you're. Well.

—Drunk.

—Yes, said Petra. Oh me too. What is it with booze and boats?

She laughed and poured out the last of the bottle. Then she swallowed. She twisted the hem of her skirt between her fingers.

—I think I might even be drunk enough to say what I've been thinking now, she said.

—What?

Petra sat up straight. She held on to my wrist with both hands and the boat wobbled. She moved her face close to mine. Her eyes were shining.

—Move in with us, she said.

—You what?

—Move in with us. Take a holiday from that depressing flat and your awful memories. Come and spend some time to recover.

—Recover? With you?

—Yes, said Petra. It'll do us all some good. Jasper especially. It'll take his mind off the coke.

—Nah. You're having a laugh aren't you? This time last week you were throwing things.

Petra blushed and looked away over the side of the boat.

—That was before I saw you in Hermès, she said.

—You're not in your right mind.

—No, said Petra. But the entire planet isn't in its right mind since May Day so for pity's sake let's just roll with it. What the hell is the use in the whole world going crazy if we can't do the same?

I was looking out over the water. People were doing nice normal things in their boats. Teenagers were snogging in their life jackets. Dads were teaching their boys to row. Everyone was laughing and putting on a brave face and sun cream. I wasn't like them any more. I didn't have a boy to teach how to row. Apparently I had a chap to distract from cocaine there's a difference. I started to cry very quietly. The tears slid off my cheeks into the Serpentine.

—I couldn't Petra. When I see Jasper I see the explosion. Again and again and again.

—Yes, said Petra. But tell me. Honestly. What do you see when you're sitting home alone?

I looked up at Petra I felt sickness rising in my stomach. I wished it was over I wished I could be far away in a caravan at sunrise I wished I'd never argued with Terence Butcher.

—This isn't fair.

Petra brushed the tips of her fingers through the tears on my cheeks and put her fingers to her mouth.

—So be brave, she said.

Our boat drifted into the shadow of a barrage balloon. It was cold out of the sun. I shivered. We never did eat that sushi. I mean why would you? All seaweed and raw tuna sushi is. More like a fishing boat accident than lunch. Petra fed hers to the pigeons. I dropped mine over the side. I cried and watched the big white rolls of rice fall out of sight in the muddy brown water. I was thinking bombs away.

Before you bombed my boy Osama I always thought an explosion was such a quick thing but now I know better. The flash is over very fast but the fire catches hold inside you and the noise never stops. You can press your hands on your ears but you can never block it out. The fire keeps on roaring with incredible noise and fury. And the strangest thing is people can be sitting right next to you on the Central Line and not hear a sound. I live in an inferno where you could shiver with cold Osama. This life is a deafening roar but listen. You could hear a pin drop.

Autumn

Dear Osama I could of been Petra Sutherland.

I looked at myself in Petra's dressing table mirror. I was putting her Sisley Lychee Glossy Gloss on my lips. I pressed my lips together mmm mmm. I am Petra Sutherland I said. I wouldn't need to work if I didn't simply adore my job. I can do whatever the hell I please.

I looked at myself and I tried to think what earrings she'd wear with those lips. I was watching the clock. 7:45 a.m. There was still an hour before I had to head off to Scotland Yard. I opened the drawer and I took out Petra's pearl earrings. I hooked them into my ears and they felt heavy and perfect. I turned my head to the side and the earrings followed like well-trained money.

I held my chin up just the way she did. I was almost there. Just my eyes to do and I was her. It was still half dark outside and there was rain beating against the window. I took her mascara. Yves Saint Laurent False Lash Effect mascara. It came in a lovely thin gold bottle. It was cold and heavy in your hand like the barrel of the gun the hit man screws together in spy films. I put it on my lashes and blinked at myself. My heart was racing. I was her. I was her. I am Petra Sutherland I said into the mirror and I smiled just so.

The real Petra was in New York. It was just me and Jasper in the house and he wouldn't be awake for hours. The poor chap was dead to the world on their bed behind me. I was all alone in Petra's life and I was thinking wouldn't it be nice if I didn't ever have to give it back. I was pretending if I could just get ever so good at being Petra then one day she'd come back from her week with American *Vogue* and I'd be all like WHAT THE HELL DO YOU THINK YOU'RE DOING LETTING YOURSELF INTO MY FLAT LIKE THAT? and I'd send her packing to the Wellington Estate.

I looked back in the mirror. I am Petra Sutherland I said. This season's colours are jade and tan and burgundy. I had one of Petra's *Sunday Telegraph* articles on the table in front of me. I was practicing talking posh. Talking posh is like anything else Osama you can get used to it pretty quick. The trick is to read one of Petra's sentences aloud and then straight away say something of your own. It's an effort but you can trick your brain into doing it. Like when me and my husband used to bump start the Astra. I picked up Petra's article and I read aloud.

—At a basic level the democratisation of high fashion is demonstrated by the hipster boot-cut pant, which is now the most common trouser shape.

I watched my lips in the mirror.

—At a basic level the democratisation of Petra Sutherland is demonstrated by the fact that I am her.

I smiled. The more I practiced the better I got. You should try it yourself Osama. This season's bloodbaths will be crimson and carmine and scarlet.

—I am Petra Sutherland. It is September now and the faces on the balloons of the Shield of Hope have faded. The summer sun turned them pale and now one has the impression that London is defended by ghosts.

I shook Petra's head at myself in the mirror. She wouldn't of said ghosts she would of said spectres. There's a difference. I tried again.

—I am Petra Sutherland and my city is protected by spectres.

There it was. I smiled.

—I am Petra Sutherland and my city is protected by spectres and my boyfriend is on a cocaine-fuelled downward spiral but I must remain cheerful.

I tried a cheerful smile in the mirror. I almost fooled myself.

—I am Petra Sutherland. I am wearing chestnut corduroys. I am wearing a bolero jacket with frilly ruffs. I am wearing myself out through overwork. I set off for the paper at the crack of dawn and I don't come back until late. I find I am happiest in the office up to my neck in fabric swatches and freelancers' copy. I have started to rather dread coming home. Jasper has turned into something ghastly. He neglects himself. He has to be goaded into the bath like a sheep reluctant to be dipped. His behaviour is monstrous and unpredictable. The morning after a really big night he cowers in bed with the pillows over his head crying like a baby. When he has sufficiently recovered he will get up and mooch around the house. He will smash crockery and guzzle coffee and sometimes even make an appearance at the paper. Where he is increasingly unwelcome. His column has followed him downhill. His words are not words any more they are 800 bared teeth. His column is a snarl against anything and anyone that is not Jasper Black. It can't be long before the paper drops him.

—I am Petra Sutherland. People at the paper have started to talk. Or more exactly they have stopped. Conversations falter when I join them. Subjects are changed. The weather has taken a turn for the worse lately hasn't it?

My lip gloss was smudged. It was the way her mouth twisted when she talked about Jasper. I wiped off the smudge with a cotton ball and started again.

—I am Petra Sutherland and the girl hasn't helped. I don't know what I was thinking. I remember hoping that once he had her up close Jasper would see how dreadfully bloody ordinary she was. But she has failed to bore either one of us. Jasper paws at her bedroom door at night. She won't let him in because she's mooning over some policeman. And then one night I walked in on her in the bathroom. On the edge of the tub her candles were burning down to stumps and she was lying quite still in the water. When she heard the door open she just stared up at me. I should have left. I stepped inside and locked the bathroom door behind me.

I had my eyes closed. I was remembering Petra forgetting herself. I heard a noise and I opened my eyes and gasped. Jasper was standing behind me. His reflection was watching mine in Petra's dressing table mirror. His stubble was thick and black and his eyes were very small in their puffy white rings of skin. He looked like a dying panda. He was wearing grey boxer shorts and black socks. Nothing else. He was starting to get a bit of a gut I noticed. When he spoke his voice was empty like a toy without batteries.

—Hello Petra, he said. I'd have thought you'd have been on your way to work by now.

I froze. I couldn't think what to say so I didn't say anything. Jasper came closer. He put his hands on my shoulders and I jumped. He smelled of nightmares and stale smoke from Camel Lights.

—Oh come on Petra, he said. Don't I even get a hello?

I looked at him in the mirror. He looked straight back at me and his eyes were as empty as his voice. You could tell he was mainly thinking about finding the Neurofen. I took a deep breath. I made sure I got Petra's voice just right. Cold and hurt.

—Hello Jasper. I imagined you wouldn't be awake for hours.

—Uh, said Jasper.

He walked into the bathroom and started going through the medicine cabinet. I heard him throwing packets of stuff on the floor. I stood up from Petra's dressing table and followed him into the bathroom.

—Oh darling I can't bear to watch you suffer.

I found the Neurofen and passed him the shiny silver box. He closed his hand over mine and he looked at me.

—Have you done your hair or something? he said.

I shook my head no.

—You look different, he said.

—It's your hangover. I'm just the same.

Jasper screwed up his eyes.

—Hangover, he said. That's what I have. It feels as if the world is ending. It feels as if mice have got into my neurons and chewed off all the electrical insulation.

He rubbed his chin.

—Oh god, he said. I was a total cunt again last night wasn't I?

—No Jasper last night you were just ordinarily awful. You've been high for 3 days. The night you really were a total cunt was Saturday.

—What did I do? he said.

—You wouldn't believe me even if I showed you the bruises.

Jasper groaned and sat down on the floor.

—Jesus Petra, he said. I'm sorry. I'm completely fucked.

—We'll talk about it when I get home from work.

—Talk about it? he said. I know what that means. You're going to leave me aren't you? Please don't. If you leave me Petra I think I'll go mad I really do.

His eyes were darting about all panicked and I wished I hadn't pretended in the first place now. I put my real voice back on.

—It's alright Jasper it's only me.

Jasper looked up at me and blinked.

—Petra's gone to New York. Remember?

He opened his eyes wide then closed them quick. I suppose the light hurt them.

—Oh, he said. You.

—Yeah. Come on. Get up.

—Jesus Christ.

He stood up and went to the sink and ran the cold tap and popped 4 Neurofens out of the pack and swallowed them. He stood there with the tap still running and looked at himself in the mirror above the basin.

—Bad Jasper, he said.

He stood there looking at himself a long time. I don't know what he was looking for. Maybe something funny to say but he seemed so sad. I went up behind him and I turned the tap off. I put my arms around his tummy and I put the side of my face against his back. He didn't move he just started crying. It wasn't much. Just some tiny sobs. He wasn't making a fuss. I stroked his tummy.

—Thanks, he said.

—You're alright. You'll feel better in a minute.

—There you go again, he said. Why can't Petra be more like that?

—I reckon she's too busy earning the money you're putting up your nose.

—Petra doesn't give a shit about me, he said. She doesn't care. I wish she'd just go.

I smiled at him in the mirror.

—No you don't. Who'd have you then?

—You would, said Jasper.

—Don't be daft.

—Why not?

—Listen Jasper you're an alright bloke but you've got to pull yourself together and let me make a new start.

Jasper turned round and put his hand on my bum and started stroking my neck with his other hand.

—So why not make a new start with me? he said.

—Cause you smell of death and I'm late for work.

He took a step back and stood there scowling at me in his socks and boxers.

—You're still seeing that policeman aren't you? he said. Mr. Timberlands.

—Yeah. I'm seeing him today.

—Isn't he married?

—We go to a hotel. Monday lunchtimes.

—How romantic.

—Says Prince Charming.

I looked Jasper up and down and Jasper looked at the floor.

—It's this godforsaken world, he said. It's brought me down.

—Nah Jasper it's the coke bringing you down. You ought to try looking on the bright side.

—Ah yes, he said. The bright side. Every week I have to write 800 words about a world that's turning to rat shit but never fear dear *Telegraph* readers because the bright side is that we can all watch the world turning to rat shit on our plasma TVs while we enjoy our ebullient housing market and our preemptive action against tyranny.

Jasper spun round and smashed the side of his hand into the mirror above the basin. A big ugly star of cracks spread across it.

—Oi! Calm down will you?

—How exactly am I meant to calm down? he said. There is no fucking bright side. Barrage balloons go up over the city? Let's do DIY! Curfew keeping us cooped up indoors? *Big Brother*'s ratings soar! How do we react when they intern the Muslims? Who cares when this year's hot new thing is threesomes!

—Jasper. Listen to yourself.

Jasper stared at me and suddenly laughed. It was a horrible laugh.

—God I'm sorry, he said. You're right. I'm ranting again. Listen you don't have any coke do you?

—You know I don't.

—No, he said. Of course you don't. Still. No harm in asking.

He sniffed. He wiped his nose with his hand all cut from the mirror. Blood dripped down onto his lips. It was real blood. It wasn't just in my head for once I didn't know whether to be sad or happy about that. The blood ran down onto his teeth while he talked.

—People have forgotten the horror, he said. Do you remember the noise of the explosion?

—Don't.

—It rattled the windows, said Jasper. It echoed and echoed through the streets. I can still hear it in my head. And then there was your face. Your poor little face when you started to realise. That's horror. You realising you had no one left to grill fish fingers for. That's what it all boils down to after all the politicking and the posturing and the 800 balanced words from pompous cunts like me. Horror.

Jasper turned round and held on to both sides of the basin. He dropped his head and blood dripped on the white enamel. I took him by the wrists and I led him out of the bathroom into the bedroom. He was muttering.

—Sleep Jasper. Try to get some sleep now there's a good boy.

I wrapped a towel round his cut hand and I tucked the duvet in around him. I stroked his hair.

—Hush now my darling boy. Hush.

He closed his eyes and I sat with him for the longest time till he seemed to sleep. His eyeballs rolled under the eyelids. His fingers twitched. There were broken things in his dreams and they were after him. I went and fetched Mr. Rabbit out of my bag and I tucked him in next to Jasper. Mr. Rabbit always was good for nightmares. I sat there for a long time stroking Jasper's hair. You never really lose the habit of looking after a boy I suppose it's like riding a bicycle. Or cleaning a Kalashnikov if that rings more of a bell Osama I mean who the hell knows what a boy like you got up to after school?

When Jasper was calm and still I went back to Petra's dressing table. I put her earrings back in the drawer. I used her makeup remover and a cotton pad and I scrubbed her face off mine. I took her clothes off and hung them in her wardrobe. I took off her bra and her knickers and I put them back in her drawers and I stood there naked and shivering. The clock said 8:45 a.m. It was time to put my own life back on.

*   *   *

I was late in at work that morning and I wasn't the only one. The buses weren't running properly and mine just didn't turn up at all. Something to do with bomb scares left a hundred of us waiting in the cold grey rain on Bethnal Green Road. There are so many bomb scares now. You can't leave a ciggie butt unattended these days without someone coming and doing a controlled explosion on it.

Everyone was late for work and complaining to people on their mobiles. Loudly so that the rest of us could all get an earful. People took it in turns. That's how the English have a good moan these days Osama. Heaven forbid we should actually grumble to our neighbours in the bus queue. We're not like you hot-blooded Arab types. That's what Terence would of said. It's the climate you see. It's the rain on Bethnal Green Road that makes Britain great and I stood in it for half an hour before I gave up and walked to the tube and the tube was closed too so it was your typical bloody London good morning.

There was nothing for it I had to walk to work 5 miles through the rain and the 3 million other people whose buses hadn't come. It was a struggle I don't mind telling you. I don't know what it is with London and umbrellas it's like everyone's trying to have your eye out. Rain makes us vicious. People were bumping into each other and giving it the old lip and stepping into puddles and all the traffic was jammed and as if all that wasn't enough it was effing Monday wasn't it.

Halfway along the Embankment I saw this man lose it. He was crossing too close in front of a bus and the bus driver hit the horn. The man jumped back and dropped his briefcase and it burst open. His computer and his papers and all his little gadgets fell out into a puddle. The man crouched down and started trying to grab all his stuff up but the crowds didn't give him a chance they just carried on walking on his papers and his iPod and his fingers. OH FOR FUCK'S SAKE the man was shouting. CAN'T YOU FUCKING ROBOTS GIVE ME A CHANCE HERE? HAVEN'T YOU HEARD THIS IS MEANT TO BE A CIVILISED FUCKING COUNTRY?

A few of the crowd gave him this look like civilisation was one thing and Monday morning was another. OH BOLLOCKS TO ALL OF YOU THEN shouted the man. He stood up and he was holding the one thing he'd managed to pick up off the road and it was his biro. The end of it was smashed and black ink was running down his hand and spreading down his white shirtsleeve with the rain. The man lifted his face up into the sky then and just screamed BOL-LOCKS TO THIS! BOLLOCKS TO BOMB SCARES! BOLLOCKS

TO THE TERRORISTS AND BOLLOCKS TO THE POLICE AND
BOLLOCKS TO COMMUTING!

The crowd around him started laughing and clapping. It was a
little miracle in the middle of a great wet misery like when the
English and the German soldiers played footie in No Man's Land.
The man was still angry at first but then he started smiling too and
bowing to the crowd and waving his smashed-up biro like a conduc-
tor's baton. You might think I was smiling too Osama but I wasn't.
The whole thing made me feel a bit poorly. One minute that crowd
was robots and the next minute it was human beings and the next
minute it'd be something else again. Ever since May Day people's
moods could change faster than the traffic lights.

When I finally got to work the sky above Scotland Yard was low
and grey and moody. You couldn't see a thing. You couldn't even see
the balloons in the Shield of Hope. You just saw the cables disappearing up into the clouds like the weather was bolted onto them.

Up in the office it was a long grey morning and one of the striplights was flashing and buzzing like an electric chair. I was getting a
headache but you can put up with a lot when you're wearing new
red knickers. Terence kept giving me these looks I don't think either
of us could wait for 1 o'clock.

*   *   *

At lunchtime Terence said not to meet him at our usual hotel he
said he wanted to go for a walk instead. I said alright but it wasn't
much of a walk at first on account of it was still drizzling and I had
to follow 10 yards behind him in case anyone saw us together out of
work. I nearly lost sight of him crossing Westminster Bridge there
were so many people. Everyone was using the bridge because the
tube was still out after the bomb scare. It always takes London
Underground hours to get all the trains back to their proper sidings
and all the buskers back in their right places at the bottom of the
escalators singing ENGLAND'S HEART IS BLEEDING with their
scratched-up old guitars. It's like an anthill the tube I mean you can

stamp on it and watch the ants charge around going mental for a bit like my boy after 3 glasses of Tizer but after a while the ants will calm down and start to fix the anthill up again and dig all the muck out of the tunnels and make everything good as new or almost. Only don't expect them to do it in 5 mins that's all.

Anyway at the other end of Westminster Bridge Terence slowed down and went off left down the steps onto the South Bank. I went down 10 yards behind him good as gold. At the bottom of the steps he stopped and turned I suppose he reckoned we'd gone far enough not to be spotted. I came and stood next to him. I leaned forward over the wall so I could look down at the Thames. It was low tide and the sides of the river were mud. Dirty gulls were paddling round the shopping trolleys and the old tampons sticking out of the slime.

—Our glamorous capital, said Terence. Not a pretty sight is it?

—Nah. Well. Best keep my eyes on you then.

I looked up at him and he smiled. You could see the London Eye behind him turning round very slow with its big glass bubbles rising up till they disappeared into the cloud about 3-quarters of the way to the top of the wheel and then popping back down out of the cloud when they were 3-quarters of the way down again. There were streaks of brown rust running down the white tubes of the Eye it looked like it could of done with a good lick of paint. I suppose there wasn't the money now there weren't so many tourists any more. The London Eye was empty as the river.

Terence followed where my eyes were looking.

—Have you ever been on it? he said.

—Nah.

—Let's go for a ride.

—Nah you're alright. I mean if I want vertigo I'll just go up on the top deck of the bus it's a lot cheaper.

—Oh come on, said Terence. Where's your sense of adventure?

—In ashes in a small cardboard box Terence they had to identify my sense of adventure from his dental records.

Terence sighed and shook his head.

—Then let's just go on it to get out of this pissing rain, he said. Please. I want to talk to you.

I said alright and Terence grabbed hold of my hand and we walked off past the Aquarium and the Dalí Museum and we bought tickets there wasn't a queue. We walked straight onto the Eye and we got a bubble all to ourselves. A guide tried to come into our bubble with us but Terence showed him an official pass and he cleared off.

—There, said Terence. Emergency police powers. They don't hand them out to just anyone you know. A year of basic training. 3 years on the beat. 20 years rising up through the ranks. I knew it would all come in handy one day.

Our bubble started to rise up into the air. It was amazing it gave me goose bumps. I wish my boy could of been there. He'd of said IS THIS THE BIGGEST WHEEL IN THE UNIVERSE? and I'd of said No darling it's not quite as big as the steering wheel on god's Astra and he'd of said HOW COME IT TURNS ROUND? and I'd of said It turns round because Harry Potter put a spell on it. My boy's eyes would of gone all wide then and he'd of been quiet for at least 8 seconds.

Me and Terence were quiet too at first. We held hands and there was just the sound of the drizzle tapping against the glass and the electric humming noise of the magic spell making the thing turn round. The people down on Westminster Bridge started to shrink.

—Tessa asked me to move out, said Terence. I'm staying in a Travelodge.

—I'm sorry.

—Don't be, he said. Travelodges aren't that bad.

—You know what I meant.

—Yes, he said.

He sighed and a little patch of mist appeared on the glass in front of his mouth and wiped out a good chunk of the Embankment.

—Is it permanent?

—Don't know yet, he said. We'll see.

—Is it me?

Terence shook his head.

—She doesn't know about you, he said. It's the job she can't stand. She says I'm married to it.

—Well she does have a point you know.

—Yes, said Terence. But that's just me isn't it? Me without the job would be like England without the penalty curse. You can't have one without the other.

I squeezed Terence's hand and he squeezed mine back and I just tried to think about that and nothing else.

The wheel carried on turning. After a while you could see over the tops of the buildings on both sides of the river and look out over North London all white stone and money and South London all dirty brown high-rise bricks. From up where we were you could see how many cables there were rising up from the north side of the river compared to the south. It was like the people who built the Shield of Hope weren't really all that hopeful about Brixton and Camberwell and Lewisham.

I held on tight and looked out east. I was trying to see those places I always lived in. I looked for my old school and the Nelson's Head and the Wellington Estate and all those streets I kissed my husband and walked my boy and let the both of them down. I looked very hard through the drizzle I was hoping my life might make a bit more sense from a great height. I squinted and stared but after a bit I had to give up because the truth was you couldn't see the East End behind all the famous landmarks.

Our bubble was rising up towards the clouds now and you could see the bubbles above us disappearing into it. Terence was just staring out over London with his sad eyes full of the endless city. He shook his head.

—There's just so much of it, he said. There's so many people. You can't put a fence around all of them.

—Yeah well it looks like you're giving it a good go.

—Yes, said Terence. We've pulled up the drawbridge. But the

bastards are already inside. That's the thing. I could tell you a hundred ways they could butcher us like cattle. They could topple those office blocks like dominoes. They could make that river run red.

We looked down at the Thames all brown and muddy starting to disappear underneath us in the first edges of the clouds.

—So do your best. That's all you can do isn't it.

—I'm just so stupidly bloody tired, said Terence. It's like the powers that be are poking sticks into the wasps' nests and my job is to run around and stop the wasps stinging us. It's never going to happen. We've simply got to stop doing just a few of the things that make these people want to murder us.

Then everything went grey. London disappeared underneath us like the whole place had been a bad dream. Our bubble had risen up into the clouds.

—Terence?

—Yes?

—Can't we just forget about it for a while?

Terence turned towards me he looked so sick and miserable I just wanted to hold him so I did. He held me very gentle with his hands round my shoulders and then his hands started to slide down my sides and I reached up to kiss him and suddenly there were tears on my face and they weren't my tears they were his. I kissed him and kissed him and I reached down to unbuckle his belt and he pushed my skirt up and it was very quiet and lonely up there in our bubble in the clouds and the light was very sad and grey and it came from everywhere and there weren't any shadows. There was a long wooden bench in our bubble and I lay down on it and I was trembling and when he was inside me I sighed and closed my eyes and breathed in his smell.

With my eyes closed I could see right through the landmarks and right through the East End I could see my boy playing in the long grass in his yellow wellies I could see everything very clearly.

—Oh god Terence oh god we can start again you and me. We can start again like new.

Afterwards I felt sad and a bit sore and we sat next to each other on the bench and smoked Terence's Marlboro Reds. We didn't look at each other we just looked out at the big grey nothing on the outside of the glass.

—This is the closest I've been to heaven, said Terence Butcher.

—You're joking aren't you? Are you telling me you've never been in a plane?

—I don't mean the height, he said. I mean the feeling.

—Oh.

I thought about heaven.

—Didn't there ought to be angels and nice food and all your old family back from the dead?

—That's Hollywood heaven.

—Oh.

—This is British heaven. It's low cost. This is EasyHeaven.

I smiled and stretched up and kissed him and when I next looked out we were out of the clouds again and we were going back down. You could see the Houses of Parliament small enough so you could of picked it up and cut your fingers on its sharp little spines.

Terence put his hand under my chin and turned my face up so I was looking at him.

—There's something I have to tell you, he said. About May Day.

—Oh Terence love let's not talk about May Day. We're in heaven remember? Just you and me. Don't spoil it.

I stubbed out my ciggie on the underneath of the bench. The ground was getting closer now. You could see the lampposts of the South Bank coming up to meet us like slow cold missiles through the rain.

—I have to tell you, said Terence. If we're going to see each other like this I can't keep it to myself.

I lit another ciggie. Terence put his hand on my shoulder but I shrugged it off.

—What are you on about?

—Decisions, he said. In my line of work you run up against

some terrible decisions. But you have to go through with it. It's your duty.

—What does this have to do with May Day?

—Your husband understood duty, said Terence Butcher.

—My boy was 4 years and 3 months old. He understood eff-all. What is your point exactly?

Terence took the cigarette out of my hand and took a drag. He sucked the smoke right down into his lungs and held the cigarette up in front of him and looked at it like he was hoping it would kill him before he had to answer. His Adam's apple was bobbing up and down.

—We knew about May Day, he said. 2 hours before it happened.

—Nah. Anyway. Look. We're nearly back down. Look my lipstick isn't too smudged is it?

I stood up and started smoothing my skirt down but Terence pulled me back to the bench.

—Sit down, he said. Listen. We knew.

—You knew? How?

—We've got a mole, he said. An agent in the May Day cell. He got a message to us while the bombers were still on their way to the match.

—Nah. Cause if you had 2 hours warning you could of stopped it.

—Yes, said Terence Butcher. But the decision was taken not to stop it.

I just stared at him.

—This is going to be so hard for you to hear, he said. If we'd acted to stop May Day then the terrorists would have known something was up. They'd have changed everything. All their people. All their places. Everything. We'd have lost all insight into what they were planning. And we couldn't let that happen. The stakes are too high. We know the May Day cell are planning another attack. A hundred times worse than May Day.

—I can't believe I'm hearing this Terence Butcher. You knew? You personally?

—Yes, he said.

—And you decided not to do anything?

—I didn't decide, he said. The decision was taken at the very highest level.

—Bollocks to the very highest level. YOU knew.

—Yes, he said. Of course I could have broken ranks and stopped it. And the reason I didn't was because I agreed with the decision. And I still do. We couldn't have known the casualties would be so high.

I stared at the glowing orange end of his cigarette and watched my boy burning to death in it. He was screaming MUMMY SAVE ME only I couldn't come and save him could I? Because I was stuck in a glass bubble with the man that killed him and I was still aching from where I'd had him inside me. I wonder Osama if you are starting to get how it feels yet?

I grabbed Terence Butcher's hair and twisted his head round so he was looking in my eyes.

—You miserable fucking bastard.

AT THE VERY HIGHEST LEVEL. That was the moment Osama. When he said those words I stopped blaming you for my husband and my boy and I started blaming Terence Butcher. He murdered them. He just used your Semtex to do it with.

—I'm sorry, said Terence Butcher. I shouldn't have told you. I thought you'd understand.

I started crying and Terence held my face and he wiped away my tears with those same fingers he used to stroke my back in cheap hotel rooms and hold mugs of tea and dial the number of the phone call that killed my boy. I took the ciggie back off him and I sat there with it. I was just crying a bit and trembling and thinking nothing much till the ciggie burned down into the skin between my fingers. Then the pain hit me and I screamed and screamed like my boy must of screamed when the flames cut into him and then I puked up all over London and the puke ran down the inside of the glass down over St. Paul's Cathedral and down towards the Thames and when our bubble reached the ground again and the door slid open I ran out and I ran along the South Bank in the rain shouting THEY KNEW THEY KNEW THEY KNEW and people were gawping at me like I was a madwoman and I suppose they did have a point Osama because they were just standing under the London drizzle but I was running screaming through falling drops of phosphorus with my little boy running after me shouting MUMMY WAIT FOR ME!

*   *   *

I didn't go back to Jasper and Petra's place I went home to the Wellington Estate instead. I just turned up like a homing pigeon I didn't really know how I got there. Up in the flat I sat very still in the lounge looking out the window. The sun went down and the sun went up the way it does. After a day or 2 the phone started ringing I suppose it must of been work wondering where I was. I just listened to the sound of the phone it never occurred to me to go and pick it up.

I'd still be sitting there now with my bones turned to dust on our old Ikea sofa but it was the hunger drove me out of the flat. There's only so much nothing your body will put up with I suppose and so one day I just sort of woke up in the corner shop on Columbia Road eating pink iced buns straight off the shelves. The woman came out from behind the till and put her hands on her hips and stood there in her dark-grey hijab watching me stuffing my face.

—You are going to pay for all that aren't you? she said.

I just looked at her with my mouth jammed full and icing dribbling down my chin I couldn't work out what she was on about. She smiled and shook her head.

—Tea? she said.

—Tea.

I knew that word it was solid it was a great comfort like the noise the handbrake makes when you pull it on at the end of a long trip. The woman took me through a curtain made of plastic rainbow strips into the back room of the shop. It was nice in there it smelled of old bits and bobs and there was a little stereo playing Radio 1. I sat on a green sofa with the arms worn through and an orange cat came and gawped at me. The woman made me strong tea with sugar and we sat there till I felt better. It was a small room and there were all kinds of posters on the walls. There was Wayne Rooney and Mecca and Medina and Avril Lavigne. I swear to god Osama that woman's head was all over the shop you could only of bombed parts of her.

—Why are you being so nice to me?

—Your husband bought the *Sun* and 20 Benson & Hedges here every day for 4 years, she said. I owe you a cup of tea.

She still made me pay for the iced buns though.

When I left the shop I went round Petra and Jasper's place and no one said anything about where'd I been for the last 3 days. Maybe they were being polite or maybe they just never noticed and after a couple of drinks I wasn't bothered anyway it was just nice not to be sitting on my sofa.

It was cannelloni for dinner that night but none of us touched a bite of it on account of I was full of pink iced buns Jasper was on coke and Petra was on the Atkins diet.

We sat round the table and drank rosé wine and watched the cannelloni going cold. There was a power cut and the fridge wasn't working so the rosé was lukewarm. Petra lit some candles but she needn't of bothered because some Bengali street gang was lighting motors in the street outside and this harsh orange light was coming in through the windows. No coppers or fire engines turned up. I suppose they must of had their hands full somewhere.

There was nothing else for it I drank 5 glasses of rosé and told them what Terence told me.

—I don't believe it, said Petra. It stretches credulity that they knew about May Day and did nothing to prevent it.

—Oh come on Petra, said Jasper. Don't be naive. They had a source to protect so they let a few football fans die. I don't see what's so incredible.

—1 thousand dead souls Jasper, said Petra. That's what's not credible.

Jasper laughed.

—1 thousand souls is pocket change, he said.

—Oh please, said Petra.

—More died at Coventry, said Jasper. November 1940. The Germans blitzed it with incendiaries. Churchill knew in advance from Ultra decrypts. Decided not to act. We couldn't let the Germans know we'd broken their code.

—Oh nonsense, said Petra. That's been totally discredited. It's a myth.

—But doesn't it ring so true? said Jasper. Don't you believe they'd do anything to protect their precious City boys?

—You're high, said Petra.

—Sure, said Jasper. But I'm right.

Another motor went up *whump* in the street outside and Jasper and Petra just sat there glaring at each other in the vicious orange light coming off it.

—Listen, said Jasper. It's the attack on the City they're really trying to stop. A thousand City suits die and it's good-bye global economy. A thousand blokes in Gunners T-shirts die and you just sell a bit less lager.

I was drunk now on the bloody rosé and I should of stayed out of it but there you go.

—Jasper's right. The government doesn't give a monkey's about people like my husband and my boy.

Petra shook her head.

—That's just paranoid, she said.

—I am not paranoid I'm working-class there's a difference.

—Oh please, said Petra. Don't make this into a class war. It's the war against terror.

—Yeah and it's no different from any other war. You ever wondered why an East End girl like me hasn't got much in the way of family? Well here's the reasons Petra. World War 1. World War 2. Falklands War. Gulf War 1. Gulf War 2 and the War on Drugs. You can take your pick because I lost whole bloody chunks of my family in all of them. That's war Petra. This one's no different. The people who die are people like me. And the people who survive. Well I'm sorry Petra but the people who survive are people like you. And you're so used to surviving you don't even notice you're bloody well doing it.

Petra stared at me.

—You know what? she said. Sod you.

—Petra, said Jasper. Please.

—No Jasper, she said. Sod you too. Sod you both. You're as bad as each other. You simply refuse to move on don't you? Hiding behind your cocaine and your conspiracy theories like sulky children. You know what I've been doing this week? Moving on. Everyone is. London is moving on. Paris is refusing to be intimidated. And New York was all about vibrant colours. Defiant colours. Thanks to New York there will still be a spring season next year and thanks to me you can still read all about it in next Sunday's paper. Helmut Lang is moving on. John Galliano is moving on. The entire Western world is able to move on apparently with the sole exception of you. What the hell have you both been up to while I've been working my arse off in New York? Moping and fucking each other? I thought you'd be good for each other but look at you. You're just dragging all 3 of us down.

She stood up from the table and went over to the window and stared out at the street. I went up to her and touched the back of her hand.

—I'm sorry Petra I shouldn't of had a go at you.

She turned to me and she was going to say something but I moved my hand around hers so I was holding it. She closed her mouth again.

—I'm sorry Petra.

Petra looked down at my hand around hers and then slowly she moved her other hand up to touch the back of mine with the tips of her fingers. Her rings sparkled orange in the light of the flames coming in off the street. Her face changed then and she looked up from our hands into my eyes.

—Oh Jesus Christ, she said. What if you're right?

Jasper laughed and leaned back in his chair.

—It wouldn't bother Helmut Lang, he said. He's moved on you see.

—Shut up Jasper, said Petra. What if she's right about May Day?

Jasper shook his head.

—Don't even go there, he said. I know what you're thinking.

Petra came forward and leaned into the table and the light from the candles made black shadows where her eyes should of been.

—Listen Jasper, she said. You should do this story.

—Petra, said Jasper. You don't believe this story. Remember?

—Well I'm beginning to change my mind, said Petra. If it's true it's the biggest scoop since the Kelly thing. Bring it in and you'll be back in favour before you can blink.

—Darling, said Jasper. You're a fashion journalist. Don't tell me what's news and what's not. Stick to hemlines and fanny waxing.

—Fuck you, said Petra. Give me one good reason why you shouldn't do this story.

—I'll give you 3, said Jasper. 1 the untold damage it would do to national security. 2 the fact that I've been fucking the principal source and 3 now let me see. Oooh yes. That pesky libel thingy that says you oughtn't to print wild accusations in the absence of any proof. Yeah. Apart from all that this story would be a great career move for me.

—Fuck you, said Petra.

—Not tonight darling, said Jasper. I'm powdering my nose.

He took a paper wrap out of his trouser pocket and opened it up on the table.

—Look at you, said Petra. You're a fucking disgrace. We work on a national newspaper Jasper. We're 2 of the very few people in this country with the power to change things. If people like us won't do the right thing with the truth what hope is there for civilisation?

Jasper laughed and shoved a rolled-up tenner into his nostril. He pointed at himself with both thumbs.

—Petra darling, he said. Do I look like the guardian of Western civilisation to you?

He grinned at Petra and a new orange flash from the window lit up his face. Outside on the street the kids had torched another motor. I'd been forgotten about. I might as well not of been there for all anyone cared. I just sat back down good as gold at the table thinking to myself Oh dear I wish my boy was here now I wish I could just hold him for one minute and smell that lovely smell of his hair and hear him say MUMMY WHY ARE YOU CRYING? and say back to him Mummy's not crying darling Mummy's fine she's just got something in her eye. I looked at Petra being furious because Jasper wouldn't do what she said and I looked at Jasper sticking powder up his nose while the cars burned in the street outside and I think that might of been the very first time Osama that I began to see your point.

*   *   *

The autumn dragged on Osama with filthy grey skies and rain every day. I moved back to the Wellington Estate for good once Jasper and Petra starting fighting about the newspaper story I couldn't handle them banging away at each other it made me nervous. I went back to work on account of I needed the money but sometimes when Terence Butcher wasn't looking I spat in his tea.

Out in the streets they started to take down some of the roadblocks and if you weren't concentrating you might of thought things were slowly getting back to normal again. People didn't talk much about May Day any more. It was like the rain was washing the memories down the drains along with the old ciggie butts and the runover conkers.

—Oh come on, said Terence Butcher. Don't look at me like that. It's been weeks. Aren't you ever going to forgive me?

—Depends. Are you ever going to bring my husband and my boy back?

I put his tea down on his desk and not too careful either. Some of it slopped out on his files I didn't care. I was thinking Ha you should of thought of that Terence Butcher shouldn't you when you left my chaps to burn.

—I did what I thought was best, said Terence. I thought you'd understand.

—Yeah well you thought wrong didn't you. You should of told me straight away. I wouldn't of come near you I'd never of let you touch me you should be ashamed.

—I'm not ashamed, he said. It was beautiful.

He spun round in his chair and looked up at me. I was still standing there in front of his desk my whole body was trembling. He smiled a little sad smile.

—Listen to me, he said. Tired old copper going on about beauty. What would I know about it eh?

I didn't say anything Osama I mean what would you or me know about it either?

—But it was beautiful, said Terence. When we were up in the clouds alone. Me and you and none of the reasons why not. No job. No Tessa. No May Day. No London. It was beautiful.

—It was a bloody lie.

—Yes, said Terence. That's when I saw I had to tell you. I couldn't have that secret between us. Not if we were going to have something together.

—Oh Terence we were never going to have something together. Not after what you did to my chaps. You should of known that. You should of never got us started I mean what the hell were you THINKING?

—I'm sorry, he said. I know. I know. I hadn't been sleeping. I wasn't rational. I thought if we loved each other that would be enough.

—Love. You said love.

—Yes. I'm sorry. But that's how I feel.

I looked right at him. His eyes were exactly the same grey as the clouds behind him it looked like someone had put 2 gloomy holes right through his head.

—Listen Terence Butcher I make your tea and I do your filing and that's all it is now right? Don't you ever get that confused with love.

He looked at me for a very long time and then he looked down at his desk. It was an empty desk apart from his 3 phones. The photo of his wife and kids was gone I suppose he might of had it by his bed in the Travelodge.

*   *   *

It was a long afternoon after that and when 5 o'clock came I just put on my anorak and walked home head down in the gloom. In England on a cloudy day in autumn it gets dark by 4 in the afternoon. A few weeks of that Osama and believe me you start to feel like topping yourself. A lot of poor bastards do. I swear to god Osama the English climate's done in more people than you ever have. If you tried living here for just 10 days in October your Kalashnikov would rust and your sandals would rot and your GP would stick you on Prozac and you couldn't hate us any more you'd just feel ever so sorry for us instead.

When I got back home to the Wellington Estate there was a power cut again so I took a couple of candles into the bathroom and ran myself a bath and lay in it and talked with my boy till the water went cold and it was time to go to bed. My boy sat on the edge of the bath. He liked the tap end best. He dangled his feet in the water and we had the nicest conversation me and him.

I got out of the bath and took my pink dressing gown off the hook next to my husband's black one. I still hadn't slung it out yet I mean it's never the right moment is it? I put on my dressing gown and wrapped a towel round my hair and my boy followed me into the kitchen making little wet boy footprints on the lino. We nattered away in the kitchen for a bit while I had a couple of glasses of vodka and a couple of some new pills the doctor put me on it was all very nice. After a while my boy went a bit quiet. I looked up from my glass and his face was very pale and I was about to say Right then bedtime for you young man but someone started banging on the front door. I turned round to check the bolt was on and when I turned back my boy was gone so I thought I might as well answer it.

I took one of the candles with me into the hallway and I didn't put the chain on before I opened the front door I mean I didn't much care what happened any more. It was Jasper Black standing there he came straight in he was all overexcited.

—Can you come over? he said. Petra's pregnant.

I just looked at him he wasn't making sense.

—Pregnant you say?

—Yes, he said. Can you come immediately?

—Um well Jasper I don't know if Mummy ever explained girls' things to you but when a woman is pregnant there isn't any hurry I mean just the opposite really you have to wait about 9 months while the baby gets bigger in Mummy's tummy first.

—Petra's frantic, said Jasper. I think you might be able to calm her down.

—Listen Jasper it wouldn't surprise me if Petra was born frantic and I hate to be the one to tell you this but if she's pregnant then it's only going to make her worse so you might as well get used to it eh? I mean why don't you go and calm her down yourself?

—She's asking for you, he said.

—Yeah well she can't have me can she? It's a bit late for all that. I mean I haven't heard a squeak out of either of you for weeks and I can't say I've missed you.

Jasper blinked.

—Christ, he said. This isn't like you. Bitter.

—Yeah well what did you expect? I wasn't put on this earth for your benefit Jasper Black I'm not some CD you can forget about down the back of a drawer and pull it out when it suits you and it still sounds just the same.

I turned and walked away from him to the kitchen. I didn't actually make it through the kitchen door on the first go. I banged into the door frame and I had to back up and have another go like something off *Robot Wars* on the telly.

—Have you been drinking? said Jasper.

—Nah. They moved the door. You been doing coke?

—No, said Jasper Black. Haven't touched it since we found out Petra was pregnant. 3 days.

I sat down at the kitchen table and Jasper came in and sat down opposite. It was hard to say in the candlelight but he looked thinner and his hands were shaking a bit.

—Drink? I said.

—Yes alright.

I poured him a big vodka it was the end of the bottle. He drank it down like it was nothing. The lights flickered on for half a minute and then they went off again and it was just the candles glowing in the middle of the kitchen table and every now and then a white flash through the window from the helicopter searchlights. I never even heard the choppers any more I was used to them now. We sat there looking at each other.

—You the father you reckon?

—Yes, said Jasper. Yes I think so.

—Good for you.

—Thanks.

More silence.

—She sick in the mornings is she?

—Yes, said Jasper. In the mornings she's sick and moody. In the evenings she's tired and moody. In between times she's moody and off at work. Thank god.

—Tell her to try a teaspoon of cider vinegar after meals.

—Alright, said Jasper.

—And tell her it helps to go for a walk in the evenings before bed.

—I will, he said.

—And tell her to. Tell her to. Oh bollocks to it I'll come over and tell her myself.

Jasper grinned and I stood up from the table and went into the bedroom and took off my dressing gown and put on my grey trackie bottoms and a grey Nike T-shirt. I mean maybe Petra was right maybe Helmut Lang had moved on but we never saw much of him down Barnet Grove anyway.

When we were leaving the flat I shouted at my boy to be good and I slammed the front door behind us. Jasper gave me a look.

Over at Jasper and Petra's place they were having the same power cut we were having in the Wellington Estate I mean you can talk as posh as you like it doesn't bother electricity. Petra was sitting on the floor in front of their sofa and she looked the way you'd love us all to look Osama. Black-eyed. Hollow. Knackered.

I knelt down and I put my hand on her tummy like you do even though there wasn't anything to feel yet. I closed my eyes and I did try so hard to feel happy for her. I mean you're meant to feel pleased aren't you? You're supposed to pretend those babies are coming into a world where no one's trying to burn them. That's the trick that lets you be pleased they're going to be born. That's the trick that lets you stop worrying and start knitting tiny boots isn't it?

Well I tried ever so hard but it wasn't any good I just couldn't do that trick any more. With my eyes closed I saw the unborn life in Petra's tummy. I felt like you knew its name before it was even born Osama. The child was doomed it floated there very lonely in the dark. It didn't know London yet but you could tell it was already nervous. It heard its mum's heart beating and each beat made it flinch like a nail bomb going off in the distance. Its little fists were closed tight and the umbilical cord was pumping it full of petrol. It was an incendiary child and when it dreamed it dreamed of sparks.

I saw its face and it was my dead boy's face. It spoke with my dead boy's voice. Mummy it said. Mummy they knew. MUMMY THEY KNEW. I stood up very quick and went over to the end of the sofa and looked down at the floor till I got my head together.

—How you feeling?

—Awful, said Petra. I'm just so bloody tired all the time.

—Yeah well you better get used to it. When your baby's a toddler you'll think these were the good old days.

—Oh thanks, said Petra. Very encouraging.

—Sorry. Don't listen to me. Honestly. It's all worth it.

Petra just sat there and stared at me. It went on too long I didn't know what to do with myself.

—Listen is there anything I can do to help?

—Yes, said Petra. You can get us some hard evidence that the authorities knew about May Day before it happened.

I looked at her.

—Actually what I meant was I've got a book on pregnancy if you want and lots of maternity clothes I don't know if they'd be your style but they're all clean and folded and then for when the baby comes I can give you all the bottles and sterilisers and that sort of thing I mean it's all up in the flat in boxes you're welcome to it.

—An audio tape would do, said Petra. But a video would be better. Get your little policeman to confess to you again. It has to be something we can show as evidence.

Jasper stepped right up to Petra and yanked her up to her feet and talked right into her face.

—Petra, he said. Bloody well stop it. We discussed this and you promised not to do it like this. I'd never have got her over if I'd known you were going to do this.

—Ha, said Petra. If you were the kind of father who did a little less coke and a little more investigative journalism then maybe I wouldn't have to do this.

—That's not fair, said Jasper.

—Fuck fair, said Petra.

She turned to me. I was leaning hard on the arm of the sofa. My brain felt like the icing on those buns all soft and pink from the booze and the pills.

—Jasper and I have had a little talk, said Petra. We think it might be best if I took the story to the paper. After all Jasper's a bit low on credibility right now. I want you to help me do the story.

—Why?

Petra shrugged.

—Because Jasper's too craven to do it. Because they'll promote me if I do it.

—I don't mean why do you want to do the story I mean why should I help you?

Petra didn't stop for a second.

—Because I'll pay you, she said. Or rather the paper will. For your collaboration. It could change your life. It could be as much as 50K.

—Nah.

—100K even.

—Petra. Listen. You're pregnant. It's always a shock. Why don't you get some rest and we'll pretend this never happened?

—Oh come on, said Petra. Don't tell me a woman in your position can turn down that kind of money.

—Listen Petra a woman in my position could wallpaper her flat with money it wouldn't make a difference. It's all just pictures of the queen to me. Without my boy to spend it on that's all your precious money is Petra. Crappy little pictures of the queen.

I turned to go but Jasper took hold of my arm very gentle.

—Then you should do it for yourself, he said.

—You what?

Jasper put his mouth close to my ear and spoke very soft.

—You still see your boy don't you? he said.

I looked at him I shook my head I made these big eyes that said WHO? ME? I mean I was in a state Osama I'll give you that but I wasn't mad enough to forget they lock you up when you start seeing people they can't.

—It's alright, said Jasper. I understand. I see things too since May Day. It's normal. It's called post-traumatic shock.

I shook my head again I was terrified. I whispered back to Jasper.

—Nah. I'm fine honestly don't worry about me I'm right as rain.

—In your kitchen just now, said Jasper. I saw the way your eyes flicked over into the corner of the room while we talked. And then when we left you actually told him to be good.

—What are you saying to her? said Petra.

—You be quiet please Petra, said Jasper.

He leaned closer to my ear.

—You're going to keep on having these troubles, he said. Until you do something to lay the boy to rest.

—I can't lay him to rest I don't have his body there's just his teeth and I'm not going to bury his little teeth am I? I mean there isn't a grave small enough.

—So do this thing Petra's asking you for, said Jasper. But don't do it for her. Do it for you. It'll help.

—Why?

—Because you need to get the truth out, said Jasper. Because if you keep it inside it's going to finish you off. I mean look at yourself.

I looked back at Jasper staring into my eyes very close and I looked at Petra watching me over his shoulder and I looked at my boy lying on his tummy trying to fish an ashtray or something out from under their coffee table. I didn't know what to think I was holding on to my head with both hands to stop it falling apart. I stepped back from Jasper I went to the corner of the room farthest from them both.

—I don't know. I don't effing well know do I? Why doesn't this thing ever just stop? Why won't you two ever leave me in peace?

—Because you know you have to do this, said Jasper. It's vital for you and it's vital for the country.

—Oh you care about the country suddenly do you?

Jasper shrugged.

—I'm going to be a father, he said. It changes everything. I don't want my child to live in a place where politicians decide who dies.

I shook my head.

—I don't know. I don't know. What about Terence Butcher?

—What about him? said Petra.

—If I do this thing won't he be in a lot of trouble?

—Do you even care? said Petra.

—I don't know. I don't know. He says he loves me.

—Loves you, said Petra. As much as you loved your boy?

—Well it's not the same thing is it? It's not the same thing at all.

Petra smiled and Jasper looked down at the floor.

—Ah, said Petra. Finally she gets it.

*   *   *

The Travelodge was near Liverpool Street and I sat in the bar waiting for Terence Butcher to come in from work. I was waiting for hours but that was alright. It was cosy and dark in the bar and they left me alone except when I asked them for drinks. I must of had 5 or 6 G&Ts and it was nice just sitting there in a bit of a fog while my boy scampered around in the lobby up to mischief I shouldn't wonder. The girl at the reception desk was very helpful when I asked her to check if Terence Butcher was staying there and the barman was very helpful when I asked him to only serve me doubles in fact all the staff were very helpful Osama so if you ever find yourself needing to break a long journey in between massacres I reckon you could do a lot worse than a Travelodge.

It was nearly 11 when Terence Butcher finally showed up. I'd chosen a seat at one of those low tables where I could see when he came in the front entrance but I needn't of bothered because he went straight to the bar and ordered a double Scotch. I got up and I went over to him. It wasn't a long way but things weren't too steady and I had to hold on to the backs of the chairs to stop the Travelodge from wobbling. I tapped Terence on the shoulder and he turned round from the bar looking tired and ill but he smiled when he saw me. It wasn't your ordinary smile it was sort of laughing and lost at the same time like when someone makes a good joke at a funeral.

—What are you doing here? he said.

—I thought you might need tea or filing.

Terence smiled and held on to my arm like he was worried I might keel over and I suppose he did have a point.

—You shouldn't have come, he said. Why did you?

—I'm not sure yet.

It was true Osama my head was in pieces from pills and gin I didn't know what I was going to do. Mr. Rabbit was in my bag and he had Jasper's video camera sewn in his tummy with this tiny lens sticking out. All I had to do was sit the little feller somewhere he could see what was going on and press RECORD and get Terence Butcher to talk. But there was a bunch of old photos in my bag too. They were of my husband and my boy and me mucking around in the flat and in Victoria Park and one of us all with ice creams on the beach at Brighton. I looked up at Terence and I held on to his arm and I giggled on account of I couldn't work out if I was there to stitch him up or talk him through the family album.

—Are you alright? said Terence.

—Nah. Are you going to take me to bed?

—Bed? he said. Last time I checked you were never going to speak to me again.

—Yeah well I'm not promising I'll speak in bed.

Terence laughed then and drained his Scotch and signalled at the barman for another.

—You're drunk, he said. Maybe you should just go home.

I blinked and rocked back and forward on my pins for a second I mean I wasn't expecting that.

—Listen Terence Butcher I'm drunk cause I've been waiting here 5 hours for you and I haven't waited 5 hours so you can tell me you don't even care.

The barman brought the new Scotch and Terence looked down into it and swirled the glass round in his hand so the ice cubes rattled. Then he looked at me and those grey eyes were flashing pink with the neon from the bar.

—I do care, he said. More than you know. That's why I think it might be best if you just went home.

—Yeah but I want to be with you.

—No you don't, he said. You told me so.

Terence Butcher put his hand under my chin and turned my face round very gentle so I was looking straight up in his eyes.

—There, he said. Look right at me and tell me you don't see a murderer.

I opened my mouth but I couldn't say anything all I could see was fire in his eyes from all those neon reflections and I gasped.

—There, he said. Tell me it wouldn't always be like that. Over coffee. Over drinks. Every night in the bathroom mirror brushing our teeth.

My legs went to rubber and I could feel the strength of him under his shirt and I knew if I kept hold of him I'd do us both wrong but I knew if I let go I'd fall down flat on the floor.

—Oh I don't know Terence I'm lost. Please won't you just hold me I'm completely lost.

*   *   *

There's a lot of things we've got in common these days Osama but here's one thing you'll never do. I bet you'll never let yourself be done in a Travelodge by the man who left your chaps to die. I bit my lip in case the pain would take my mind off the shivers that were racing up my back. I bit until the blood came but it wasn't any use. In my head I was hating Terence but my body was still in love. I wanted to say I hate you you vicious lying coward YOU KNEW but you still left my chaps to die. YOU KNEW in that time we had together in the clouds. For months and months YOU KNEW. I was trying to make my mouth say all that Osama I swear to you but all that came out was moans.

I gasped and I twisted my head on the pillow and my eyes were rolling back in my head and then nothing. I lay on the bed with Terence on top of me and the flames flickered out in his eyes and there was nothing. Just grey smoke smouldering and my boy sitting on the edge of the empty bath next door and kicking his heels on the enamel bang bang bang.

Afterwards I let Terence lie inside me for a little while. Nice and quiet with his head on my shoulder while I stroked the back of his neck. Mr. Rabbit sitting watching us from the chair beside my bag.

—Lovely Terence. I missed you so much.

—Mmm, he said.

Silence.

—Terence. I've been thinking. If you had another chance to decide what to do on May Day. Would you make the same choice again?

Terence sighed and I felt his muscles go all tight again.

—Do you really want to think about it now? he said.

—I have to know.

Terence Butcher pulled out of me and rolled on his back. He reached over for his Marlboro Reds and he lit one and I lit one too.

—It's hard to say if I'd do the same again, he said. There were so many factors.

—Tell me all about it.

He nodded and gave a little smile and took a drag of his ciggie and blew smoke out very slowly up towards the ceiling. He turned towards me and gave me such a sad look then. I think he knew what was going on. He looked at me like our old dog looked at me and my husband the day we reckoned the kindest thing we could do for him was give him his favourite food and wrap him up in his favourite blanket and drive him one last time to the vet in the boot of our old Astra.

—Do I have to? he said.

I couldn't look at him and my voice came out very quiet.

—I have to.

Terence Butcher nodded. Then he lit another ciggie and sat up in the bed and told me everything very slow and careful and clear like his voice was typed in capital letters. When he'd finished he didn't even look at me he just lay down and slept like I reckon he hadn't slept since May Day and there was this strange expression on his face while he slept very sad and calm like the stone men you see in churchyards.

*   *   *

It was 5 a.m. when I left it was still dark. The courier was waiting outside the Travelodge just like Jasper and Petra said he would be. I gave him Mr. Rabbit with his camera inside and the courier got on his bike and I got on the number 23 bus. I got off at Piccadilly Circus and I checked in at the Golden Square Hotel. I chose it because I saw it once when I took my boy to the Trocadero and I thought it looked quite fancy. Actually it's a filthy place Osama but it is cheap. I stayed there for 4 days just waiting for Sunday and no one knew where I was not even Petra and Jasper. Jasper said it'd be best that way.

I stayed in my room and ate crisps and sandwiches and drank the rusty water from the hand basin. It was weird just stuck there doing nothing. Knowing I could never go back to Scotland Yard again. I tried to sleep as much as I could so I didn't have to think about it all. Every day I dozed on the bed and watched flames licking up the wallpaper and every night I lay awake listening to the backpackers laughing and shouting in the corridor. In the early mornings when there wasn't anyone about to watch I crept out of the room and walked through the piles of cold puke to the bathroom at the end of the hall. It was a lonely 4 days Osama but I didn't mind because after a while my boy turned up and we had a good talk.

—Mummy, he said. Where are we?

—We're in a hotel darling.

—Why are we? he said.

—We're hiding.

My boy's eyes went wide.

—Why? he said.

—Because it's safest that way. Mummy helped Petra to write a story for the newspaper where she works. The story is going to be published on Sunday. When that story comes out it's going to be very bad for the men that hurt you and Daddy. Lots of people are going to want to talk to your mum.

—So we're hiding! he said.

I smiled at my boy. It was so nice to have him there. He was beautiful with his bright ginger hair and his stubby little teeth. There wasn't a scratch on him. I said he could eat all the crisps he wanted but he wasn't very hungry.

On Sunday morning very early I checked out of the hotel and walked out onto Piccadilly Circus. I had one of those travelling suitcases on wheels that Petra lent me. I was dragging it behind me with the boy riding on top of it. He looked up at the huge electric billboards with his eyes all wide and his mouth open and his breath steaming in the cold morning air. The poor chap was only wearing his jeans and his Arsenal away shirt.

—Aren't you cold? Don't you want Mummy to find you a jumper?

The boy shook his head. He was too excited to be cold and I was just the same. At the first newsagent's I found we were going to buy our copy of the *Sunday Telegraph*. I couldn't wait to see our story splashed across that big front page under those nice gothic letters. I was so nervous I had the shakes and my tummy was going mad. I wondered what the headline was going to be. How I'd of done it was I'd of had a huge photo of that vicious tower of smoke above the Emirates Stadium with just 2 words over the top THEY KNEW. That's how I'd of done it but then what would I know? Like I say Osama we always had the *Sun* in my family.

There were a few other people walking round Piccadilly Circus. I watched everyone's faces to see if they'd heard the news yet but none of them looked like they had. We walked past a group of girls giggling on their way home from the clubs. Then there was a pair of tourists videoing the big electric Coca-Cola sign and the huge barrage balloon floating above with the faces of the dead Arsenal players on it. Then we went past a traffic warden. He looked more like he would of known what was going on.

—Morning. You heard the news yet?

The traffic warden stared at me.

—What? he said.

—About May Day.

—What about it? he said.

—You haven't seen the papers yet?

—No, he said. What's in them?

—They knew. They knew May Day was going to happen but they didn't do anything to stop it.

The traffic warden looked at me for a moment with my Adidas trackies and my suitcase and then he shook his head and smiled.

—You look after yourself alright love? he said.

—I'm not bonkers or anything. It's the truth.

—Of course it is, he said. You take care now alright?

The traffic warden turned away and walked off towards Regent Street. My boy looked up at me.

—That man didn't believe you Mummy, he said.

—No love. You can't blame him. He will when he has a sit-down with the papers.

I smiled at him and we headed off up into Soho. On Warwick Street I took a deep breath and I went into a newsagent's.

I stood there looking at the front page of the *Sunday Telegraph* for quite a while. There was something wrong with it you see Osama. The picture on the front was a row of houses all with For Sale signs on them. The headline was HOUSE PRICES SLUMP AS BUYERS FEEL THE PINCH. I shook my head. I didn't see what that had to do with May Day. I checked the date on the top of the paper. Then I opened it up and looked on every page. Nothing about May Day. I felt sick. I kept wishing I'd wake up and still be in the hotel. Only once I'd started thinking like that I thought if this really was a nightmare then I might as well wake up in bed with my husband before May Day ever happened. When I thought about my husband I wanted to scream and I started to pull all the other papers off the racks to see what was in them. They were all the same. It was all HOUSE PRICES PLUMMET except for the *Sunday Mirror*. The *Sunday Mirror* said £ MILLIONS IN OUR LIFE-CHANGING GIVEAWAY and it had a photo of a family on the front page lounging around on deck chairs by a pool. There was a mum and a dad in the photo and it looked like they'd spent some of their £ MILLIONS on fancy cocktails and instead of faces they had shiny silver foil so you could see your own face there. THIS COULD BY YOU IN THE MIRROR the paper said and there was a little boy with ginger hair larking about in the pool. I suppose he must have been about 4 years and 3 months old. I threw the *Sunday Mirror* down on the floor and I screamed and the newsagent came out from behind his counter.

—Oi darling, he said. You pay for them papers or you put them back.

I fell on my knees and looked at the headlines laid out on the floor all around me and I just went off on one I don't know if I was screaming or laughing.

—Oh for fuck's sake, said the newsagent. This is a newsagent's not a nuthouse. Go on piss off.

I stood up and ran out of the shop dragging my suitcase behind me. My boy was hanging on for dear life while the suitcase banged up and down on the pavement.

—Mummy! he shouted. What's wrong?

I stopped running and looked at my boy and then I put my hands up to my mouth and screamed. It was his face you see Osama. His lovely ginger hair was burned to thick black tar dripping down his face. His skin was raw with burns and one of his eyes was boiled white as an egg. I screamed again and left the suitcase where it was and ran up Warwick Street with my boy running after me and all the cardboard boxes and the homeless in their cheap nylon sleeping bags going up in flames as he brushed past them.

I stopped at the first phone box I came to and jammed 30p in the slot and called Jasper and Petra's flat but it was just the answering machine and the phone ate my money. Both their mobiles were off too. I tried again and again all through that day to call Jasper and Petra. I spent all the money I had in phones. I should of still had the wad of cash Petra and Jasper gave me only that all went on drinks in the Travelodge and the Regent Palace Hotel. They told me not to use my bank card so that was still under my mattress. I was too scared to go back to Bethnal Green till I knew what was going on so I just wandered round Soho. You wouldn't like Soho Osama I reckon there can't be one single place in it that isn't forbidden by your prophets for one thing or another except maybe Soho Square and the trouble with that is it gets pretty crowded. It was the longest day.

By the time it got dark I was hungry and my boy was so starving he'd given up howling and he was just sitting there on the pavement very quiet and pale. Even the flames on him were starved. It was just his fingertips burning with flickering little flames like candles. I had to get some food for him but I was skint. So we just sat there for a while in some doorway or other getting hungrier and colder and just hoping something would turn up. But nothing did turn up and when my boy started to shiver I started to beg. I wonder if you know what that felt like Osama to have my poor boy's eyes on me while he watched his mummy kneel down on the pavement on Wardour Street with a McDonald's cup in front of her to beg spare change off the old pervs coming out of the sex shops.

People must of taken pity because I scraped together a fiver. I spent it on a Happy Meal for my boy and an extra-large Fanta and we sat at a table in the corner of McDonald's. My boy was sulking and I couldn't blame him Osama I mean no boy should have to see his mum on the cadge like that. He wouldn't touch his Happy Meal and in the end I had to eat it for him.

We spent the night in a doorway in Berwick Street. I found a big sheet of bubble wrap and tucked it round us but it didn't do any good against the cold. I didn't sleep much. My boy sparked and smouldered all night but somehow there wasn't any heat coming off him.

*   *   *

In that doorway tucked up in my bubble wrap I had a dream where the terror was over. In my dream Osama I wrote you this letter and you read it and then you went off behind a rock where your men couldn't see you and you cried and you wished you hadn't killed my boy. It made you too sad now. You didn't feel angry any more you just felt very tired. I wrote to the others too Osama like I promised you at the beginning. I wrote to the president and the prime minister and now they felt sick and tired too. None of you wanted any more small boys to die 4 years and 3 months old who still slept with their rabbit whose name was Mr. Rabbit. So all you men just told your people to pack it in and go home. And that was it. It was over. There was just a load of old foxholes filling up with rain and empty basements with the jihad graffiti slowly going black with mildew. There were a million old chewing gum wrappers and fag butts where the terror used to be.

They untied all the balloons in the Shield of Hope and let them float away. I held on to the cable of my boy's balloon and I hung there under his smiling face getting carried higher and higher in the night sky. It was lovely looking down on London shrinking till it was just a tiny spark in the darkness. It looked like all you had to do was spit and you could of put the whole city out. In my dream I smiled and I wondered where my boy would carry me. We floated very high above the world and the moon was very bright and I saw it all. All the rivers and the mountains were lit up with silver and the forests were full of creatures hunting and hiding and thinking nothing much. There was a warm wind pushing us and we swooped down low into the valleys and there were little villages there where the windows were lit up and all the colours glowed and you could smell food cooking. And from inside all the houses you heard mums singing their children to sleep and their love was stronger than bombs.

When I woke up it was raining and I sat in that doorway just shivering. I watched everyone in the Monday morning rush to work I was thinking how last Monday I'd been one of them. After I'd watched for a bit I got up and walked to a phone box. My boy followed along after me with the tarmac of the road melting under his feet.

I stuck my last coins into the phone box and dialled Jasper's mobile. It was the longest time before he picked up.

—Jasper! It's me. What's going on? Can I come back to the flat yet?

—Wouldn't be wise, said Jasper. There are people looking for you.

—I looked at the paper. I looked at all the papers. Where's our story?

—Our story is nowhere, he said. Our story is dead. Petra killed it.

—What do you mean?

—Petra claims she changed her mind, said Jasper. She called me from the office late on Saturday night. Said she no longer believed the story was in the national interest. Bless. As if Petra's ever given a fuck about the national interest.

—Look Jasper I haven't got much time my money's going to run out. If Petra doesn't want to go with the story then you'll just have to do it yourself.

—No, said Jasper. I'll tell you what's happened. The paper's sold out to the government and Petra's sold out to the paper. Now the government has your videotape and the paper has first dibs on the next big Downing Street leak. God knows what deal Petra's cut for herself. I'm guessing she'll come back from maternity leave as deputy editor. Everyone's a winner. Oh. Except you. And me. And the British public of course. You do have to hand it to Petra Sutherland. She's fucked an entire nation.

I couldn't get my head round it. I leaned back on the wall of the telephone kiosk and watched the glass melting where my boy was pressing his nose against it.

—Are you still there? said Jasper.

—Yeah. What happens now?

—Oh, said Jasper. Now the fun really starts. I get sacked from the paper and blacklisted as a drug addict. No one else hires me. Petra moves to one of her family's charming homes in Primrose Hill and has my baby and gets a court order barring me from seeing it. I fester. My cocaine dealer and my local off-licence garner a modest living from me for a short period of time. One day my neighbours ring up to complain about a nasty smell and the fire brigade turn up to remove my rotting corpse from the flat.

—You're high aren't you?

—Very very high sweetness, said Jasper. It's 8 in the morning and good old Jasper Black is high as a motherfucking kite.

—I need to come back Jasper. I need my bank card and my clothes. Who are these people looking for me? What do they want?

—Nothing good, said Jasper. But maybe nothing too bad either. You're small fry. They'll probably just threaten you. Tell you what'll happen if you try taking the story elsewhere. If it's any consolation anything they can do to you and me is small beer compared to what they'll do to Terence Butcher. They'll chain that poor fucker down a well so deep you could throw a packet of fags down it and he still wouldn't have anything to smoke till Christmas.

—Listen Jasper we've got to be quick this phone's flashing at me. What are you going to do now?

Jasper laughed down the phone. It was a sharp and vicious laugh and it hurt my ear through the receiver.

—I'm going to do what any self-respecting Englishman would do in my position, he said. I'm going to blow up the Houses of Parliament.

—Please Jasper this isn't the time to muck about I—

—Want to watch? he said. Meet me in an hour on Parliament Square. Do you want me to bring your—

The phone went dead.

*   *   *

I didn't have the bus fare so I walked down to Westminster. It was only a couple of miles. It was raining a bit and the sky was so black and heavy it gave you a headache but it felt good to be going somewhere finally. I couldn't wait to see Jasper even if he was off his rocker. My boy was feeling better too. When we walked through Trafalgar Square he laughed and chased the pigeons and singed their wet tail feathers with his hands.

Jasper got to Parliament Square before me. He was sitting on a pink suitcase under the big black statue of Churchill. There was a little dry patch there sheltered from the drizzle. I ran across the road and Jasper stood up and we hugged for a long time while the traffic roared past on the wet roads. He smelled of whisky. After a bit we stepped apart and looked at each other. Jasper got out his Camel Lights and we both lit one and I stood there smoking with my hand shaking like a sewing machine.

—You look like fucking shit, said Jasper.

—Thanks.

—So, said Jasper. Petra stitched us up.

I shrugged.

—Yeah.

—I'll miss her you know, said Jasper. I'm surprised. What with me being heartless and everything.

—You've always been kind to me.

—Not always, said Jasper. I've always fancied you but don't mistake it for kindness.

I smiled at him.

—I didn't bring your bank card, he said.

—Oh.

—I brought you my bank card instead, he said. I won't be needing it. Pin number's scratched into the back of it. It's good for a few grand. Not a king's ransom but it should get you back on your feet.

He reached in his pocket and handed me his card. I just stared at him.

—What's going on?

—I'm not ecstatic with how I've lived my life, he said. I was born with a certain amount of talent and I've snorted it away. I let the system absorb me. But even a man like me has a point beyond which his pride will not allow him to go. I will not let them screw us like this. I've decided to make a stand.

He looked down at the suitcase by our feet.

—See this? he said. This is what the authorities are scared shitless of. This is six sticks of dynamite packed around a jam jar full of Strontium-90 and Caesium-137 painstakingly stolen from hospitals and factories across the Middle East by Al Qaeda operatives.

—No it isn't Jasper. It's Petra's Louis Vuitton suitcase.

—You know that, said Jasper. And I know that. But as far as the rest of the world is concerned it's a dirty bomb. If this thing goes off the whole of Westminster will glow in the dark until well into the next ice age. I'm about to call the police and tell them. And they'll believe me because I'll use the code word the May Day cell used. The one Terence told you about in your little pillow chat. And as soon as I get off the phone with the police I'll call the BBC. That should get everyone's attention.

—You're off your nut. What do you want to do all that for?

—I'll threaten to set off my nasty little bomb unless they bring me a camera crew. And then on live unexpurgated TV I'll tell the world what really happened on May Day.

—No Jasper. Please no. You know what they'll do to you.

—Oh yes, said Jasper. I'm hoping they kill me outright. I've never been much tempted by prison.

I stepped up close to Jasper and put my hand on his cheek.

—Why are you really doing this?

Jasper grinned.

—Well, he said. Would you believe me if I said I think you've been through enough and you deserve some kind of justice?

—No.

—No, said Jasper. Must be your tits then.

I started laughing then and so did he. It must of been on account of he was on coke and I'd had no sleep but we were in hysterics.

—Oh Jasper. We're fucked aren't we?

—Oooh yes, he said. Petra's really done a number on us. We're as fucked as it's possible for two individuals to be in Great Britain at the start of the 21st century. We have finally done it. We have achieved terminal fuckedocity.

He hugged me. We were having a right old time of it there under good old Winston Churchill with the morning rush hour roaring on all round us but it didn't last long because soon Jasper stopped laughing. He reached down and unzipped the suitcase. It wasn't a dirty bomb in there it was Mr. Rabbit.

—Here, he said. I thought you'd want him back. Take care of him now won't you?

Seeing Mr. Rabbit reminded me it was all real what was happening to us. The rain felt cold again and I shivered.

—Jasper. That's enough silliness now. Let's just get out of here. Let's disappear. We'll get on a train and just go.

—Where to? said Jasper.

—I don't know. Anywhere that isn't London.

Jasper stroked my cheek.

—Everywhere is London, he said. For us. Don't you see? We are London. Anywhere we could go you'd always be grieving and I'd always be. Well.

—What?

Jasper looked down at the rainy pavement and the pigeon shit and the old black discs of chewing gum.

—Disappointed, he said.

The roar of the traffic was quieter now. Rush hour was nearly over. Anyone who had work to go to was either there already or hoping their boss wasn't. I reached up and kissed Jasper very quick on the mouth.

—Jasper?

—Yes? he said.

—My boy would of liked you.

—Go on, he said. You'd better get out of here.

Then he got out his mobile and dialled the Metropolitan Police. I walked off down St. Margaret Street and I didn't look back.

Jasper Black never did get to say his piece on camera and I never saw him again except for the TV pictures of that moment when he's climbed up with that silly pink suitcase onto the statue of Churchill and the police sharpshooter gets him in the back. I expect you've seen those pictures too Osama they're pretty famous. It's the way that great big smile comes over his face as he's falling.

*   *   *

I hadn't got far when the panic started. I don't blame people for panicking with the telly reporting a dirty bomb in Parliament Square. If I'd been them I'd of legged it too. I was on Millbank halfway down the Victoria Tower Gardens when people started running out of their offices. Once it started everything happened so quick. The panic was like a living thing Osama it had a smell and a voice. The smell hit me in the guts it was the smell of bodies sweating and struggling. Then there was the horrible noise. It was grown men screaming and sirens going berserk and the crunch of cars reversing into legs and bollards and railings. It was a panic like the darkest dream and the more people ran out onto the streets the bigger the panic got like a monster made of human beings.

I lost my boy and I was running in all directions screaming and looking for him but then the crowd got too thick and I couldn't choose my direction any more. I was in the middle of all these young blokes in office suits and they were shouting and barging everyone out of their way so I just had to run with them. Then I couldn't keep up any more and I fell. I lay on the streaming wet tarmac and they all ran over me in their hard leather shoes. I curled up into a ball and when it was finished I got up and walked on down towards Lambeth Bridge.

When I got to the Horseferry roundabout there was this woman in a green Range Rover and there were 2 blokes in suits trying to take it off her. She'd locked all the doors and she was gripping on to the steering wheel and screaming at these blokes to go away but you couldn't hear her. You could just see her face white and terrified behind the windscreen like a telly with the sound turned off. These blokes wouldn't let go of the door handles and the woman couldn't drive off because there were people all around. The 2 blokes started rocking the Range Rover. They were screaming at the woman to let them in.

—My wife! shouted one of the blokes. My wife is stuck at home! I have to get to her. Let us in you bitch you've got 4 empty seats in there.

The woman collapsed over the wheel. She was holding her head in her hands and wailing at the pedals by her feet. The poor cow probably didn't have a clue what was going on. One minute she'd been worrying about house prices and the next minute she was in the middle of a panic. Then one of the blokes lost it. I saw this expression come over his face.

—Right then, he shouted. I'll show you you fucking bitch.

You could see the spit coming out with each word and splattering across the windscreen. He went round the back of the Range Rover and opened the petrol cap.

—Oh Jesus oh please god no.

The bloke took a Zippo out of his pocket and looked at me and there wasn't anything in his eyes at all. He flicked the Zippo on and shoved it down the fuel pipe of the Range Rover.

—There you go bitch, he shouted.

The flames shot out of the fuel pipe in a jet and they blew the bloke off his feet. He went down with his suit in flames. It was soaked in petrol it burned white and fierce. It was shocking and the crowd pulled back and made a circle around him. You could see everyone's faces very white against the grey rainy sky and their eyes glistened with the flames and the shadows of their noses were very sharp and black.

The other bloke who'd been trying to get into the Range Rover just ran off. I smelled my hair singeing and I pushed myself back away from the heat. The woman got out of her driver's seat and stood with the crowd watching the man burn. The flames went 10 feet up in the air with the bloke twisting and flailing at the bottom. He was screaming for his mum and after a while he was just screaming and if you looked carefully towards the end you could see him lifting his head up and thumping it down on the tarmac again and again. He was trying to knock himself out and I hope he did.

After the longest time the bloke stopped moving and then someone shouted for us to get away before the Range Rover went up. There was another rush then and everyone was kicking and punching each other to get out of the way. I didn't see the Range Rover go I just heard the *whump* and I felt the heat of it on my back. There were more screams and then I was running again. A hard black line of riot vans was keeping us from turning west up the Horseferry Road and they were laying into us with water cannons and teargas. One of the canisters exploded by my feet and then I was running blind and choking.

Every breath with teargas is like dying the shock is horrible. The crowd streamed onto Lambeth Bridge and I ran with the snot pouring down my face. Then things got worse because there were too many people for how narrow the bridge was. You could tell we weren't all going to get across at that speed but there was no stopping on account of there must of been 10,000 people coming along behind us and there was no way they were slowing down. There was a lot of fighting and shoving and when my eyes cleared from the teargas I saw a lot of people getting trampled. The bridge got more and more jammed. I was pushed towards the edge and I started to see people going over into the river. I fought and kicked like everyone else but I was getting nearer and nearer to the edge. When I finally went over myself it was quite a relief because there was no more screaming and crushing. Just the rush of air while I fell and then the sharp cold splash of the Thames.

I went in feet first and I went very far down. I can't swim Osama I never learned. I mean there wasn't much call for it in the East End. We never saw more water than you needed to pour on tea bags. The Thames was cold and it was the colour of the dishwater at the end of the washing up. I remember looking up through it and seeing the light pale brown and far above and wondering if I would sink farther or float up to it. I stayed down for the longest time Osama. I wouldn't of minded drowning but I did float up in the end. Somehow I always seem to.

When I came up I was right next to one of the pillars of the bridge and I hung on to the stones while people fell from far above me and splashed down all around. The ones that could swim took themselves off to the banks and the others were either lucky like me and found something to hang on to or else they just thrashed around for a bit and went under.

I hung on to the stones for god knows how long. There were gaps between them maybe half an inch wide. It was just enough so you could push your fingers in and wedge your toes and cling on with just your head out of the water and the current trying to suck you away. It was so cold my head hurt and my arms and legs went dead. I don't know how I hung on but I did and I wasn't the only one there were lots of us hanging there. A girl with curly red hair was next to me. She was wearing a pinstripe office suit and a white shirt with big collars. She wasn't wearing a bra and you could see her tits through the wet shirt. She had a tattoo on her left tit. One of those Chinese letters. I remember thinking how strange love I've seen your tattoo when all the people you worked with for years probably had no idea. It's funny the things you think about when you should be thinking about dying.

—I can't hold on much longer, the red-haired girl said.

—Well you're going to have to.

—I can't, she said.

—Yes you can.

She looked right at me and her eyes were furious and exhausted.

—And how the fuck would you know? she said.

She lost her grip and I saw her go under. Her bright red hair sank last of all like a clown's wig. I was getting so cold I couldn't feel my fingers it felt like I was holding on with little dead sticks. There was green slime on the stones and you had to keep forcing your fingers and your toes back into the gaps and they kept on slipping out again. When I did think about dying I got so angry. The only thing going through my head was my boy screaming with Mr. Rabbit in his pocket and his Arsenal shirt in flames.

I was so angry Osama I was shouting THEY KNEW THEY KNEW and the other people were staring at me. My shouts were echoing all under the arches of the bridge. That's when the police boat came. I suppose someone must of heard me shouting. It was only a small boat with one copper driving. I don't suppose he realised how many of us were under there. You could see the expression on his face when his boat swung round the pillar of the bridge and he clapped eyes on us all. His mouth opened wide and he spun the wheel to turn away but it was no good. The current swept him nearer to the pillar and then the people closest to the boat grabbed hold of it and pulled themselves in. There must of been 20 of us hanging on to those stones and I reckon nearly everyone grabbed on to the boat. The only reason I didn't was I couldn't make my fingers let go of the bridge. The police boat started to lean under all that weight. You could see the sides of it dipping close to the water. The driver was shouting no more please no more. He had a long pole with a hook on the end of it and he jabbed it at the people who tried to get in. It was no good. People just kept climbing on and the sides of the boat went lower and lower until the water started to pour in all quiet and brown and deadly.

When the boat flipped over nearly everyone was trapped under it. I didn't see many people come back up. Maybe just 2 or 3 and they went straight back down again. And then that was that. There was just me clinging to the arch all alone with the police boat floating upside down next to me. The underneath of it was orange and glossy and I suppose it stuck up from the water maybe 6 inches in the middle. There were waves breaking over the boat and it was starting to drift away in the current.

The roar of the crowd was getting louder from the bridge above me now and more people were starting to splash down into the water very nearby. I reckoned if I didn't do anything now I was finished. I smashed at my hands with my forehead till my fingers let go of the bridge and I pushed myself out through the water to the upside-down boat. I was already starting to sink when I grabbed hold of it. My hands slid and I thought Right that's it then but I was lucky because my fingers hooked round the propeller. I pulled myself right out of the water and I lay on my tummy on the underside of the boat with the Thames slopping all around me.

I drifted all day till it got dark and no one came to help me. I suppose everyone had their hands full. I was so cold it was agony. I kept my eyes closed most of the time on account of I couldn't bear to watch all the bodies floating down the river with me.

Once when I did open my eyes it was hours later and I was going under Southwark Bridge with the sun setting very sick and yellow through the Shield of Hope. It was a seagull squawking that made me open my eyes. There was an Asian boy maybe 16 or 17 years old floating in between my boat and the sunset. The boy was 2 feet from me he was floating face up in a McDonald's uniform. Grey polyester trousers maroon short-sleeved shirt and a maroon baseball cap. The seagull was sticking his head in under the peak of the baseball cap to eat the boy's left eye. The boy had a name badge it said HI MY NAME IS NICK HOW CAN I HELP YOU TODAY? He had 2 out of 5 merit stars on his badge and they glistened in the sunset.

I think I fell asleep after that. It was a miserable sleep because every time I drifted off I felt my fingers lose their grip on the boat and I snapped back awake. That must of gone on for hours until I opened my eyes for good because my boat hit something and I felt a bump. It was dark and there was a huge thing looming over me. I screamed and put up my hand to push the dark thing away from me till I realised it was Tower Bridge. It was low tide and my boat was stuck on a mud bank on the north side of the river.

I let myself slide off the boat into the soft sucking mud. It was a disgrace that mud. It was as old as London and I swear it stank of diseases people forgot the names of 500 years ago. This whole city is built on plague pits and murder holes and I sank into it right up to my thighs and I puked and cried and puked again. When I couldn't puke any more I struggled through the mud up to the stone wall of the bank. There was a ladder there made of rusty iron hoops and I pulled myself up it. I had to keep stopping. I was so cold and tired and I never was what you'd call sporty.

I came up right under the Tower of London. Everything was quiet. There was no one about at all. I'd lost my shoes in the river and I walked with my arms hugged round me and my bare feet on the cobblestones. I was so cold I was shaking like our washing machine on a spin cycle. I walked past the high walls of the Tower with the stinking mud all over me. Black rats were scuttling and squeaking around my feet. The streetlights were out and it was dark as you like. It had stopped raining. There were gaps in the clouds where you could see a new moon and the stars very bright.

I kept on walking quick as I could to get warm. I kept my head down. You couldn't see where your feet were going and I was trying not to tread on anything nasty. The churches started chiming 10 o'clock. You could hear their big bells booming through the sound of helicopters. Those choppers were all over the sky and one came down low over the Tower. It came along the street towards me with its searchlight flashing off the wet cobbles. I pushed myself right up against the Tower wall and I watched the circle of light move over the spot where I'd been walking. It carried on down the street and then it stopped because there was a bloke caught in the beam.

This bloke was naked and his skin shone blue white in the searchlight. He was a young chap maybe 20 years old and there was blood pouring down him. The blood was coming out of his mouth and you could see why because he'd bitten his tongue half off and he was still chewing away at it. With one hand he was holding a butcher's knife and with his other hand he was playing with himself. When he saw he was caught in the searchlight he looked right at the place where I was hiding in the darkness and he screamed with rage. Then I suppose someone in the chopper shot him. I didn't hear the shot over the racket of the rotors but I saw the chap's neck explode in a burst of red and I saw his body sit down on the cobblestones. He sat down very neatly on his dead bum with the one hand still holding on to his thing. The searchlight stayed steady on him till the first of the rats started to move in through the edges of the beam. Then the helicopter pulled back up into the night.

Nowadays I suppose that chap was just some lunatic who escaped in the panic but at the time I didn't know what was going on. I thought maybe everyone had gone like him. So I went very careful after that Osama and you can't blame me. It took me 2 whole hours to walk back to Bethnal Green. I didn't take the streets I took the footpaths and the back alleys and I went across gardens like a fox. When I did catch a glimpse of the main streets there were soldiers standing all along them. The soldiers had machine guns and armoured cars and I even saw some tanks though god knows what they were in aid of.

There were a few other people in the alleys on the way home but this time none of them was trying to rape me or eat me thank god. I started to feel a bit better because they were just ordinary people like me in Nikes and Pumas trying to get home through the curfew. We looked at one another in the half-light from the helicopters and you could see this same expression on everyone's face. It was the look of people who'd woken up expecting one sort of day and got something completely else.

Barnet Grove when I got there was dead quiet. No people out on account of the curfew and no lights anywhere because the electric was off. Half a dozen cars were burning and there was no one to put them out. Melted rubber from the car tyres was running down the gutter at the side of the kerb. It boiled and bubbled like the lava when a volcano erupts and it disappeared hissing down the storm drains. The stink was horrible.

My boy was waiting for me in the street outside the Wellington Estate. He waved hello to me.

—Oh my boy oh my poor little boy are you alright?

My boy grinned and climbed into one of the burning cars and sat down on the bare white-hot springs of the passenger seat. He smiled out at me while the flames licked around him and the windscreen popped and shattered.

A helicopter was hovering low at the far end of the street. It was coming our way. Its rotors whipped the orange flames of the burning cars into this roaring white. My boy looked up. He was excited. The helicopter was getting closer. You could hear its rotors over the roar of the flames. My boy twisted his head out through the melted glass of the passenger window to look at it. Chopper he said. Chopper chopper chopper. He always loved that word.

The searchlight came onto us and it stayed there. It was a bright white light like a camera flash and you couldn't look up into it. A megaphone voice came down out of the sky. STAY WHERE YOU ARE it said. YOU ARE IN VIOLATION OF CURFEW. DO NOT I REPEAT DO NOT MOVE. Yeah right. Like I was just going to hold still while the coppers got a good steady aim. I just legged it and ran into the Wellington Estate with my poor boy screaming LEAVE MY MUMMY ALONE up into the burning sky.

I sat down in the stairwell of our tower block to get my breath back. I sat there for half an hour shivering till I found the strength to climb the stairs to our flat.

Someone had shoved a letter under the front door and I picked it up after I let myself in. I put the letter down on the kitchen table and lit a couple of candles and they started flickering on account of there was a nasty breeze in the flat coming from the windows which were all smashed in. There was broken glass all over the floor and the smell of burning tyres coming in from the street. I went into the bathroom and turned the battery radio on. THERE IS NO CAUSE FOR ALARM it was saying. I started the bath running and I went back into the kitchen and popped 4 of my pills out of their packet and drank them down with vodka. Then I opened the letter.

My brave friend, what can I say, except let us remember the happier times? I did so enjoy choosing those clothes with you and I will never forget how stunning you were in them. Please wear them sometimes and remember I wasn't always a bitch to you. You must loathe me for the choice I had to make. I searched my heart and decided it would not have been helpful to the country for us to run the story. The paper has been very supportive of me as I made this difficult choice and they have offered me some wonderful opportunities, which will mean security for my son when he is born. I hope you will find it in your warm heart to understand and forgive me one day. As someone who has been a mother I know you will understand that we must always do what is best for our children. Your friend, Petra Sutherland.

I burned the note and dropped the ashes on the kitchen floor. I took the candles into the bathroom. The radio was saying INITIAL ESTIMATES PUT CASUALTIES AT 100 TO 120. A HOTLINE FOR CONCERNED FRIENDS AND RELATIVES HAS BEEN—

I turned the radio off and got into the bath and lay back with my ears underwater listening to the sound of helicopters rumbling through the plumbing. I lay there till the water went cold and the candles went out.

Winter

Dear Osama I taped newspaper over the broken windows to keep the draughts out but still it's been a cold winter. There is comfort in the small things of course I do like to watch the pigeons fly up over the roofs I do like the frost on the motors on a bright early morning. I got 1 letter from Terence Butcher on very thin blue paper his handwriting was shaky and it got worse towards the end so you couldn't make it out. I would of liked to write back but there wasn't an address.

Since I got that letter I get nervous they'll come for me next and take me off somewhere in the back of an Astra. Whatever it is that makes your writing go to scribbles I'm scared they'll do it to me. I did get a visit from 2 plainclothes men quite early on but they didn't stay long they wouldn't even have a drink. I showed them my boy and said Look you can't take me away what would become of him then? The men just looked at each other and then back at me and one of them said In consideration of the circumstances madam I don't think it would be appropriate for us to press charges. I said Oh fair enough then. Then the other man said However madam it has been decided that you will no longer receive your widow's pension. I said You're joking aren't you why's that then? How am I expected to live? and the man said Perhaps you should have thought of that madam before you passed official secrets to the press.

There wasn't much to live on after that. Jasper's bank card was no use it was lost somewhere in the dark mud at the bottom of the Thames. I pulled up the carpet and got out all those fivers I used to stash when my husband was gambling. We had a high old time for a month me and my boy. He had choc-chip every day and I had vodka and not just the own-brand stuff either it was real Absolut but by the end of last month the money was gone. So I went out and I did the exact same thing you'd of done in my situation Osama I got myself a job stacking shelves at the Tesco metro on Bethnal Green Road.

I had to fill in an application form to get the job. It asked why I specially wanted to work at Tesco's and I wrote BECAUSE MY HUSBAND AND MY BOY WERE RECENTLY BLOWN UP BY ISLAMIC TERRORISTS AND THIS HAS CAUSED A NUMBER OF PROBLEMS FOR ME BUT THE MOST URGENT NOW IS MONEY AND THAT IS WHY I WANT TO WORK AT TESCO'S ALSO BECAUSE IT IS CLOSE TO MY FLAT AND I WOULD MUCH RATHER STACK YOUR SHELVES FOR MONEY THAN GO ON THE GAME and then I threw that application form away and I took another one and wrote BECAUSE I AM A TEAM PLAYER AND I BELIEVE TESCO'S IS AN EXCELLENT COMPANY THAT RESPECTS TEAMWORK and they gave me the job just like that.

Stacking shelves is excellent Osama you shouldn't knock it till you've tried it. It does not vex your brain very much and it is a great comfort taking the out-of-date tins off the shelves and putting new ones there till all the shelves in your section are very neat and all the labels face the front. If you got the job they'd give you a uniform so you'd never have to worry about what to wear and they'd give you lots of training I mean they even have a course in anger management and if you could get through the trial period without butchering any of the difficult customers and broadcasting their executions on the Internet then they'd give you a very nice name badge to pin on your red dungarees with your name printed out on a Dymo tape and your badge would say

TESCO
O S A M A
HERE TO HELP

The day I got this job was the day I started writing this letter to you Osama. I'm on 7 pound 20 an hour which is to say I can either afford food or booze but not both so it's true what they say I suppose life is full of choices. Back at the flat I can't afford the electricity to turn the telly on so after my boy goes to bed I just write. I've been writing to you till after midnight most nights and if it's a quiet day then I write at work too. Part of this shelf-stacking job is that you have to walk up and down with a clipboard taking stock and so that's just what I've been doing. I count up all the tins of beans and I write them all down and while I'm at it I write down what you've done to me Osama I just think you ought to know.

Sometimes late at night I get too tired or too sad to write any more and then I just sit on the sofa all wrapped up in blankets and watch my breath steaming in the lounge. It can be a bit sad just to see the telly sitting there all dead and blank so I Blu-Tacked some of my boy's drawings up over the screen and I sit watching them. Sometimes I put music on or I make myself laugh very loud so the upstairs neighbours can't start feeling all superior. You may think that's funny Osama but you never can squeeze every last bit of pride out of a human being. It's like a tube of toothpaste. You can twist it and you can crush it but there's always a tiny bit left isn't there?

Sometimes I fall asleep on the sofa. When I wake up it's 5 in the morning and still dark. I go into my boy's room and tuck the blankets more close around him. Then I pick up my biro and carry on writing to you for an hour or 2 until it's time to get dressed for work. Is it any use Osama has any of it changed your mind or would you do the same things all over again tomorrow?

Just before I leave for work I walk over to the window in the early morning light. I look out and see my boy walking down the white line in the middle of the road. He balances on the white line with his arms out to the sides like the tightrope man in the circus. He's concentrating. His tongue sticks out the way it always does when he's busy. Sometimes black smoke pours off him and sometimes there's just these little wisps.

In the evenings when I get home from work the first thing I do is look at the post if any's come. I only ever get 2 kinds of letters in the post these days. The first kind says they're going to repossess the telly and the second kind says they're going to repossess the flat. Since the beginning of December both kinds have been arriving in red envelopes. I'll tell you honestly Osama I don't know what I'm going to do.

Sundays are a bit different from the normal routine. First thing in the morning I go out to the newsagent's and buy the *Sunday Telegraph*. I take it back to the flat and lay it out very careful on the kitchen table but I don't read it straight off. First I have a shower and then I go to the wardrobe and get the outfit Petra bought for me. I put it on very gentle so as not to stretch it. First the bright white underwear. Then the white silk slacks and the Hermès tunic top. Last of all those lovely Fendi heels. Next I go to the bathroom and put Petra's face on very slow and careful. It took me a long time to save up for that makeup.

My boy sits on the edge of the bath and bangs his heels on the side of it bang bang bang watching me get ready. When I'm done I look at myself in the mirror above the basin.

—You look lovely Mummy, says my boy.

—I am not Mummy darling. I am Petra Sutherland.

My boy giggles and we go to the kitchen and we sit down at the table and open up the *Sunday Telegraph* to the Lifestyle section. Petra's column is at the front of it and there's a little photo of her next to her name. My boy always touches that photo with his stubby little fingers.

—That woman looks just like you Petra, he says.

I smile back at my boy.

—Yes. Isn't it adorable?

Then I read Petra's column aloud. I haven't forgotten how. I can still do her voice perfect. I flick my hair back when I speak. Just the way she does. For half an hour every Sunday morning Osama I am Petra Sutherland. I forget all about the cold and the dirt and my poor dead chaps. With my beautiful accent I tell my empty kitchen all about how I'm coping with my very public bereavement by focusing every ounce of positive energy on my pregnancy. How thrilled I am by the letters of support from ordinary members of the public. How I don't think I'm being particularly brave. I'm just doing what any mother-to-be would do. One has to face the future.

Talking to the landscape gardener about my new house in Hampstead is a wonderful distraction and helps me connect with the eternal cycle of nature. And no I absolutely do not think one should be obliged to dress in a tent just because one happens to be pregnant. Chloë and Prada both have some terribly clever maternity frocks that make me feel sexy and glamorous.

In the spring my baby will be born in a holistic birthing centre and I will go straight back to work. My column won't even miss a beat. Did I mention I recently won the Columnist of the Year award? And I am delighted to be able to inform my readers that I have my own television show starting next month on the BBC. Impending motherhood has broadened my horizons. I feel I now have more to share than just lifestyle ideas. I want to talk about life. In the broadest sense. And I am lucky enough to have the opportunity to do so. The fabulous thing about being a mother these days is that all your hard-won wisdom doesn't need to stay with you in the kitchen. You can go out and shout about it. I'm fortunate to have discovered a wonderful nanny. She's a great find.

Every Sunday morning Osama I am just so happy being Petra Sutherland.

*   *   *

It is Christmas Eve Osama and there is a new release of ENGLAND'S HEART IS BLEEDING in the charts with bells on it.

They've hung lights on the Shield of Hope. Each balloon has its theme there are huge stars and candles and snowmen. It looks amazing at night there are a million electric bulbs glowing where the sky used to be. The only thing is you can't see the faces now. My husband isn't there any more there is a red-and-white Santa Claus instead. My boy's been replaced by Rudolph.

It is Christmas Eve Osama and this morning I decided you were right after all. I mean I've been thinking about it a lot what with not having much to do of an evening. Some people are cruel and self-ish and the world would be better off without them. You were absolutely right the whole time some people only deserve to burn.

It was 7 this morning when the bailiffs came to evict us from the flat. It wasn't their fault they were just doing their job and it didn't look like they got the same satisfaction out of it that I get from neat-ening up rows of tins. They were sorry for what they had to do. They looked so miserable I told them to cheer up and I made them a cup of tea. It's funny I mean I'd been dreading them coming for so long that it was quite a relief to finally have them in my kitchen. They said I could take all the time I wanted to pack my things up but I told them not to worry. I put my makeup and my Harvey Nick's clothes into a Nike bag along with Mr. Rabbit. Then I took my boy's hand and we left the Wellington Estate.

It was cold and crisp this morning with a bright blue sky and ice on the pavements. On Bethnal Green Road we had a McBreakfast at McDonald's and I changed into Petra's clothes in their toilets. I put Petra's face on in their mirror and I shoved my old Adidas tracksuit down their khazi. So if you ever wondered Osama why the McToi-lets are always blocked well there's one of your reasons anyway. Then I took the boy to the Shell garage and I told them my motor was run out of petrol. They let me buy a 5-litre red plastic can and they filled it with unleaded for me. People are ever so helpful when you're shivering in Hermès cause you left your coat in the car. Before I left the garage I bought a nice silver Zippo lighter. I got the man to fill it with lighter fluid for me I said I didn't want to get the stuff on my clothes. The man flicked it on to test it and it made a nice bright flame till he snapped the lid back on and handed it over.

Outside the garage I put the Zippo in my pocket and I put the petrol can inside my Nike bag. We walked to Cambridge Heath and got on a D6 bus and went up to the top deck and sat right at the front. My boy always loved the top deck of a bus. He was jumping around and shouting he was so excited but I was very calm I knew what I had to do. At Mile End we changed onto the 277.

It wasn't any problem getting in to the tower at Canary Wharf. The security blokes just nodded me through. I was Petra Sutherland after all. As seen on TV. I took my boy into the lift and we rode up to the *Sunday Telegraph*'s floor. At the reception desk the girl was a bit confused because she thought she'd seen me go in already that morning. I smiled and told her I'd had to pop back to the car for my gym kit. I held up my Nike bag and she smiled and buzzed me in.

Petra was on the phone when I stepped into her office with my boy. She had her back to me and she was saying NO I DID NOT SAY PLAID I DISTINCTLY REMEMBER SAYING TARTAN. She didn't turn round till she heard the click of me locking her office door behind us. Petra's office was gorgeous. It was right on the corner of the tower and you could see the whole of London laid out behind her with the buildings glittering under the blue morning sky.

Petra's mouth opened wide but I didn't give her a chance to speak. I thought she'd said enough. I just picked up the solid glass Columnist of the Year award off her desk and smacked her across the side of the head with it. She fell back stunned into her office chair. I turned round to look back through the glass walls of her office. No one was watching. There were venetian blinds on the glass and I twisted them shut so no one could see us.

I looked down at Petra it was obvious one of her cheekbones was broken and I felt sick I remembered kissing that cheek. I remembered stretching up out of the bath to do it while the candles flickered low. I didn't want to think about Petra's broken cheek so I just got the 5-litre can out of my Nike bag and I started pouring petrol. I poured it all over the carpet round Petra's chair and I poured it all over Petra's chair and I poured it all over Petra till her white cashmere sweater was soaked and heavy with the stuff and clinging to her skin. You couldn't breathe for all the petrol fumes and Petra started choking and coming round. Her eyes were streaming and there was blood and snot running out of her nose.

—Oh no oh fucking Jesus Christ no please no you're not going to murder me are you? she said.

I didn't say anything I just got the Zippo out of my pocket and opened the lid of it and held it up and Petra Sutherland was squirming in her chair but she couldn't stand up she was saying no no NO NO NO. My boy wasn't taking any notice he was laughing and running round the office banging on the glass windows and looking out over the whole of London in flames underneath us. LOOK MUMMY he was pointing. WHAT'S THAT BURNING? It's the new Swiss Re building darling. AND WHAT'S THAT BURNING? It's St. Paul's Cathedral. AND WHAT'S THAT BURNING? Shush now just for a second darling Mummy's very busy.

I looked back at Petra I looked right in her eyes.

—God you're fucking crazy, she said. There's no one fucking there you're talking to yourself oh god oh god oh you need help I can help you you don't have to go through with this please oh please just put that lighter down and we can get you some help oh please and you won't get into any trouble I promise.

I just looked at her I couldn't believe she was promising again.

—Why are you doing this? said Petra. Please? WHY?

—It's like you said yourself Petra. We must always do what's best for our children.

Petra went very scared and pale then she was just trembling and whimpering. I took a couple of steps back towards the wall of the office so I'd be out of the way when all that petrol went up. I called to my boy. He had his nose pressed up against the windows gawping at the waves of flame rolling over London so all you could see was the very tops of the tallest towers crumbling in the heat.

—Come on darling come back here with Mummy out of the way.

I held up the Zippo and I put my thumb on the spark wheel. I stayed like that watching Petra cry for a very long time. My boy looked up at me.

—Mummy what are you waiting for?

Kids will ask questions won't they Osama? I took a deep breath.

—I'm waiting till I don't feel anything for her any more not even a tiny bit.

—How long will that take Mummy?

—I don't know.

—Oh.

I just stood there and Petra was crying and I was crying too even through all the pills.

—Mummy I'm bored can't you just do it anyway?

I sighed.

—Nah.

I looked at Petra Sutherland one last time with London burning behind her and then I took my thumb off the wheel. I folded the lid back on the Zippo very slow and careful and I put the Zippo down on the desk very gentle. I thought about it for a moment and I reached down and I took Mr. Rabbit out of the Nike bag and I sat him down nice and comfy next to the Zippo. Then I took my boy by the hand and we walked out of Petra's office and we closed the door behind us.

*   *   *

That was this morning Osama and now I'm back at work I mean it's not as if I've got anywhere else to go is it? I changed into my uniform and the manager had a go at me for being 2 hours late but it's not as if she was going to sack me. I mean it's Christmas Eve and they need all the staff they can get. I don't suppose you know much about Christmas Osama so let me explain it's the holiest day in our religion so half the East End is in here today stocking up on lager and fairy lights.

I'm on my lunch hour. I would of thought the coppers would of been here by now to take me away but they haven't turned up yet so I'm sitting in the staff room eating Tesco's Value mince pies and finishing off this letter. It's nice in the staff room there's Christmas songs playing on the stereo and some of the other girls are in here laughing and nattering. My boy is playing on the tabletop making claws with his hands and going RRRR! RRRR! he's a prowling jungle tiger I think or maybe a JCB digger. There's a little window in here and you can see out into the store and you can hear the Christmassy customer announcements over the loudspeakers. JOY TO THE WORLD. GOODWILL TO ALL MEN. KAREEM TO CHECKOUT 4 PLEASE.

You can see my section from here Osama. I am very proud of my section all the tins and packets are inside their sell-by dates and all the labels are facing front and everything is very neat and tidy. I wish you could see it. I think it is beautiful all that neatness. Tidiness almost hides the horror. This is love Osama this is civilisation this is what I'm getting paid 7 pound 20 an hour for.

The coppers will find me here soon and they'll take me away and have me banged up. I don't blame them I mean you can't have people like me strolling around with petrol cans. They'll put me in prison for a bit or maybe in the nuthouse although I think I'd prefer prison on account of the nutters would just upset my boy. Don't worry about me Osama I'll be alright I'll just keep myself to myself and it's not as if I'll get bored I've got more letters to write like I said.

When I get out of prison Osama if you're still outside too then I want you to come and live with me. Please don't laugh please just think about it it could be a new start for both of us. We could get a decent place in the nice part of Hoxton or somewhere else if you prefer. Anywhere not too pricey would be alright although not South London if it's all the same to you. Come out of your cave Osama and come to me I can't hate you any more. I am weak from hate I don't even have enough hate left to turn the little spark wheel on a Zippo. I know I'm just too stupid to know better but look at me.

I'm like a broken jukebox the only tune I play is looking after my chaps. Won't you let me play it?

I will comfort you when you have bad dreams in the night. I will cook your tea just the way you like it. I will make our upstairs neighbours wish they'd never been born. I will try very hard to be faithful. I will hide you from the law and put all your CDs back in their right boxes with their labels facing front. We'll make a new start the 2 of us. Everyone should be allowed a new start. Come on Osama my boy needs a dad and it's about time you grew up too. I've told you all about the sadness of bombs so now you must give them up. I know you are a clever man Osama much brighter than me and I know you have a lot of things to get done but you ought to be able to get it done with love that's my whole point. Love is not surrender Osama love is furious and brave and loud you can hear it in the noise my boy is making right now while he plays. RRRR! RRRR! he says I wish you could hear him Osama that noise is the fiercest and the loudest sound on earth it will echo to the end of time it is more deafening than bombs. Listen to that noise Osama it is time for you to stop blowing the world apart. Come to me Osama. Come to me and we will blow the world back together WITH INCRED-IBLE NOISE AND FURY.

The work was carried on with diligence, and London is restored; but whether with greater speed or beauty, may be made a question.

—Inscription on the Monument to the Great Fire of London, south side

ACKNOWLEDGMENTS

Thank you

Rebecca Carter, a brilliant, generous, and inspiring editor. Laetitia Rutherford, a perfect agent. Hannah Dawson, who got things started. Alex Cleave, the man and the legend.

Toby Eady and everyone at Orme Court. Jessica and Rosie Buckman. Karolina Sutton. Vanessa Kling. Alison Samuel, Dan Franklin, David Parrish, Paul Baggaley, Roger Bratchell, Rachel Cugnoni, Beth Coates, Suzanne Dean, Claire Wilshaw, Tom Drake-Lee, Lorelei Mathias. Sonny Mehta, Maya Mavjee, Leyla Aker, Thomas Ueberhoff, Elik Lettinga, Anna Pastore, Stefania De Pasquale, Charlotte Weiss, Maggie Doyle, Ana Maria Barros, Tone Torp, Anand Tucker, Andy Paterson, Sharon Maguire.

Louis and Clémence. Rosemary and John. Mary, David, Sue, Fennella, Keith, Susanna, Duncan, Reuben, Amy, Nick, William, Sally, Emily, Anna, Libby, Catherine, Adrienne, Alice, Ben, Catherine, Julien. Chloë, Mike, Becs, Matt, Olivia, Jake, Grace, Mark, Dan, Martha, Vlad, George, Jonathan, Lucy, Jonas, Tanya, Emelyne, Siobhan, Chris. All the people who saw me home on the nights when I wouldn't have made it.

Chris Cleave, London

ABOUT THE AUTHOR

Chris Cleave took a degree at Oxford and worked for the British newspaper The Daily Telegraph. *He lives in Surrey with his wife and son.*

A NOTE ON THE TYPE

This book was set in ITC Esprit, a typeface designed by Jovica Veljovic in 1985. Veljovic was born in 1954 in Suvi Do, Yugoslavia, and worked as a type designer, calligrapher, and teacher in Belgrade. He currently teaches in Hamburg, Germany, and conducts workshops throughout Europe and the United States.

Composed by Stratford Publishing Services, Brattleboro, Vermont
Printed and bound by R. R. Donnelley & Sons, Harrisonburg, Virginia
Designed by Anthea Lingeman